DEAɪH
AT THE DANCE

DEATH
AT THE DANCE

VERITY BRIGHT

Bookouture

Published by Bookouture in 2020

An imprint of Storyfire Ltd.
Carmelite House
50 Victoria Embankment
London EC4Y 0DZ

www.bookouture.com

ISBN: 978-1-83888-755-1
eBook ISBN: 978-1-83888-754-4

'Every saint has a past, and every sinner has a future.'
Oscar Wilde, *A Woman of No Importance*

CHAPTER 1

Eleanor cowered at the end of the bedstead as shattered glass rained down on her head. 'Oh, botheration!' She shook the larger shards from her flame-red curls, her sharp, green eyes peering up at the ceiling now devoid of its ornate chandelier, the plaster rose sprouting only a wire.

'Double botheration!' She hurled the long bamboo cane responsible for the damage onto her bed, pulled on her slippers, and crunched across the glass. In her grey, silk pyjamas and with her slender figure she looked every inch the martial-arts student. She opened the door and jumped back. 'Clifford! Please don't lurk outside like that! You frightened the sense out of me.'

Her butler dropped his white-gloved hand, which had been raised ready to knock. 'Apologies, my lady, but I rather fear that happened a long while ago.'

'What? Now look here.' She glanced up at him and caught that twinkle in his eye. She found herself grinning back. He had not only been her late uncle's butler but also, despite the class difference, his friend. And so it was proving with her.

'In fact, don't come in. Well, actually, you'll have to, I suppose.' She opened the door for him to see. 'You may have heard a teensy noise.'

'Indeed, my lady. Mr Penry called from his butcher's shop in the village to ask if we would be good enough to keep the noise down.'

'Very funny.'

Clifford pulled the bell sash at the head of Eleanor's bed twice. 'Not to worry, the ladies will do a swift job, given the circumstances.'

'Circumstances?'

'That you have precisely thirty-seven minutes before we need to leave.'

'Oh golly, that's not long. But wait, need to leave for where?'

Clifford adjusted his perfectly aligned shirt cuffs. 'If you remember, my lady, the Fenwick-Langhams are holding a masked ball and I will be driving you there in the Rolls.'

Eleanor picked up her uncle's fob watch from the bedside. She'd found it when she'd inherited Henley Hall after his unexpected death, and kept it as a memento of the rare times she'd spent with him. 'Thirty-seven minutes is' – she looked down at her pyjamas – 'ample. And I'm sure the ladies will… ah! Here they are.'

'Oh, my stars!' Mrs Butters, the housekeeper, flustered in and stood peering at the mound of glass and silver fittings. 'Thank goodness Master Gladstone wasn't in here, his paws would be full of cut chandelier crystal.'

Gladstone was the elderly bulldog Eleanor had inherited along with Henley Hall, and much else besides, from her late uncle.

Mrs Butters looked up from the mess on the floor. 'More importantly, are you alright, my lady?'

'Yes, I'm quite fine. Do come in, Polly.' Eleanor didn't need to peer round the door to know her young maid would be waiting on the other side.

Polly loped in on her willowy legs and looked around the room. 'Oh lummy!'

'Yes, Polly, oh lummy indeed,' Clifford said. 'But not to worry, her ladyship has finished her martial-arts training for the moment, so kindly clear up the aftermath.'

Eleanor cocked a questioning eyebrow at him. How could he possibly have known? 'Look here, Clifford, I just thought it would be a good idea to be better prepared, given the events of the last few weeks. Hence a dash of self-defence training.'

'Indeed, my lady, assuming, of course, your assailant was planning to pounce on you from the chandelier.'

'Very droll. Actually, I think it's a shame Baritsu died out so quickly, I rather like it. Sherlock Holmes practised it, you know.'

Clifford cleared his throat. 'Sherlock Holmes did indeed practice a form of martial arts, my lady. I believe, however, the correct name is actually *Bartitsu*, with a middle "T", being a blended word of the surname of the gentleman who invented it, Mr Barton-Wright and jiu-jitsu. Unfortunately, the Bartitsu Club closed seventeen years ago in 1903, my lady, even though Mr William Barton-Wright is still teaching it I believe.'

Eleanor never stopped marvelling at just how much her butler seemed to know on any subject under the sun. With the mess cleared away, Mrs Butters bobbed a half curtsey. 'Will there be anything else, my lady? Shall Polly help you dress?'

'Good heavens, no!' Eleanor replied a little too quickly. 'I mean, no thank you. I have yet to work out which of these silk brocaded apparatuses of torture I will choose as my penance for this evening.'

The housekeeper chuckled and winked over her shoulder as she ushered Polly from the room. Clifford gave a polite cough. 'Perhaps getting one's skates on, as I believe the expression is, would be advisable?'

'Tsh, tsh, skates are hardly the appropriate footwear, silly.'

'I am given to understand that there will be several people there you have met previously at the rose garden luncheon Lady Fenwick-Langham put on two months ago.'

She groaned and flopped backwards onto the bed. 'Great! A stern old dowager and her soppy niece and a henpecked husband and his American wife who delights in ribbing my lack of fashion sense.'

'And, of course, a certain gentleman…'

Eleanor sat up. 'What! Oh no, not Colonel Bardifoot-Puttleton. Whatever I do, he seems to disapprove of.'

'It's Colonel Puddifoot-Barton, my lady. He is a highly decorated soldier. Admittedly, he can be a trifle… caustic on the surface, but if you dig—'

'One has to dig very deep to find any redeeming traits in the man. And, frankly, I am not in the mood for digging. I've tried to get on with him, but he has an unmatched skill for turning even a simple "Hello, Colonel, how are you?" into a declaration of open war!'

Clifford picked up the two dresses hanging on the door of her wardrobe and laid them carefully on the bed next to her.

'True, my lady, but I wasn't actually speaking about the colonel, rather a younger gentleman.'

She coloured at his last remark and tried to sound disinterested. 'Oh yes, Lancelot.' She peered at the dresses. 'Which do you think he would like?' She slapped her forehead. 'Oh, I didn't mean for that to come out aloud.'

Clifford smiled. 'I should think, my lady, that the gentleman will be delighted to see you in either. However, since you've asked, I would suspect the blue dress will catch his eye most assuredly.'

'Right, then I'll wear the red! I'm not having him goggling at me all night. I'm supposed to be a lady.'

'Well, we live in hope,' Clifford muttered as he left the room.

Alone, Eleanor yanked off her house pyjamas, throwing them in a heap on the bed. She couldn't help smiling on opening her wardrobe. Mrs Butters had surprised her the day before by making an exquisitely detailed set of hanging storage pockets. Made in duck-egg blue silk voile, they were perfect for her stockings.

Choosing a middle denier pair in glossy black, she yanked them on and grabbed the red dress from the bed. With one leg in, she paused, frowning. Clifford was bound to have guessed that she would pick the one he hadn't suggested. Oh what a fool, she'd nearly fallen for it. He obviously thought she should wear the red one. She reached for the blue gown. But wait, supposing it was a double bluff?

*

Thirty-five minutes later she pulled her bedroom door closed and tried to step elegantly down the stairs, the train of her gown tripping her feet and nearly defeating her efforts. She had finally chosen an emerald-green-and-gold gown. It had been her mother's, but it fitted her perfectly. After her parents' disappearance, her uncle had kept her mother's clothes at the Hall, much to Eleanor's delight when she unexpectedly came across them after inheriting the estate.

Mrs Butters, Polly and Mrs Trotman, the cook, stood in line in the hallway.

'Will I do, ladies, do you think?'

'Oh, m'lady, you look a princess.' Mrs Butters took Eleanor's hands in hers and pulling her arms to the side, clucked as proudly as a mother hen.

'The perfect choice, m'lady. You'll be the star of the ball and no mistake.' Mrs Trotman smiled.

Polly wiped tears from her cheeks as Mrs Butters reached round and pushed the maid's gaping jaw up.

'Thank you, ladies. I sincerely hope, however, that I won't be the star at all. I intend to sneak in at the back and loiter in the shadows, hoping not to catch anyone's eye and thus avoiding all the tedium of social niceties.'

'Well, perhaps just one set of eyes would be fine,' Mrs Trotman muttered.

'Trotters!' Mrs Butters said. 'Decorum, please. Sorry, my lady, I'll go boil her tongue so as it doesn't happen again.'

They all chuckled, Polly jiggling excitedly on her long legs.

'Right, wish me luck,' Eleanor said. 'Let's hope this gown fools them and they don't realise I'm as unladylike underneath as a frog in wellington boots.'

She stepped to the front door.

'Enjoy yourself, my lady.' Mrs Butters patted her arm as she held the door open. 'You look absolutely exquisite, definitely the most beautiful frog I've ever seen.'

'Thank you.' Eleanor's eyes twinkled with warmth for the kind-hearted housekeeper she wished had been there when she was a child.

Clifford had brought the Rolls Royce around and was waiting patiently. It was an early June evening, with a warm, damp breeze threatening rain. As she reached the gravel, Mrs Butters called out, 'Gracious, your train, my lady!'

With a grateful nod, Eleanor swished up the tail of her gown and stepped to the driver's door.

Clifford raised an eyebrow. 'My lady?'

'Now, none of that. I'll drive, thank you, Clifford. I'm in need of some more practice.'

He looked her up and down. 'In that gown? Are you sure that is wise?'

'Of course, why ever not?'

'I fear, my lady, you are sure to snap your heels off as you stamp on the brakes, and rip the train of your dress as you wrench the gear stick back and forth.'

She stared at him. 'You are a terrible man, you do know that.'

'Kind words, my lady. Shall we?' He gestured round to the passenger side and led the way without waiting for her response. Sliding into the driving seat, he pointed to the glovebox. Inside was a mask that matched her dress perfectly.

CHAPTER 2

Clifford pulled round the grand horseshoe entrance of Langham Manor and stopped at the base of the sweeping stone staircase that led up to the colonnaded stately entrance. Lights shone from every window and lanterns burned brightly on each step, illuminating the lush garlands of roses twirled along every inch of the balustrades on either side up to the front door. Eleanor sighed at the fairy-tale atmosphere.

'Here we are, my lady. The invitation said seven to half past, so quarter to eight is close enough.'

'Wish me luck, Clifford,' Eleanor said.

Clifford smiled. 'You'll be fine. Perhaps just steer clear of politics, religion and colonels.' He nodded at a footman and her car door opened like magic.

Sandford, butler at the Manor, was waiting for her at the top of the steps.

'Good evening, Sandford. How are you?' Eleanor called as she tried to make sense of the yards of fabric that made up the train of her gown.

Clifford coughed from the driver's seat. 'And perhaps try to avoid fraternising with the staff. Think "lady".'

Eleanor frowned as she finally managed to get out of the car. 'You know, Sandford, I'm planning to send Clifford back to butler school to learn how one should address the lady of the house.'

Sandford's eyes twinkled as he suppressed a laugh.

'Please watch out for Lady Swift this evening, Mr Sandford,' Clifford called to his friend. 'If things get ugly you know where to find me. However, if she needs bail money, well, then I've moved and left no forwarding address.'

Sandford's shoulders shook, but he quickly regained his composure. 'Very good, Mr Clifford. Lady Swift will be in the best hands.'

Eleanor rolled her eyes as she started up the stairs. 'Sandford, Clifford really is a monster. You don't speak to Lady Langham in that way I'm sure?' At his horror-struck expression, she nodded. 'Just as I thought. Now, let's get this thing underway. The sooner we start, the sooner we finish, that's my motto.'

'With respect, my lady, the ball is well underway. All the other guests arrived some time ago.'

'Yes, well, you can blame Clifford for that too. He made such a fuss about which dress I should wear and then there was a row about me driving.' About halfway up the staircase, Eleanor peered over her shoulder and groaned. 'You couldn't grab the back of this infernal frock, could you? It's in such a tangle I can barely move my legs.'

Sandford disentangled the mass of fabric, spreading it out down the staircase. 'Should be fine now, my lady.'

He escorted her into the hallway, which was adorned with huge bowls of white lilies and gardenias. As they walked past the sweeping double staircases, the sounds of a chamber orchestra wafted along the scented air.

Arriving at the ballroom, Eleanor gasped. The oval room rose to the height of two floors, the walls a rich cream. Gold plaster reliefs decorated each of the arched doorways before scrolling up to the ceiling. Between each of the doors a sculpture was displayed in a deep alcove outlined by more gold carving of swirling branches and leaves. Crystal chandeliers dotted the domed ceiling. On the floor, veiled ladies in a rainbow of colours chatted with masked gentlemen in black to the sounds of the orchestra. She went to step forward.

'My lady, perhaps you will be good enough to permit me to announce you?'

'Oh, yes, of course.' Eleanor had been brought up abroad by bohemian parents and despite attending a strict girls' boarding school after their disappearance, she had never mastered social etiquette.

Sandford gestured to the leader of the small orchestra who indicated to the musicians to play sotto voce. The room quietened as all heads turned her way.

'Lady Eleanor Swift of Henley Hall.' Sandford nodded to the leader and the music resumed full volume.

A tall lady in her fifties with tight, greying curls and deep-blue eyes glided across the marbled floor with arms outstretched. 'My dear Eleanor, there you are, you poor lamb! Whatever happened?'

'Good evening, Lady Fenwick-Langham,' Eleanor said. 'Um, nothing terrible happened that I'm aware of.'

'But you're the last to arrive by quarter of an hour. We've held over starting the dancing so you could be announced. And do call me Augusta, dear.'

'Ah! Yes, do forgive me on both accounts.' Eleanor looked around for a change of subject. 'What… what an exquisite setting.'

Her host's frown dissolved instantly. 'Oh, do you like it? It is wonderful to see it filled with swirling gowns and black ties. I keep saying to Harold that we should do this more often.'

At the sound of his name Lord Fenwick-Langham bowled over. 'Eleanor, my dear, how are you?'

'Very well, thank you, er, Harold.' Although she loved them both, Eleanor felt more comfortable around this old coot, with his informal ways, than his high-society wife with her airs and graces.

'Still in one piece and not too many scorch marks on your pretty frock.' He turned and patted his wife's arm. 'Well done, my love.'

'Whatever are you waffling about, Harold?'

'Nothing, flower of my life. Just congratulating you on not giving Eleanor too much of a roasting for being so unforgivably tardy, eh?'

He clicked his fingers at a footman and grabbed three flutes of champagne. Passing one to Eleanor he whispered, 'Have some bubbles, it will make everything run so much more smoothly.'

Eleanor suppressed her giggles and took the offered glass. 'You know, it must be such a task arranging an event like this.'

Lady Langham's eyebrows shot up to meet her hairline. 'Well, strictly between you and me, my dear, I've had the most awful nightmare trying to pull this show off. You wouldn't believe the list of disasters I've averted since four o'clock this afternoon.'

Lord Langham nodded. 'Isn't she the most marvellous duck?'

Eleanor struggled to know where to look. 'Forgive me, "duck", Harold?'

'Yes. Serene, perfectly poised on the surface. But below the dress, she's paddling like billy-oh! That's why her skirt is so simply enormous!' He roared with laughter at his joke and plopped an arm round his wife's shoulders.

To Eleanor's relief, Lady Langham tutted good-humouredly and patted her husband's portly stomach. 'Do go and find Lancelot, dear. Tell him Eleanor's arrived… finally.'

'Good plan, Augusta, old fruit. Boy's been skulking in and out for the best part of an hour pretending he's not looking for you, Eleanor, my dear.' Before he could set off in search of Lancelot, he caught sight of Colonel Puddifoot-Barton. 'Pudders! Your glass is empty, man, shame on you! Still, best lay off the champagne. At your age, too many bubbles will be the death of you. Let's get you a brandy…'

The elderly, balding colonel saluted him and, catching Eleanor's eye, pursed his lips and nodded stiffly from a distance.

She returned the less than cordial greeting and turned back to Lady Langham, who took her arm.

'Don't worry about the colonel, my dear. He's simply had military drills coursing through his veins for forty years and no good lady wife to soften him up. Harold really is most fond of him… for some reason. Oh, look there's Viscount and Viscountess Littleton. You remember them, of course?'

'Of course,' Eleanor said more enthusiastically than she felt, they being the couple she had slated to Clifford as the henpecked husband and his rude, fashion-obsessed American wife.

'Lady Swift, if indeed it is you under your mask.' Viscount Littleton strode up and took her hand.

Viscountess Littleton trailed behind her husband. 'Cuthbert, you chowderhead, you can't say that to everyone. Your joke's flatter than a tyre nailed to a wall.' Mangling most words to end in 'uh' or 'aw', her Bostonian accent caused Lady Fenwick-Langham to stiffen.

Eleanor laughed. 'It seems I'll have to wear more than a mask to disguise myself, Viscount Littleton. Maybe I should have come in full costume?'

At this moment, Lady Langham caught the frantic eye of a servant and jumped into martyr mode. 'I do apologise. It seems I need to save us from another crisis. Must dash.'

Left with the viscount and viscountess, Eleanor tried to make polite conversation. 'How are you both?'

'All fine, quite marvellous,' the Viscount said. 'Delia's patience is perhaps a little blunter than when we last met and her allergy of all things countryside has escalated I fear, poor thing, but otherwise quite alright.'

He winced at the slap to his arm.

'Ignore Cuthbert, Lady Swift. He really was a fine catch in every regard except his manners,' his wife said.

Eleanor peered round the room, desperate for a lifeline. 'Would you excuse me for just a moment, I need to… say hello to the colonel. He'll think me frightfully off if I don't.'

Viscountess Littleton sniffed. 'That old goat thinks everything and everyone is off. Do you know I have never actually seen him smile?'

'Delia, please!' Her husband shook his head.

'What? He's like soured halibut. Stiff as a corpse.'

At that moment the colonel himself appeared. Lord Langham followed, humming loudly while balancing two generously filled glasses of brandy. The colonel was scowling.

'Disgraceful, this country is in significant trouble. Men mincing about in costumes and feathers. How's that going to look when the Boche gets up to his old tricks again?'

Feathers? Maybe that's Lancelot! She wondered about asking the colonel where he saw the feathered guest, but changed her mind. If she told him she was looking for Lancelot, the whole world would know by the end of the next dance.

Lord Langham chuckled. 'Used to be worse, old boy. What about that Regency mob? All that dandifying themselves with face paint and high heels... What do you think, Sandford?'

Eleanor started. The Langham's butler had the art all butlers seemed to have of materialising exactly when they were required and appearing as if they'd been there all along.

Lord Langham continued. 'You butlers, after all, are the arbitrators of fashion downstairs, what?' He chuckled as he took a large swig from one of the glasses and then spluttered as most of it came out of his nose.

Lady Langham appeared at his side, looking flustered. 'What are you all doing skulking around here, Harold? Sandford?'

Lord Langham waved his glass. 'Let the man reply, Augusta. We're having a most diverting conversation about male fashion. Sandford is about to enlighten us.'

Sandford cleared his throat. 'Well, with respect, my lord, as you have asked, I believe that those in the Regency period were in fact trying to simplify and refine men's fashion after the excesses of the Macaronis.'

'The confounded Maca-whats?' Lord Langham stuttered. 'That's a type of pasta, what?'

'Macaronis, my lord. A group of gentlemen who frequented the streets of Mayfair in four-inch scarlet heels, sporting two-foot wigs, multiple diamonds and such accessories as muffs and fans.'

'Hear, hear!' cried the colonel. He turned a disapproving rheumatic eye on Sandford and then back to Eleanor. 'Can't stand such prissy affectation, ponsing about in decorations like that.'

'How does one reconcile that with military costumes and decorations, Colonel?' Eleanor asked. 'Ostrich plumed helmets and such?'

The colonel snorted. 'Completely different!'

Lady Langham gestured vehemently behind the colonel's back for her husband to remove his old pal to a far corner of the ballroom.

'Good evening, by the way, Colonel.' Eleanor smiled sweetly. 'I do believe we forgot to greet each other properly.'

'Harrumph! Evening.'

Lord Langham swung the colonel around and shoved him forward with a loud, 'Oh spiffing, look there's Barty and his new wife. Smile, Pudders, it's a party, old boy.'

Eleanor took her chance. 'I say, Sandford, do you by any chance know where Lance… young Lord Fenwick-Langham is?' Lancelot was the only son of Lord and Lady Langham. Even though he wouldn't inherit the title until after his father's death, as was customary he had the cursory title of 'Lord'.

Sandford looked down at his gloves. 'Young Master Lancelot retired to the garden, along with Lady Coco and Lady Millicent Childs, Mr Seaton, Mr Singh and Mr Appleby. It may, however, be a little difficult to recognise him, my lady. Like a few of the other guests, he has come in full costume.'

'Typical Lancelot, but that should make him all the easier to spot.'

'Indeed, although several other guests have taken the same approach and attired themselves in the same full regalia, as it were.'

'Golly! Good job they're not women, that would be a disgraceful faux pas. What sort of costume is it?'

'I believe it is some sort of pirate. The most prominent feature being a cutlass. And strangely, feathers.'

Ah, feathers, Ellie!

'Now, shall we?' Lady Langham gestured at the ballroom. 'There are your old acquaintances, the Dowager Countess of Goldsworthy and her niece, the delightful Cora Wynne. Let's go say hello and then I have some other guests to introduce you to.'

Eleanor followed her hostess, looking out for one particular young gentleman. One adorned with feathers and brandishing a cutlass.

CHAPTER 3

Outside, the threatened rain had arrived. Big, fat drops fell lazily onto the ballroom's rows of floor-to-ceiling windows. Inside, the music swirled, the dancers whirled and Eleanor's eyes blurred with the myriad faces Lady Langham passed in front of her. But then, in working round the room, her hostess stopped at a group of young people, several of whom were in full costume. 'And these are Lancelot's… friends from Oxford. Good evening, everyone, enjoying yourselves?' Lady Langham forced a smile.

'Rather!' a Harlequin said.

'Absolutely spiffing,' an elegant Cleopatra replied.

'It's simply sublime, *so* kind of you to invite us,' an exotic bird of paradise cooed as she stroked her headdress.

'Yes, thank you, Lady Fenwick-Langham. I'm quite inspired by the colours of this spectacle to write a poem.' This came from a homespun costume to the bird of paradise's left.

Lady Langham smiled weakly. 'Everyone, this is Lady Eleanor Swift.'

A wave of hands met the introduction.

'Oh, we've heard about you, of course.' Cleopatra stepped forward. She laughed in a manner that Eleanor wasn't sure was good-natured.

'Sis, don't be mean!' the bird of paradise hissed.

Lady Langham patted Eleanor's arm. 'I'll return for you in a moment, dear. Duty calls.'

As Lady Langham vanished into the crowd, Eleanor was left feeling conspicuous. Lancelot had obviously told his friends about her, but what had he said?

'Speaking of making an entrance,' she said, which nobody had been, 'have you seen Lancelot? I rather expected him to come roaring through in his plane or balancing on the rear wheel of his motorbike.'

The Harlequin nodded. 'Oh, that would be so typical of Lance. Always up for a caper. By the way, I'm Johnny, Cleopatra here is Millie and the exquisite bird of paradise is Coco, her sister.'

Eleanor smiled at them.

'Oh dash, sorry, Albie old chum.' Johnny nodded at the unintroduced member of the group. 'And this is Albie, or Albert if you catch him in a particularly poetic mood. We've got a wager on what exactly he's come as.'

Millie leant against the wall and folded her arms. 'I had him pegged as a vagabond.'

'Millie!' her sister hissed. 'Why do you have to pack your claws every time? Albie, I told you I think you look great. I guess you've come as a cleric of some sort?'

Johnny shook his head. 'Honestly, Albie, it beats me. I've plumped for Lord Mayor of London… whilst at the barbers, munching on a snack.' He pointed to the apple hanging from Albert's wrist.

Eleanor had to stifle her giggles.

'Philistine!' Albert said. 'Actually, I'm Raphael's *Young Man with an Apple*.'

'I think it's brilliant! Very original,' Eleanor said.

Millie slapped him on the back. 'Brilliantly stupid, Albie, but don't worry about it. No one else has noticed.'

Eleanor turned back to Coco. 'Did you all come over from Oxford tonight?'

Coco nodded. 'Yes, although you just missed Lucas, the last of our number. He had to leave a few moments ago.'

Millie leaned forward. 'It's *Prince* Lucas, actually.'

'Leave it alone, Millie,' Johnny said. 'What's the point of him being in good old Blighty if he's still shackled by all the expectations of his title? He prefers plain "Lucas Singh".' He smiled at Eleanor. 'And how do you prefer to be addressed?'

She laughed. 'Just plain Eleanor is fine.'

'Plain indeed,' Millie muttered.

Coco slapped her sister's arm. 'Stop it!'

Millie yawned affectedly. 'Yes, I never got a dance with him because old Lady Fenwick-Langham wouldn't let anyone start until you had finally arrived.'

Coco moved her mask and glared at her sister.

Eleanor decided to ignore Millie. 'Oh, so I won't meet Lucas then?'

Millie waved at a servant and took another flute of champagne. 'No. What a shame. He particularly wanted to meet you.'

'Meet me?'

Millie downed her champagne without replying.

Bored of Millie's sniping, Eleanor glanced round and caught sight of a pirate, replete with cutlass, winding his way through the revellers.

'Excuse me a moment, won't you?' She gathered up her skirt and hurried after her quarry, but by the time she'd reached the other side of the ballroom, he'd vanished. She spent the next few minutes hunting everywhere. As she was about to give up, she spun round, forgetting about the train on her gown, and fell flat on her face.

'Oh, bother!' she said to the polished marble flooring.

Lord Langham, who was waltzing past, stopped and bent to help her up. 'Nice work, old girl. You've obviously got stuck in on the champagne. That's the spirit!'

Viscount Littleton hurried up. 'Are you alright, Lady Swift?' He kept a firm grip on her elbow as she stood up. His wife appeared, her face betraying her horror at such a public embarrassment.

The dowager countess then appeared with Cora in tow. Cora, eyes wide, echoed the Viscount's concern. 'Are you alright, Lady Swift?'

Eleanor smiled at the ring of concerned, and not so concerned, faces. 'Oh gracious, I'm really quite alright. Just a little bruised dignity, no harm done.'

The men laughed and discreetly rolled their eyes.

She brushed down her dress and thanked Viscount Littleton for retrieving her headband. She placed it back on her head and straightened up. Eleanor saw Sandford watching from the side of the hall. He caught her eye and moved across the floor to meet her. 'Do you require a poultice, my lady? I shall call on Cook immediately.'

Eleanor shook her head. 'No, really, I'm fine, thank you. Unless Cook has a cure for mortifying embarrassment?'

'I fear not, my lady.'

Lady Langham appeared and took her arm. 'Now, my dear, I came to check you weren't in tears?'

'Tears? Thank you, but why would I be in tears?'

'Well, you fell.'

'Oh that, it was nothing.'

'Nothing!' Lady Langham bent towards her and whispered, 'My dear girl, the *whole* party saw you fall!'

'Yes, well, not my finest moment, I agree.'

'Mortifyingly embarrassing, I'd say.'

Eleanor wondered if Lady Langham was referring to her own feelings. It was then she became aware that the music had stopped and the entire ballroom was staring at her. She coughed and announced to the onlookers, 'It's called a Parisian pancake. Really, all the ladies are doing it.'

*

She told her hostess that she needed to fix her make-up, and made her escape. A movement caught her eye. A pair of striped trousers replete with cutlass was disappearing round the sweeping bend of the side stairs. She smiled. She'd have to tell Lancelot tight trousers really didn't flatter his legs. He'd be devastated.

With her skirt held high, she skipped up the remaining stairs realising she had no plan when, and if, she did catch Lancelot. *Oh well, Ellie, you can't make any more of a fool of yourself tonight than you already have.*

At the top step, she paused and looked left and right. 'Dash it!' No striped trousers. No cutlass. No tousled blond hair and blue-grey eyes. Randomly she turned right and started down the corridor.

A few minutes later and she had to admit she was lost. The place was a labyrinth compared to Henley Hall. How did the servants ever find their way around? She imagined being found weeks later in a far-off wing of the house, living off dead flies and brackish radiator water.

A small crash further down the hallway made her jump. She tiptoed forward, listening intently. A sharp cry rang out, 'Oh bally heck, no!'

Was that Lancelot?

Pushing open the panelled oak door to her right, she saw the pirate she had followed up the stairs. He was hunched over someone lying at a peculiar angle on the floor of what appeared to be a study. Eleanor just had time to take in the walls covered in books.

'Lancelot?'

The figure turned round, a large silver candlestick in his right hand.

'Sherlock, what the hell are you doing here? You should leave. Now!' The masked man spoke in an urgent whisper.

'But what...? Who...?' She started as she recognised the crumpled figure at the pirate's feet.

The double doors at the far end burst open, the handles smacking against the wood panelling. They both spun round and froze as half a dozen policemen ran in and surrounded them. A broad-shouldered man then strode in, accompanied by two more policemen.

Eleanor gasped. 'Inspector! What are you doing here?'

'Lady Swift!' For a moment they stood staring at each other. Then he looked across at the masked man. 'Stand aside, please.'

He turned to the two policemen on his left. 'Cuff him, Brice. Peters, check the casualty.'

Once Lancelot was handcuffed, Detective Chief Inspector Seldon stepped forward and pulled the mask off the man's face.

'You!'

Unmasked, Lancelot stared coolly at DCI Seldon.

Eleanor's mind was racing. 'Inspector? Lancelot? What...?'

DCI Seldon walked around Eleanor to the far wall. Mounted in the wall was a safe, its door wide open. Up to that moment, Eleanor hadn't noticed it. DCI Seldon looked inside. 'Empty!' He turned back to Lancelot. 'Lord Fenwick-Langham, you are under arrest for the theft of Lady Fenwick-Langham's necklace and on suspicion of being responsible for a series of related burglaries.'

Eleanor felt as if she was in a bad dream.

'Now wait a bally moment,' Lancelot finally spoke. 'I'm being arrested for stealing my own mother's necklace? That's rich!'

The policeman Seldon had referred to as Peters stood up looking ashen. He nodded at the crumpled figure on the floor. 'He's... dead, sir.'

Everyone looked at the body. Seldon kneeled and checked for himself. Standing up he turned his gaze on Lancelot.

'I am also arresting you for murder. You will be read your rights before a judicial officer down at the police station. Brice, take Lord Fenwick-Langham out the back way to save the hosts' embarrassment.'

Lancelot stared coolly at the inspector. 'The hosts, as you put it, are my parents. They aren't going to be terribly impressed that you've arrested not only the wrong man, but their son in his own house. This isn't going to look good your end.'

DCI Seldon held his gaze. 'From where I'm standing, your lordship, it's *your* position that doesn't look good. Caught at the scene of a theft and a murder. And' – he indicated the candlestick – 'holding the murder weapon, I warrant. You are advised to remain silent until you have representation present. Take him away, Brice.'

Eleanor's brain whirled. 'But, Inspector, you can't think—'

'Lady Swift, please don't leave. I will need a full statement from you.' He nodded at another uniformed officer who stepped over beside her.

Lancelot drew level with her as he was led out by the constable and whispered, 'Play it cool, Sherlock, you know what these uniformed johnnies are like. You've beaten them to the punch once already. But it wasn't me, I swear to you.'

As Brice pushed Lancelot through the door, Eleanor made to go after them. DCI Seldon clicked his fingers at a young officer and gestured towards Eleanor. The policeman blocked her way.

She swung round to face the inspector, green eyes blazing.

Out in the corridor, there was a loud commotion. 'Open this door immediately or Harold will thrash the buttons from your uniform, you idiot!'

'Who told the Fenwick-Langhams before I did?' Seldon growled. He strode to the door just as it burst open.

Lord Langham charged into the room and confronted the inspector. 'What the hell have you done, man? I will have your superintendent—' He froze on seeing the body crumpled against the far wall.

'Pudders!'

Lady Langham appeared at her husband's side. 'Colonel Puddifoot-Barton?'

'Constable!'

Before the officer could reach her, Lady Langham had slid to the floor in a faint.

CHAPTER 4

'Do you think I'll need to wait much longer?' Eleanor had to raise her voice to be heard above the rain now pelting against the windows.

The nervous young policeman who had escorted her to the library shrugged apologetically.

'Couldn't say, m'lady.'

'Is Inspector Seldon staying here or returning to Oxford?'

'Chief Inspector, m'lady. And I couldn't say.'

'Will Lance— Lord Fenwick-Langham be permitted visitors this evening?'

'I couldn't say, m'lady.'

Hopeless! What was keeping the inspector? They had first met only a few days after Eleanor had arrived at Little Buckford to inherit her uncle's estate. She had reported seeing a murder, but as the body had disappeared, the inspector had refused to investigate further. By the time the case was solved, however, the gruff inspector had become a firm ally.

Eleanor groaned. She wanted it to be over. For Lancelot to be released and for him to be back at Langham Manor. Even for the colonel to be alive and his usual unpleasant self. Her stomach rumbled. Champagne and dead bodies weren't the happiest of bedfellows. The smell of musty leather-bound books and over-polished wood wasn't helping either.

Voices came from outside the door. 'Make sure no one leaves.'

A muttered response eluded Eleanor's ears.

'Just do it, man!' DCI Seldon called over his shoulder as he entered the room. He offered Eleanor a thin smile as he stepped across to the table where she waited, drumming her fingers. He nodded at the uniformed officer who nodded back and left the room. Pulling out a chair, he sat, folding his long legs awkwardly.

'Lady Swift.'

'Inspector.'

He took a deep breath. 'I am sorry to detain you. I wish we were meeting under different circumstances.'

'So do I. I hope this awful misunderstanding can be cleared up quickly.'

'Misunderstanding?'

'Don't play coy, Inspector, please. You can't possibly think Lancelot stole Lady Langham's jewels. She's his mother, for goodness' sake. Why would he steal her jewels?'

He held up his hand and consulted his notebook. 'The accused was discovered standing by the open safe which, on inspection by myself, was found to be empty.' He looked up at her.

'That's as may be, but we can't be sure the jewels were even in the safe. The real thief could easily—'

The inspector held up his hand again and read from his notes. 'I verified the presence of the necklace in question at precisely seven forty-five.' He flipped the front of the notebook back and forth with his thumb. 'And given that the safe wasn't blown and the short timescale between my verifying the presence of the jewels and my men entering when they heard voices, whoever stole those jewels, in my professional opinion, knew the code.'

As she had no answer, she switched tack. 'And it's inconceivable that… that he killed the colonel. The poor man was a close friend of Lancelot's family. What possible reason would he have? Be realistic, Lancelot's a clown, not a killer. He hasn't the wherewithal, or the malice, to do something so terrible.' Eleanor's face flushed. 'And why were your men there? Why were they, or you, even at the ball? If I didn't know better, I'd say this reeks of a police set-up!'

DCI Seldon stiffened. 'I am acutely aware of how you feel about authority in general, Lady Swift, especially the police, but—'

She cut him off. 'Hardly surprising, given that they were covering up a murder and wholesale corruption last time I dealt with them.'

'Indeed.' The inspector ran his hand over the back of his neck. 'But this isn't the same department. These are *my* men. This is my investigation and I am in charge, Lady Swift. I hardly need to remind you that this is a murder investigation not a grudge match with authority.'

She had the good grace to look embarrassed. Last time she had met the inspector, she'd practically accused him of being involved in a police cover-up. 'Quite so. I am sorry, Inspector, I wasn't suggesting you were… I mean, I am still very grateful for your help in catching the killer from the quarry. But perhaps not showing it very well,' she ended, with another flush to her cheeks.

He nodded. 'I understand, it has been quite a night for you.' He spun his pen. 'By the way, no need to be grateful for that… all part of the job, you know. Although, well, it was a genuine pleasure to do so.'

He held her gaze for a moment and then returned to his notes. For the first time since the terrible events of that evening, she felt herself relax a little.

DCI Seldon coughed. 'Where were we? Yes, we've established no underhand police activities were conducted this evening.' He glanced at Eleanor. 'And that the facts of the case are that the accused was found hunched over the deceased, Colonel Puddifoot-Barton, holding a silver candlestick.'

Eleanor felt the tension flood back through her body. 'Has it been proven that the candlestick was indeed the murder weapon, Inspector?'

'Not yet. The lab chaps have to analyse it but there was a substantial amount of blood and some matted hair on the top and along the side. I'm quite certain it will match that of the deceased.'

Eleanor desperately tried to think of anything else that might throw doubt on Lancelot's guilt. 'Okay, but the colonel could already have been dead, couldn't he?'

'When the deceased was examined, his wristwatch was found to be broken. The glass had been smashed. Fragments were found on the edge of the fireplace. I therefore deduce the colonel was hit on the back of the head by a heavy object, I presume, at the moment, the candlestick. He then fell forward, his watch hitting the edge of the fireplace. The impact broke the glass and mechanism. The time recorded on the watch was eight twenty-three. My men entered the room at exactly eight twenty-five. So there's no way anyone entered the room between the time of the colonel's death and my men arriving. Except…'

She groaned and covered her face with her hands. 'Except me.'

DCI Seldon turned back to his infernal notebook. She wanted to grab it from his hand and toss it in the fire.

'What has Lancelot said? Surely he can explain everything.'

'Young Lord Fenwick-Langham refuses to do anything except repeat his original statement.' He turned over a couple of pages in the notebook. 'To quote: "I came into the room and saw the colonel lying on the floor. I knelt down to see if I could help and noticed the candlestick by his side. I heard a noise and thought the killer was returning, so I picked the candlestick up to defend myself. Then I heard the door open and Lady Swift came in, followed by you lot."' The inspector looked up. 'He means the police. And he swears he didn't know the candlestick had been used to murder the colonel.'

'But what did he say about why he was upstairs?'

'He has not given a clear explanation. He merely said that it is his house and why shouldn't he be anywhere that he damn well pleased?' DCI Seldon tapped his pen on the notebook. 'Excuse the language.'

'Not at all. I'm surprised his language wasn't more colourful, given the gravity of his situation.' She rubbed her eyes. 'The stupid fool. Does he think this is a game?'

DCI Seldon cleared his throat. 'Lady Swift, I need to ask you what you were doing upstairs.' A muscle twitched in his jaw as he waited for her response.

She frowned. 'I was looking for Lancelot.'

'Why were you looking for him, Lady Swift?' There was that twitch again.

She leaned forward, her elbows on the table. 'Because, Inspector, I was a little overwhelmed by meeting so many new people. I wanted to see a... familiar face.'

'Familiar face,' DCI Seldon repeated as his pen scratched across the paper. He glanced up at her. 'Please continue, Lady Swift.'

'Well, I had taken a small... tumble on the dance floor and was just going to fix my make-up when I spotted him disappearing up the side stairs.'

DCI Seldon looked at her strangely. 'Yes, I am well aware of your small "tumble", as was everyone else, including my men.' He looked back down at his notebook. 'So, you followed him upstairs?'

'Yes, as I said, I followed him up the stairs.'

'And what did he do?'

'Honestly, I don't know. When I got to the landing, he'd disappeared.'

DCI Seldon stroked his jaw. 'Did he know you were following him?'

'No, he was quite a way ahead of me.'

'You didn't call out to him, then?'

'Inspector, I appreciate you refraining from remarking on my unladylike behaviour in following him in the first place, but was I really likely to bellow his name out? I was trying to be discreet.'

The corners of Seldon's lips curled upwards. 'Being discreet,' he mumbled as he wrote. 'So whilst discreetly creeping around the upstairs, you…?'

'Wandered around for a few minutes, if I'm honest.' She studied the tabletop. 'I can understand how this sounds, Inspector, but I had the idea and just ran with it. All that doing the right thing at the right time doesn't come naturally to me, you know.'

'Yes.' He stared at the paper. 'I do know.'

She tried to gauge this response. Was he laughing at her? *Oh, this was all so ludicrous!* 'Yes, well, anyway I wandered around and then heard a noise coming from *that* room so I went in.'

'Without knocking?'

She stiffened. 'Inspector, are you making fun of me?'

He looked up. 'I'm just establishing the facts of the case. If you had knocked, the accused would have had time to react.'

She tugged at the yards of fabric swaddling her legs. 'I-I'm sorry, I'm a little on edge. Yes, without knocking. I wish that I had knocked.'

DCI Seldon leaned forward. 'Lady Swift, it is my duty to remind you, again, that this is a murder investigation and that your statement will be the most pertinent in the case. You may wish to stick to the facts.'

Eleanor was tired and confused. With every word of her statement she seemed to be incriminating Lancelot even further.

DCI Seldon cleared his throat. 'If you would like to continue from "heard a noise coming from that room so I went in"?'

'So I went in…' Her chest tightened, pulling the air from her lungs.

'And saw?' DCI Seldon coaxed.

She pursed her lips. 'And saw Lancelot crouched over… a body that was lying on the floor.'

'And was the accused holding anything?'

She nodded slowly. 'Yes, a candlestick.'

She sat up as the detective's notebook snapped shut.

'Thank you, Lady Swift. You are free to go but we will obviously need you to call in at Chipstone Police Station and sign your statement within the next day or so. I will also need to talk with you again once we have corroborated your story.'

She frowned. 'Corroborated my story?'

He pushed his chair back and stood up. 'Lady Swift, you were found in the room with the accused. Lady Fenwick-Langham's jewels were missing and there was a dead body! You are as close to a suspect in this affair as that blasted young Lord Fenwick-Langham.'

Eleanor gasped. 'You can't be serious!'

The inspector held her stare. 'As I said at the beginning, I wish we were meeting under different circumstances.' He opened the door.

'But this is preposterous!'

He spun round. 'For goodness' sake, you and the accused were the only people in the room. Alone, damn it! As the detective in this case, I have to consider the possibility that either you were working together, you are protecting him or...' He looked into her eyes. 'He is protecting you.'

CHAPTER 5

'Mrs Trotman's sent me in with your favourites, my lady, fresh from the griddle.' Mrs Butters made space on the breakfast table for the covered plate she held. 'Master Gladstone seems to think as they're for him, mind. Followed me all the way from the kitchen.' She gave the bulldog a gentle look of reproach as he leaned on Eleanor's leg, breathing heavily and waiting expectantly.

Eleanor brightened as she lifted the cover. 'Mrs Trotman's famous crumpets! Just what's needed. I shall pop down and thank her as soon as I have eaten the lot.'

The housekeeper smiled and pushed the mustard and jam closer to Eleanor.

'Look at that! It's supposed to be summer.' Eleanor gestured with a half-buttered crumpet to the morning room's French windows that normally gave a wonderful view of the formal lawns and colourful herb borders. But the rain of the night before had died out to be replaced by a blanket of grey, oppressive fog. 'Mrs Trotman couldn't have timed a welcome plate of comfort food any better. What do you say, Clifford?'

Clifford straightened his cuffs. 'I should think that finishing a full complement of crumpets would see one in a flour-and-sugar-induced coma, my lady.'

'Tosh, I'll rise to the challenge. Half with egg and gammon, and half with Mrs Trotman's fine home-made jam. Besides, a hearty breakfast is essential to aid concentration.' She reached for another crumpet. 'It would be entirely ungrateful of me to let them go stale after all her efforts.' She looked down at Gladstone and tickled his chin. 'Don't think that means you can share them, greedy old chum.' His eyes implored her to think again.

Mrs Butters stifled a giggle and pulled a fresh serviette from her apron pocket.

Clifford stepped to Eleanor's side. 'Would you care for more coffee to accompany your substantial breakfast?'

Eleanor nodded as she swallowed another mouthful, savouring the salty butter contrasting with the sweetened damsons. 'Yes, indeed.'

Mrs Butters took the coffee pot. 'I'll bring a fresh pot, Mr Clifford. I'm sure you and the mistress have plenty to discuss this morning.' She threw Eleanor a sympathetic smile before leaving them alone.

'So, a busy day for us then, if not an easy one.' Eleanor ignored the proffered tongs as she helped herself from the silver egg decanter Clifford held for her. 'Yikes, they're super hot!' She dropped the boiled egg into her cup at an angle. Clifford set it upright with the tongs. 'Oh, and Clifford, thank you again for appearing so promptly at Langham Manor to collect me yesterday. Very timely. I was positively itching to leave.'

'You have Mr Sandford to thank. He telephoned me when Detective Chief Inspector Seldon started interviewing you.'

'Yes, gosh that was a horribly awkward business.'

'Being involved in a murder investigation tends to be a trifle… unsettling.'

She eyed him over her coffee cup. 'I meant it was awkward with the inspector. He was, well, odd, most odd. Honestly, it's like he'd already decided that Lancelot was guilty.'

Clifford cocked an eyebrow.

'Seriously, I have a suspicion the inspector is struggling to balance his professionalism in this case. It's as though he disliked Lancelot for some reason.'

Clifford cleared his throat. 'Indeed, it is hard to be objective when one is emotionally caught up in a case.'

Eleanor paused in adding a gammon ring to her crumpet. 'What do you mean, "emotionally caught up in a case"?'

Mrs Butters broke the awkward silence by arriving with the fresh coffee pot. Sensing something was hanging in the air, she set it down without a word. The door closed behind her. Gladstone let out a quiet grumble at the lack of crumpet and dropped into an ungainly sprawl on the floor.

Eleanor stared at her butler. 'Clifford, please don't dance around the maypole on this. What were you insinuating?'

'If I might offer a contrary opinion, my lady, I was not insinuating, it was a statement of fact. The inspector has a challenging task in meeting the demands of two powerful forces pulling him in opposite directions.'

'Riddles, all riddles! Be clear, man! What forces?'

Clifford poured her a cup of coffee and set the pot down on its mat.

'In my experience, Detective Chief Inspector Seldon has always been a very dedicated officer. But, beneath the policeman and the commitment to justice, lies a man.'

Eleanor stared at the tablecloth puzzled. Then it dawned. 'Are you suggesting that... that he likes me?'

'I suspect more than likes, my lady.' Clifford straightened his collar and stood silently.

Eleanor vigorously stirred several lumps of sugar into her coffee. 'No, no, no! Don't you see? This is a disaster.' Her cheeks coloured. 'How on earth is he going to see justice done for the colonel if his brain is clogged up thinking about... well, anything else?'

'I think the problem is larger still, my lady, given the circumstances in which the chief inspector found young Lord Fenwick-Langham. The accused was not alone at the scene of the crime, I understand?'

'No, the inspector basically said I'm as much a suspect as Lancelot. Something about us being in it together or that I'm protecting him.'

Clifford nodded. 'As I suspected, which means…'

Eleanor groaned. 'Which means I have to clear Lancelot's name to clear my own.' She turned her fork in her hands. 'The thing is… I found Lancelot standing over the poor colonel… with the apparent murder weapon. I don't know what I would do if he was found…'

Clifford tidied the condiments on the table, lining up the jam, mustard, breakfast relish, salt and pepper in a neat row. 'Guilty, my lady?'

Eleanor buried her head in her hands. 'You know the worst part of it all? I felt that every time I answered one of the inspector's questions, I was hammering another nail into Lancelot's coffin.'

'You had no choice, my lady. You had to tell the truth.'

She looked up. 'I know, but Lancelot isn't a killer. He didn't, wouldn't, couldn't… kill.'

Clifford straightened his shoulders. 'Forgive the directness of my question, my lady, but how can you be sure?'

'Because it's Lancelot we're talking about! Come on, Clifford, you've seen him grow up. Ask Sandford, he's terribly fond of Lancelot. Do you think he would have any doubts about Young Master Lancelot's innocence? Of course he wouldn't.' She stared at her knife.

'My lady, I share your thoughts about the accused. In my experience—'

'Do you mind if we don't refer to him as "the accused"? It has a horrible, sort of, well, finality to it.'

'My apologies. It is also my experience that young Lord Fenwick-Langham is not of the disposition to commit such a heinous act as that of taking a man's life. But' – lines furrowed his brow – 'even if you and I signed affidavits to that effect, it isn't going to sway a jury. We need some evidence.'

Eleanor hung her head. 'I realise that,' she murmured. 'Oh, why did he get himself into such a situation, the monstrous fool!' She slammed her spoon onto the crown of her soft-boiled egg with the last word, imagining Lancelot's infuriating face grinning up at her as the shell smashed.

Clifford dabbed a serviette over the tablecloth to remove the worst of the splashed yolk.

'Sorry, Clifford. I'm not quite myself this morning.'

'Normally you do manage to contain your breakfast mostly on your plate, my lady.'

She appreciated his attempt to make light of her outburst. 'Clifford, can I talk to you?'

'I rather imagined we had been conversing for nigh on half an hour.'

'I mean really talk to you. I've only got you to confide in. And Gladstone, of course, but he's absolutely hopeless. All that turning his head to the side and pretending he's listening when all he's really doing is wondering if I said "biscuit".' Gladstone shot up at this and dropped his comforting, if rather heavy, head in her lap.

The corners of Clifford's mouth turned up perceptibly. 'I appreciate the compliment that I am the preferable choice for a confidant over an elderly, greedy bulldog.'

'You know what I mean. Your natural aptitude for logic and reason is what Lancelot needs. I've already made things so much worse.' She slumped back against her chair.

'It is my belief, my lady, that one cannot make things worse by telling the truth. If, that is, it is a situation where the truth should be told, which I devoutly believe this is. Your statement to the chief inspector was accurate and true, was it not?'

Eleanor nodded glumly.

'Then you have done young Lord Fenwick-Langham the best service possible in, what I admit, is a perilous situation for him. You have presented one of the country's finest investigative minds with the facts as you know them.'

'But all the facts point to Lancelot being... guilty.'

'This is true.'

'And the inspector doesn't like Lancelot because... oh, dash it! Because he thinks I like Lancelot and the inspector likes me, according to you.'

'This is also true.'

'Then please explain how you see any hope for Lancelot when I've basically stood on a dais and pointed him out as the murderer.' She held her hands up in despair. 'And when it seems the inspector is dying to get him out of the way.'

'One does not have all the answers immediately.'

'Come on, Clifford. We both know the real killer is currently walking free and we made a great team over that dratted murder in the quarry case.'

Clifford coughed pointedly. 'After, that is, you'd stopped accusing me of trying to kill you.'

Eleanor waved the objection aside. 'There was a tiny matter of that, yes. But after that, I thought it all went swimmingly well.'

Clifford nodded. 'However, I have a grave concern that we are up against an even bigger hurdle this time.'

'Don't worry, Clifford, I shan't accuse you of trying to murder me again, I promise.' Eleanor paused, frowning. 'Assuming, of course, you don't try and kill me. I know on rare occasions I can be a tad annoying.'

'I shall, my lady, practise the art of self-restraint.' Clifford bowed magnanimously. 'However, I refer us back to the opening of our conversation and the difficulties of being objective when one is emotionally caught up in the case.'

Eleanor closed her eyes and nodded. 'I know, I know. I'm in the same place as the inspector, dash it.'

Clifford poured her another coffee. His voice soft, he continued, 'Nevertheless, I believe young Lord Fenwick-Langham is most fortunate to have such a lady as yourself fighting his corner.'

Eleanor was taken aback. 'How so?'

'I have had ample chance to observe your dogged pursuit of justice, combined with your ceaselessly enquiring and resourceful mind.'

'Thank you.' Eleanor smiled. 'But I think you meant stubbornness?'

'Indeed. And, of course, you like to be proven right.'

'Who doesn't?' She laughed. 'Seriously though, where do we begin?'

'Perhaps the most informative source might be young Lord Fenwick-Langham himself?'

'Good idea! I'll shove some more appropriate togs on.' She looked down at her silk pyjama bottoms and housecoat. 'And we'll go talk the inspector into letting us see Lancelot.' She dropped a quick kiss on the top of Gladstone's head and then jumped up and instantly frowned at the ring of the doorbell.

'Excuse me, my lady, the door,' Clifford said needlessly.

'Well, whoever it is, please send them away sharply, we're too busy for visitors.'

A moment later, as Eleanor was draining her coffee cup, Clifford returned. 'Lord and Lady Fenwick-Langham to see you, my lady.'

CHAPTER 6

A few minutes later, Eleanor entered the drawing room. Lady Langham rose from the Regency striped sofa.

'Eleanor, my dear, we're most dreadfully sorry to call unannounced.'

'Yes, apologies, old girl.' Lord Langham stared at Eleanor's teal silk blouse and silver pleated skirt. 'Dragged you out of your pyjamas by the look of it.'

'Harold!' Lady Langham slapped his hand.

Eleanor smiled. 'It is a delight to see you. How are you holding up?'

'Oh, my dear, it's so awful.' She pulled a flowered, lace handkerchief from her sleeve. 'We haven't slept a wink. And I can't seem to eat the merest morsel.'

Lord Langham took his wife's arm and guided her back onto the sofa. 'Very bad business. Simply don't understand what that Seldon fellow is up to.'

'Er… Clifford, tea!' Eleanor said.

He nodded and stepped from the room, failing to stop Gladstone from shouldering his way in.

Lady Langham dabbed at her nose. 'Eleanor, my dear, we didn't know where else to go. It's such a delicate business and… oh, I am sorry, perhaps we shouldn't have come.'

Lord Langham put his hand in her lap and closed his fingers around hers.

'Yes, we bally well should. Eleanor, old fruit, look, it is dashed awkward, as the old girl has just said, but we need help and you've proved yourself such a resourceful girl.' The couple looked at each other and nodded.

Eleanor looked from one to the other. When she had first arrived at Henley Hall she'd known no one. The Langhams had invited her over to the Manor and treated her as an old friend from the very beginning. Now she wanted to return the favour. *But how?*

A tap at the door heralded Clifford's return with a full china service tea tray. Finger pastries delicately cocooned in lace paper doily cases filled the tiers of the silver stand.

'Thank you, Clifford. Please do continue, Augusta.'

Her guests seemed to hesitate. She glanced at them, and then at Clifford. Of course, her butler was present and they had come to discuss a very personal matter. 'That will be all, Clifford.'

Lord Langham jumped up. 'I say! Perhaps Clifford might stay, what? Might need the both of you, eh? Brains and bravado, so to speak.' He laughed uneasily and sat back down.

'Absolutely!' Eleanor said with relief.

'Oh, Harold!' Lady Langham took his hand in hers. 'Perhaps I should do the talking.' She paused, then seemed to make up her mind. 'Eleanor, we were so impressed with all that you achieved back during that terrible business…'

'Rotten business!' her husband mumbled.

'Yes, well, you and Clifford solved both murders and put the murderer away at great peril to yourselves.' She paused and smiled weakly.

Eleanor nodded at Clifford who set about serving the tea. 'That's very kind of you to say.'

'Well, the thing is. Would you be willing to help us? It's absolute rot that Lance could have killed Pudders, and we're desperate to see justice done for both of them,' said Lord Langham.

'Of course, Clifford and I will be delighted to look into the matter. We're rather a team when it comes to, well, that sort of thing. Please do go on. Rest assured the conversation will not leave this room.'

Clifford offered Lord Langham a second milk jug.

'Top hole, Clifford, much obliged.' He winked at Clifford who poured what looked suspiciously like a large whisky measure into his tea.

'So,' Eleanor said, 'shall we forget any awkwardness about whatever needs to be said? The whole situation is quite wretched, but isn't that what friends are for?'

Lady Langham rose and hugged Eleanor tightly. 'So like your uncle, my dear girl. So like him.'

Clifford passed the cake stand around. Lord Fenwick-Langham reached for one, hesitated, and then took two.

'I say, Eleanor old thing, can you send your marvellous cook up to the Manor to teach ours how to make these simply delicious little beasts?' He took a bite and nudged his wife. 'Launch in, dearest, no point in beetling round the bush.'

Lady Langham stared at her tea. 'It is the most awful thing to happen to the family since… well, I won't bother you with our family tragedies.' She took a deep breath. 'I… fear that we've brought all this catastrophe on Lancelot's shoulders ourselves.'

Eleanor looked from one to the other. 'But how?'

Lady Langham laughed nervously. 'There's no easy way to say it, my dear. Regrettably, we're… in temporary straitened circumstances. You know how it is when a few investments go awry.'

Eleanor nodded even though she had never had any money to invest in anything. Until, that is, she had unexpectedly become lady of the manor, inheriting her uncle's modest fortune.

Lord Langham thumped the armrest, making Gladstone look up from beside Eleanor's feet. 'And then the tax ogre comes banging on the blessed front door demanding his pound of meat. Just when things are already on the wonk money-wise. Bally nuisance, especially when it upsets my good lady wife so.'

His wife smiled fondly at him and took up the story. 'I decided the only answer was to sell my necklace.'

Eleanor caught her breath. *Straitened circumstances indeed!* 'Isn't that the one…?'

Lady Langham nodded slowly, her chin on her chest. 'Yes, the one Harold gave to me on our wedding day.'

Lord Langham's face flushed. 'I feel dreadful that we're in this bally awful position. Poor Augusta shouldn't be troubled by nonsense like this. Couldn't let her send the old sparkles to auction and then have to face the rah-rah set looking down their sniffy noses, gossiping behind our backs. So I told her there was no way we were going to sell it.'

Eleanor waited for one of them to continue. But finding only silence, she spoke first. 'Please do excuse my fluffy brain. I don't quite understand the connection with your unfortunate situation and Lancelot's current predicament?'

Lady Langham accepted another cup of tea from Clifford with a nod. 'Well, that's just the wretched point, you see. We can only imagine he heard us twittering on about what a ridiculous ghastly mess it all is with the finances and… and if we held a ball we might strike lucky, as it were… with a burglar.'

'And not just any burglar. The best!' said Lord Langham. 'You know, that fiendishly brilliant safecracker who's been looting the Home Counties for the past goodness knows how many months.'

Eleanor looked blank.

'Oh, come on, old fruit, you can't play the new girl in town over this. Even you must have heard about it. He's got away with literally thousands, if not tens of thousands, of pounds' worth of shiny trinkets.'

Ah! That explains why the inspector arrested Lancelot on suspicion of similar burglaries, Ellie. He must think he's this thief.

Lady Langham tutted. 'They're far from trinkets. This man knows his jewels. He only targets the best. I'm sure Clifford is aware of this burglar's crime roll so far.'

Clifford nodded. 'I have read the reports, my lady. The rogue in question seems to be most accomplished indeed.'

'Hence you believing he would be tempted to… steal yours?' Eleanor finally felt she had caught up.

'Precisely!' Lady Langham pointed at her. 'Do you see why we presumed there was a fair chance he might target us if we held a masked ball and, well, advertised?'

Eleanor sat back in her seat. 'I'm clearly missing something most pertinent. I get that Lancelot possibly heard you planning that the ball might be a target for this jewel thief, but you'd have lost your jewels. How would that have helped?'

'The insurance, my lady,' Clifford said.

'Ah, of course, silly me.'

Lord Langham sighed. 'Well, it wouldn't have been fraud, you see. The necklace would have been stolen, that was the supposed genius of it all. Of course, putting on the ball cost us a packet of money we never had, but we hoped the insurance money would cover that as well.'

'Very neat,' Eleanor mused. 'But supposing the thief hadn't shown up?'

'That was a possibility,' Lady Langham said. 'But it would appear he never got the chance. Lancelot seems to have taken it upon himself to beat the thief to the punch, the poor, silly darling.'

Something in her sadness pulled at Eleanor's chest. 'Look, I'm struggling to grasp all this, but one thing I'm sure of: Lancelot might have planned to take your jewels to help you out, but he'd never have… hurt the colonel. He simply wouldn't.'

Everyone concurred on this point except Clifford, who busied himself with the tea.

Eleanor remembered that Lord Langham had been a friend of the colonel's. 'And my sincere condolences, Lord, er… Harold. He was a most extraordinary gentleman.'

Lord Langham sighed. 'Thank you, my dear. Truth be told, he was a total pain in the rump most of the time, silly old fool. But he was a decent sort beneath it all. Not his fault you know, never found a good wife like I did to shake some sense into him.'

Lady Langham rubbed his shoulder. 'It's such a tragedy. And it was supposed to be a party. Even if it was one planned with an ulterior motive.'

'You really mustn't blame yourselves for any of it,' Eleanor said. 'Honestly, I don't even believe Lancelot did steal your jewels.'

The Langhams shared a quick look.

'How so, my dear?' Lady Langham said quietly.

'I was in the room.' She glanced at Lord Langham, and hurried on, 'You know, after the poor colonel had been killed. And the safe, well, it was swinging wide open. I didn't notice until the police thundered in and the inspector declared the safe empty and the jewels gone. The point is, they searched Lancelot on the spot and no one passed me on my way to the room. Furthermore, despite the inspector's boorish insinuation, I know I am not Lancelot's accomplice.'

Lady Langham's hand flew to her mouth. 'He didn't! You mean he actually accused *you* of being involved? Oh, the mess we've caused. I am *so* sorry, my dear.'

'You don't have to apologise, Augusta. The point I'm trying to make is this: Lancelot didn't get a chance to steal the jewels. Someone else must have beaten him to it. And... and I believe that someone else also killed the colonel.' She thought back to DCI Seldon's words. *There's no way anyone entered the room between the time of the colonel's death and my men arriving.* She groaned inwardly.

Clifford cleared his throat. 'Forgive my interjection, but one thing stands out as being most irregular. If I might enquire, how was it that the chief inspector and his men happened to be at the ball? They were not guests, but on duty I understand.'

Lady Langham sprang up, stepped to the window and stared out. Everyone waited. 'It was the dratted invitations! You appreciate how it is. When you hold a ball, you have to invite all the right people. It would have been a dreadful faux pas not to have done so. But if we'd just not sent… that one.' She sniffed again. Gladstone stole over and nuzzled her hand. Her fingers hung limply against his cheek.

Lord Langham picked up the reins. 'My bish totally, didn't think about it at all. I included Lord Cavendish-Wraith in the guest list, naturally.'

'Er… naturally,' Eleanor said. *Who the devil is Lord Cavendish?*

As if he read her thoughts Lord Langham continued, 'Cavendish is the bally Chief of Police, old girl. So naturally he tells Inspector Seldon to set up a sting for these wretched jewel thieves at the ball. Messed up the entire plan and got our boy cuffed into the bargain.'

Clifford nodded. 'Lord Cavendish would have been aware that Chief Inspector Seldon had been after this jewel thief for some months. I imagine they both agreed with Lord and Lady Fenwick-Langham that the thief would not be able to pass up the opportunity to steal such a prize as Lady Fenwick-Langham's necklace.'

'Exactly, Mr Clifford!' Lady Langham turned, her eyes rimmed red. 'We decided all we could do was plough on with the ball. We just hoped that the burglar would be as clever as he had been at the other events and that he'd elude the police and escape with the necklace.' She put down her cup. 'Please excuse us, dear Eleanor, but there's really nothing more we can tell you. We must be going. This business has caused such great upset, we really aren't ourselves.'

She began shooing her husband from the room. Turning back to Eleanor she kissed her on the cheek. 'Thank you, my dear, you've given us both hope. With you and Clifford on Lancelot's case, he'll fare much better than in the hands of so-called Law and Justice.'

'Of course. Clifford and I will soon have him back at Langham Manor where he belongs.'

Eleanor hoped she sounded more convincing than she felt.

CHAPTER 7

As Clifford returned from seeing Lord and Lady Langham out, Eleanor flopped full-length on the sofa.

'Clifford?'

'Yes, my lady?'

'What did you make of all that?'

Clifford pursed his lips. 'As Mr Burns would say, "The best-laid schemes o' mice an' men gang aft agley."' At Eleanor's look, he translated. '"Often go awry", my lady.'

Eleanor snorted. 'Well, I'd hardly call this one of the best-laid schemes I've come across. I'd say this was one of the worst, whether laid by man or mouse. What *were* they thinking of? I mean, who would dream up such a ridiculous plan, Clifford?'

A discreet cough was his only reply.

She groaned. 'Okay, maybe it has all the hallmarks of something I might have come up with, but we need to get serious. What's our first move?'

Clifford looked thoughtful for a moment, and then nodded as if to himself. 'If we are to aid their lord and ladyship, not to mention young Lord Fenwick-Langham, perhaps we should establish the exact events that evening leading up to the theft of the jewels and the colonel's murder.'

'You're right, Clifford, let's get everything clear in our heads first and then we can see what's what.'

She fetched her notebook, and set about jotting down a rough timeline of the evening, explaining her calculations to Clifford as she went.

'Lady Langham said I was the last to arrive by about quarter of an hour. Now, I arrived around seven forty-five, so Lancelot's friends must have been there by seven thirty, but I don't imagine before around seven fifteen, as I can't imagine they'd have wanted to be the first to arrive. And then me at seven forty-five.'

She looked up and caught Clifford's expression. 'Don't say a word, Clifford! I'm just not naturally good at arriving on time for, well, anything really.'

'Very good, my lady,' he said, in most butlery tones. But his eyes were twinkling. 'What of the colonel?'

'I don't want to speak ill of the dead, Clifford, but the colonel really was a most difficult man. I spoke to him before I went upstairs to look for Lancelot and he did talk a load of nonsense.' She sighed. 'But we can't allow his killer to walk free. So, onwards.'

'What of the colonel's death?' Clifford asked. 'Didn't you tell me that Chief Inspector Seldon found a stopped watch in the study?'

'Ah yes, you're right. I assume the colonel was killed sometime around this time as the inspector said the colonel's watch stopped at eight twenty-three.' She added it to the list and showed it to Clifford.

7 p.m. Ball starts

7.15–7.30 p.m. Lancelot's friends arrive – Child sisters, Singh (Prince), Seaton and Appleby

7.30 p.m. Lord Hurd arrives?

7.45 p.m. I arrive
Sandford tells me Lancelot was in garden with his friends. Lancelot dressed as pirate – time?

8.05 p.m. Prince Lucas Singh leaves

8.15 p.m. See pirate and go to follow him but fall on my face!

8.20 p.m. Go to repair my make-up and pride. Spot pirate legs going upstairs and follow

8.23 p.m. The colonel's watch stops.

8.24 p.m. Go into room, see Lancelot and body!!

8.25 p.m. Police come in

Eleanor stopped writing and looked up. Despite her gut feeling that Lancelot couldn't have stolen the jewels, let alone murdered the colonel, she found her mind, and her jottings, telling her a different story.

'Oh, Clifford, what have we got ourselves into? How on earth are we going to prove a man innocent when he's caught red-handed and all the evidence points to his being guilty?'

CHAPTER 8

The following day the sun had decided to stop hiding and show itself. Despite this goodwill gesture, not being market day, Chipstone High Street was half empty. The Rolls glided past groups of women gossiping on street corners while bored shopkeepers cleaned their front windows and swept the shop steps.

As Clifford pulled into a parking space next to the police station's signature blue lamp, Eleanor noted there were none of the usual uniformed men smoking in the adjoining alley. Perhaps after she and Clifford had brought the corruption at the station to light, a shake-up had occurred.

As he opened her door, she stepped out. 'Thank you, Clifford, please wait for me. This is a battle I need to fight on my own.'

'Of course, my lady. But do you feel that going into battle is the best attitude with which to approach such a delicate matter?'

'No, not at all, but it's the one I've got.' Without waiting for a reply, she strode up the steps.

Inside the station the atmosphere felt altogether different to when she'd last been there. A gentle hum of activity filled the building, boots echoed on polished floors. The officer behind the reception desk stood smartly as she approached.

'Good morning,' she said.

He looked at the large wall clock opposite. 'Actually, it's afternoon, miss.' Recognition dawned. 'Oh, it's you, Lady Swift. Apologies, what can I do for you?'

'Constable… oh, sorry, I believe it's Sergeant Brice now, isn't it?'

'That's right, Lady Swift.' He swelled with pride. Brice had been recently promoted after the previous sergeant had been removed for incompetence and suspected corruption. 'May I ask the nature of your visit?'

'Yes, you may. I wish to speak to Lance... Lord Fenwick-Langham, please.'

Brice gave an involuntary low whistle that he tried to turn into a cough. 'Prisoners held for serious offences aren't permitted visitors.'

Eleanor's stare bore into his skull. Few had survived the Swift Stare.

He shuffled behind the counter. 'It's the rules. You can leave a message and I'll ask Detective Chief Inspector Seldon if I can pass it on to the... accused.' He glanced up at her and hurriedly looked back down. 'That's the best I can do.'

'The inspector?' She frowned. 'He's still here? I rather hoped he would have been dragged back to London or Oxford.'

'He's in charge of the investigation, Lady Swift. He'll be with us until the verdict is reached.'

'Verdict? Now just you hold your horses! None of you should be thinking about verdicts, or trials at this stage. You haven't even established the facts yet!'

Another voice interrupted. 'Good afternoon, Lady Swift. Have you stopped by to offer the police advice on how to run a murder investigation, or is there something else we can do for you?'

She turned to the newcomer. 'Inspector.'

'It's Detective Chief Inspector,' Brice whispered.

She couldn't help notice DCI Seldon's eyes seemed warm, despite his smile being not much more than a thin line across his strong jaw.

He tilted his chin. 'Can I help you?'

'Yes. As you most likely overheard, I would like to see Lord Fenwick-Langham.'

'I'm afraid he is not permitted visitors.'

'I did tell her that, sir,' Brice said.

DCI Seldon shot him a look. 'Tea, Sergeant. We'll be in my office.'

'I thought you was going out to…' The sergeant tailed off at the inspector's glare. 'Yes, sir.'

'Hot and in scrubbed cups, mind,' Eleanor couldn't help calling after him.

Brice whirled round and then caught her drift. Shaking his head, he disappeared through the door behind him.

DCI Seldon raised a questioning eyebrow.

'Oh, it was that buffoon Sergeant Wilby's favourite command. "Brice! Tea, hot and in scrubbed cups!"'

'Ah, yes, Sergeant Wilby. Well, as you know he is no longer at this station.'

'Or any other I sincerely hope.'

DCI Seldon rubbed his forehead and gestured to the half-open door behind him.

'Lady Swift, as you are the main witness, I was going to call and ask that you came and signed your statement, but it appears you have saved me the trouble.'

He marched into the office, ducking under the doorframe as he did so. She followed and stood as he closed the door behind her. The office had a temporary feel; boxes crammed with files littered the floor while the bureau stood empty, its door ajar. He threw his blue wool overcoat and bowler on the corner stand and pulled a chair out for her.

She smiled as she sat. 'Inspector, I just need to talk to Lancelot. It's very important.'

'As is answering some pertinent questions.'

She leaned across the desk. 'Fine. And then you'll take me to see Lancelot?'

He flopped in the chair behind the desk, folded his long legs under the seat and wrestled them out again. 'Lady Swift.' He sighed.

'As I said I have some further questions to ask you.' He pulled his notebook from his pocket.

She removed her gloves, unpinned her hat and dropped them in front of him. 'I have some things to ask you too. You first.'

'Right.' He shifted a mountain of files to the corner of the desk. 'First off, what precisely did you see on entering the room on the night of the murder?'

'Didn't we cover this already *on* the night of the murder?'

'Lady Swift, please just answer the question.'

Eleanor marshalled her thoughts. 'I pushed the door open and saw Lancelot. Well, I wasn't sure it was him at first. So I suppose, to be accurate, I noticed a figure standing over another figure lying on the floor.'

'Did you notice anything particular about the victim?'

'I did think he was lying at a most peculiar angle.'

'And what did you do next?'

Eleanor scrunched her eyes shut. 'I called out to Lancelot.'

'What were you trying to warn him of?'

'Warn him? I wasn't warning him of anything. As I said, at that point I wasn't certain it *was* him. So I called his name and he stood up.'

'What exactly did you say, please?'

'His name.'

DCI Seldon sighed. 'Specifics, please. Did you use his first name, his full name?'

Eleanor frowned and tried to peer at his jaw. Was it twitching again? 'Lancelot. I just said "Lancelot". You know, because that's his name.' *Ellie, just answer the questions!* She shook her head, aware that DCI Seldon was staring at her. She didn't mean to be difficult, but she'd struggled with authority, especially the police, since her parents' disappearance. A thought struck her. 'But surely you must have heard me? Isn't that why you and your men then charged into the room?'

'My men and I entered just after that point, yes.'

'Because you heard me?'

A fumble at the door handle appeared to bring him relief. 'Ah, here's the tea. Enough questions for a moment.'

He rose to open the door.

'Thank you, Brice.' DCI Seldon indicated for the cups to be set down on the one clear spot on the desk. 'That will be all.'

'Er, sir, would you like me to telephone and cancel your appointment? You were supposed to be at—'

'I know where I was supposed to be, Sergeant. It will be obvious by now that I have been detained.'

As the door closed behind Brice, Eleanor leaned her elbows on the desk. 'Is it my turn now, Inspector?'

'Not yet.' He grunted, running his finger along the handle of the mug. 'I haven't finished.' He took a sip of his tea and winced. 'There was a moment between you calling the name of the accused and my men and I entering the room. Can you describe what you remember?' Pen at the ready, he held her stare.

'Um, was there? It all happened so fast, I'm not sure I can remember.'

'Let's see if you can try.'

'Okay, well I think Lancelot stood up and turned around.'

'And did he respond to you calling out to him?'

'But you must have heard…' At Seldon's pursed lips, Eleanor paused and took a deep breath. 'He said something, I don't quite remember what.'

'Let me remind you.' Seldon flicked back through the pages of his notebook. '"Sherlock, what the hell are you doing here? You should leave. Now!" Does that sound familiar?'

'Yes, he may have said something like that.'

'He seemed surprised to see you?'

'Of course he was. I told you he had no idea that I'd, you know, followed him up the stairs.'

'And he ordered you to leave?'

'As there was a dead body in the room, I imagine any gentleman would try and spare a lady that unpleasantness.'

At the word 'gentleman', Seldon stiffened. 'And what is the reference please of "Sherlock"? Is it code for something to do with the crime?'

Eleanor blushed. 'For pity's sake, you know full well it isn't code! Just as you know I'm not Lancelot's accomplice, and he isn't guilty of stealing the jewels or of finishing the old colonel off!'

Seldon leaned towards her, his tone terse. 'Sherlock?'

She shrugged. 'It's a… pet name, if you must know.'

'Thank you. That is the end of questioning, for now. I will ask Sergeant Brice to bring in the fingerprint kit.'

'Fingerprint kit? For me? But I didn't touch anything.'

'Perhaps not, but we need to match all the fingerprints found at the murder scene, including those discovered on the candlestick, which we are now certain is the murder weapon. The murder weapon you failed to disclose was in the accused's hand as he turned and called you Sherlock!'

Stay calm, Ellie! She took a deep breath. 'Did you find any other fingerprints on the candlestick? Apart from… Lancelot's, obviously.'

'The only other fingerprints were the maid's, who Lady Fenwick-Langham confirmed cleaned the room the day before.'

Eleanor leaned forward. 'And has she an alibi for the time the colonel was killed?'

'Yes, she was in the parlour with two other servants, who corroborated her statement.'

She leaned back in her chair and groaned.

He strode over and pulled the door open. 'Brice! Fingerprints, now!'

A scurry of footsteps saw the sergeant back in the room. One look at DCI Seldon's face brought a stuttered, 'Shall I take them here, sir?'

'I'll do it. Just leave it.'

DCI Seldon flipped the lid of the inkpad and hesitated before asking Eleanor for her hand with his own outstretched. She offered the left first. His hand was warm, strong and surprisingly soft as he rolled each of her fingers in the ink and then onto the accompanying paper. When it was done, he completed the boxes at the bottom of the form.

She felt her chance of helping Lancelot slipping away. 'Inspector, can I ask if Lancelot has said anything that explains what happened?'

DCI Seldon grunted again. 'He still refuses to say anything other than the statement he gave at the scene, which I read out to you on the night of the murder.'

'Look, just ignoring the colonel for a moment, what possible reason would Lancelot have for stealing his mother's jewels?' She blushed. 'Or for being your notorious jewel thief?'

'Young Lord Fenwick-Langham had got in with a bad set, I have been told. Maybe his habits were costing more than his doting parents gave him?'

To Eleanor the detective's tone seemed scornful. 'Inspector, I don't believe this investigation is entirely about justice. I suspect something may be clouding your judgement about the accused.' *Oh, Ellie, what are you doing?*

DCI Seldon's neck reddened. Before he could reply, a uniformed officer bowled into the room and strode over to DCI Seldon, then jerked to a halt on seeing Eleanor. 'Oh, sorry, sir, I didn't realise you weren't alone.'

'What is it?' DCI Seldon's voice was as cool as his glare. The officer whispered something in his ear. 'Right, get the car.' DCI Seldon waved his hand.

Eleanor waited until they were alone again. 'A development in the case?'

'Lady Swift, as you are acutely aware, you are too involved in this case for me to discuss any details with you.'

She swallowed hard. 'Can I ask one question?'

DCI Seldon rubbed the back of his neck. 'Which is?'

'When you searched the study immediately after arresting Lancelot, did you find Lady Fenwick-Langham's jewels?'

He shook his head and reached for his hat and coat.

Eleanor decided to chance her arm even further. 'And do you still believe the thief had an accomplice?'

DCI Seldon looked her in the eye. 'Lady Swift. I am officially warning you to stay out of the investigation. And please ensure that Mr Clifford does too. I won't remind you again that this is a police matter, one where we will act upon evidence and facts in line with the law. And as you are also a suspect…' He let the sentence hang. 'Now, if you'll excuse me, duty and justice call.' He placed his bowler squarely on his head.

His footsteps reverberated down the hall, the walls echoing as he barked, 'Brice! Give Lady Swift five minutes with the accused. Don't leave them alone. And no more than five minutes. Now, where's my blasted car, for Pete's sake?'

CHAPTER 9

'Come with me, please, Lady Swift.' Sergeant Brice hovered in the doorway.

Eleanor followed him to the end of the long corridor where a formidable steel door blocked their path. He slid open the narrow hatch and called out, 'Sergeant Brice with a visitor for cell thirteen, Langham-Fenwick.'

As the door rumbled open, Eleanor snorted. They could at least get Lancelot's surname right!

'Sergeant Brice, sir.' A fresh-faced officer in a perfectly turned-out uniform saluted.

'This is the police, not the army, Lowe,' the sergeant muttered.

'Constable Lowe?' Eleanor peered over Brice's shoulder.

'Good afternoon, Lady Swift.' Lowe yanked off his cap and smoothed his hair. 'I've been promoted to a full-time position, now Sergeant Brice is no longer a constable.' His chest threatened to pop the buttons from his jacket as it swelled with pride.

Eleanor smiled at the eager young man. 'Congratulations!'

Brice rolled his eyes. 'Lowe, I am escorting Lady Swift to the prisoner, not to Sunday school for a natter. Door!'

The young constable jumped into action and slammed the door shut, making Eleanor's ears ring. 'This way.'

Their footsteps clattered down the corridor. The public rarely visited this part of the station and it had missed the refurbishment of the front; the half-height orange paint that ran the length of the corridor was faded and scuffed, the floor tiles chipped and dirty.

They passed a row of empty cells with iron bed frames and paper-thin mattresses with a decidedly thin and itchy-looking blanket bundled on the top of each. Eleanor shivered.

Stopping outside the second to last cell, Brice pulled out a ring of keys. 'Five minutes. That was the DCI's order.'

Lancelot lay sideways on the bed, repeatedly throwing an apple into the air, his legs stretched out, feet against the wall.

'Visitor for you,' the sergeant called as he locked the door noisily behind Eleanor.

Lancelot's head turned languidly. 'Sherlock!' He jumped up, his rumpled shirt hanging out of his creased trousers. 'Good show, old girl. How the bally heck did you persuade Seldon to let you in?'

Eleanor smiled. 'It's a secret.' She peered at his face. 'How are you bearing up?'

Lancelot laughed. 'You sound just like Mater. Why the dramatics?'

'How about because you're in prison? Well, in a police cell, accused of theft and…' She glanced at Brice leaning against the wall outside and whispered, 'Murder!'

A shadow crossed his face and he slumped back down on the mattress. He held out the apple. 'Hungry? Not much to offer in the hospitality stakes, I'm afraid.'

'Lancelot, listen—'

'What happened to Goggles? I rather liked him.'

She sighed in exasperation. Goggles was the pet name she had given him when they first met and he was clad in his motorcyclist gear. 'Goggles, then. This is bad. *Really* bad. You're in a proper heap of trouble. We both are, dash it!'

He frowned. 'Wait up, how are *you* in trouble?'

'Because the inspector has a nasty suspicion.' She checked if Brice was listening. He seemed to be far too busy shining his shoes on the back of his trousers. 'That I might be your accomplice.'

'What!' Lancelot sat straighter and rubbed his forehead. 'That imbecile, how dare he! Next time I meet him, I shall punch his bally lights out!'

She groaned. 'Please don't, you... you dullard. Can't you understand that assaulting a police officer really isn't going to help?'

He shrugged. 'I suppose not. But, honestly, what a wretched cheek accusing you. I tell you that man is *so-oo* tiresome. I guarantee he's no fun at parties.' He glanced sideways at her with a look she couldn't decipher. 'Sherlock?'

'What?'

'Why did you come?'

She stared straight ahead at the wall. 'You know perfectly well why.'

'To... clear your name?'

'You impossible oaf! No, to try and clear yours. Oh, you are too much.'

'No, you are too much. Too... special. And sitting here with you, in these delightful, elegant surroundings is enough to make it all worth it.' He tucked a stray curl behind her ear.

'Goggles, this is a bit awkward.'

'I know. We've got a peeping tom and' – he whispered in her ear, his soft stubble brushing her cheek – 'he's disguised as a policeman, the fiend!'

Eleanor smiled, but then her face clouded over. 'Lancelot, what can you tell me about what really happened?'

He held her gaze. 'Nothing more than I've told Seldon and his goons, ad nauseam.'

She took hold of his shoulders. The tingling down her arms made her words tumble over each other. 'There has to be more. Something that proves you aren't a... that you didn't do it.'

Lancelot sighed. 'It would be amazing, wouldn't it, if there was? Truth is though, Sherlock, I've told them exactly what happened. I came into the blasted study and saw the colonel on the floor. I trotted over and knelt down to see if I could help the old buzzard. Then I heard a noise. I was in shock and panicked. I thought it was the killer returning, so I grabbed the nearest thing I could to defend myself.'

'The candlestick,' they chorused.

'Exactly. I didn't bally well know it was the murder weapon. I wouldn't have touched it if I had.' He looked at her almost eagerly. 'Did they find anyone else's fingerprints on the dashed thing?'

'Only the maid's, who cleaned the room the day before, and she has a cast-iron alibi for the time the colonel was killed.'

'Blast! I suppose the jewel thief wore gloves, of course.'

'But why were you in the study in the first place and not in the ballroom?'

'Well, my favourite guest was vulgarly late and everyone else seemed horribly dull, so I decided to kick my heels upstairs. I heard a… an odd noise and went to investigate.' He tilted his head. 'More to the point, why were you upstairs?'

'How about because my favourite host was nowhere to be seen? He couldn't even be bothered to be my knight in shining armour when I fell flat on my face in front of the entire blasted party. So I resorted to sneaking after him when I saw his silly pirate legs running up the stairs.'

Lancelot's shoulders shook. 'Only you could face plant at a ball! Monster shame I missed it. But you know you've got to stop chasing after me like that. First at the airfield on some spurious tale of a non-existent murder, then at the rose garden luncheon. And now here. People are going to talk, it's not very ladylike.'

'Well, I'm not much of a lady.'

'I've noticed.'

She slapped his hand, then checked Brice was out of earshot. 'Look.' She lowered her voice. 'I know you're not telling me the whole truth. Your parents came to see me.'

He started at her words. 'So… you know?'

She nodded. 'Look, I understand you can't tell Seldon about planning to steal the jewels to help your parents out, you'd look even more guilty, but we need to find a way to prove you're innocent. Is there anything you think might be a clue as to who the real thief and killer is?'

Lancelot sighed. 'No one knows the identity of the jewel thief, even the police haven't been able to find that out.' He grinned without amusement. 'He does seem to pick parties we're at, though, which just goes to show how in demand we are at all the top society events. A party simply isn't a success without us there.'

Eleanor frowned. 'You said "we"?'

He shrugged. 'My "bright young things gang", as so many dull, tiresome types have dubbed us.' He lapsed into a frown again. 'I suppose, if you think about it, that does make them suspects, though. That blasted— I mean, the poor old colonel as much as said so more than once.' He looked up at her. 'But everyone knew about Mater's jewels, and a lot of people with highfalutin titles are short of a bob nowadays, as you know Mater and Pater are, so the jewel thief could be one of the titled guests who were at the ball even.' He sighed. 'Doesn't really narrow it down much, does it?'

Brice tapped the bars of the cell and rattled the key on the ring. 'Time's up, Lady Swift.'

Eleanor glared at him before turning back to Lancelot. 'Don't worry, Goggles, you've given me some ideas to follow up and I'm going to do everything I can to get you out of this mess. *I* know you're innocent.'

'Well you're probably the only one who does.' Lancelot ran his fingers through his tousled hair.

'Lady Swift, *please*,' Brice called from the door.

Ignoring the urgency in his command, she stared at Lancelot. 'What do you mean the only one?'

'Look, Sherlock, thanks for the offer to help but I don't want you to get into any more trouble because of me. Your Inspector Do-Goody-Two-Boots will frame me anyway, just to have you to himself, the wretch!'

She looked away remembering Clifford's words. 'Rubbish, the inspector isn't interested in me.'

He held her chin gently, his voice was quiet. 'Darling fruit, you'll never see it, will you? You're irresistibly… peculiar. You have a way of making us chaps go, well, a bit giddy, if I'm honest. I saw it in Seldon's face when he ordered his officers to cuff me that night. He looked at you in that way. He's not very subtle for a detective!'

'But he's a professional!'

Lancelot shrugged. 'Maybe. But why the bally heck was he even at the house on the night of the ball, anyway?'

'Look, I haven't got time to explain, but it makes sense that he was there.'

Brice stepped into the cell and took Eleanor's elbow.

'Unhand her, you brute!'

Brice shot Lancelot a look but let go and gestured towards the door. Eleanor led the way and felt her heart sink at the sound of the lock turning.

Lancelot called from behind the bars. 'Sherlock? Has the great detective found the jewels yet?'

She shook her head and turned to see him wink before flopping back onto the bed.

The dull thud of an apple thrown repeatedly against a wall followed her and Brice down the corridor.

CHAPTER 10

'Good morning, my lady. Her ladyship is expecting you.'

'Morning, Sandford. How is everyone holding up?' Eleanor gave him a warm smile.

Sandford hesitated. 'I have to confess, my lady, the Manor has seen happier days. However, we are greatly indebted for your dedicated efforts.'

'Fingers crossed.' She followed him up the grand entrance steps and into the drawing room where Lady Langham was waiting.

'Eleanor, my dear, come sit. Sandford, fortified tea, please.' As the butler closed the door behind him, she sat beside Eleanor. 'It is so kind of you to throw yourself into proving Lancelot's innocence, my dear. Really, we're eternally grateful.'

'It's the least I could do for all your kindness,' Eleanor said. 'I only hope I can.'

'As we all do, my dear.' Lady Langham patted the back of Eleanor's hand.

'How is Harold coping?' Eleanor asked.

Her hostess gave a wan smile. 'Even he is showing the signs of the terrible strain this situation is placing on us all. Yesterday I found him in Lancelot's room, sitting on our son's bed, fiddling with the arms of the teddy bear my brother sent over from America on Lance's fourth birthday.'

'Oh golly!' Eleanor couldn't move the lump from her throat and was grateful when Sandford knocked at the door before settling the tea things before them. With a lifetime in service, he sensed the emotional cloud in the room and left without offering to pour.

Lady Langham turned back to Eleanor. 'You know, Sandford is such a gem. For some peculiar reason, he is very fond of my son. I remember one particularly wet day when Lancelot was six and his governess had scolded him repeatedly.' She smiled wistfully. 'I'm sure he deserved it, he usually did. I can't tell you how many governesses we went through. Anyway, she banished him to the other side of the house. A little later I happened along the corridor to the butler's pantry to check on something for dinner and you'll never guess what I saw.'

Eleanor shuffled forward. 'I'm intrigued, do tell.'

'I saw Lancelot balancing on two flowerpots with string handles, walking along like a puppet, giggling his heart out. And behind him, Sandford on his own set of stilts.'

Eleanor roared at the image. 'Sandford does seem a genuinely kind-hearted soul and a most valuable asset to the staff. Much like Clifford, really.'

'We are both lucky in that respect. And they're quite the chums, you know, on the quiet.' Lady Langham stared into the distance. 'But where was I?'

Eleanor set her cup down and turned to face Lady Langham. She was pouring a small glass of sherry that obviously constituted the fortified element of the requested tea. She offered Eleanor a glass.

'No, thank you.' Eleanor took a deep breath. 'Perhaps I should begin with interviewing the staff. Not that there is any suspicion there,' she hurried on, 'simply that they are, as we know, the eyes and ears of the household.'

'A splendid idea, my dear. I always think it takes a woman's guile to get a man to confess.'

'Or a woman.'

'A woman? You surely don't imagine it could be a *woman*? What callous creature could ignore her natural sensitivities and commit such an act?'

Eleanor frowned. 'Well, we are now firmly in the nineteen hundreds, not the eighteen hundreds. If women are to have equal rights that should include the equal right to be suspected of murder. Although, I confess, that probably isn't in the Suffragettes' charter.'

'I'm sure you'll think me the most frightful dinosaur but I do not hold at all with this women's equality nonsense. Standing for Parliament? Whatever do they think they are doing?'

Eleanor said gently, 'I believe you'll find a woman can do just as good a job as a man.'

'That, my dear, is precisely the problem.'

'Forgive me, Augusta, I don't quite follow.'

'It's like this, my dear. Once you put someone in a position of political power, it swells the head, and the ego elbows out all sense of reason and moderation.'

Eleanor laughed. 'I definitely agree on that point.'

'For centuries,' Lady Langham continued, 'the only voice of reason has been the wife or mistress. Behind the scenes they have kept men from their own worst foolishness and everyone else from the catastrophic effects of that foolishness.'

'And you believe that when such foolish acts *were* made, the lady was ignored?'

'Exactly!' Lady Langham's voice betrayed an underlying bitterness. 'When a politician declared war, or levied a tax that resulted in families having to sell off their cherished possessions, it was the act of a man without conscience. For a woman is a man's only true restraining influence. So this equality talk is a fine sentiment, but what is to become of this country if all the women are slandering and fighting each other in public and whoring and gambling in private like the men?'

Eleanor thought for a moment. 'Well, on the upside, we'd be able to pass a law banning these dratted corsets!'

Lady Langham stared at her, then burst into peals of laughter. She downed the remaining sherry in her glass and rose. 'Now, to business. Come. Our Lancelot's fate is in your hands!'

With those words still ringing in her ears, Eleanor followed Sandford to a small sitting room at the far corner of the ground floor. A well-worn settee sat lengthways against the oak panelling at one end, while a bright tapestry of a family playing croquet filled the opposite wall. A deep-pile pink wool rug added an extra warmth to the cosy atmosphere.

'This is perfect,' Eleanor said. 'I want the staff to be relaxed when I interview them.'

'I fear, my lady, that with the mark of recent events, that will be a difficult task to accomplish,' Sandford said.

'I'll be gentle, I promise. Whom do you suggest I interview first?'

'Perhaps myself, my lady? I can then loudly declare in the servants' hall that you were most agreeable and sympathetic.'

'And if you find my interrogation methods terrifying?'

'I will keep the waver from my voice as I tell them a tall tale.'

She laughed. 'Thank you, Sandford.' Making herself comfortable on the sofa she continued, 'Why don't you tell me all that you remember of the evening?'

'Certainly, my lady. As is customary at such an event I greeted the guests. The last to arrive were the financial gentlemen. They tend to spend the major part of their time in London. I was then dispatched by Lady Fenwick-Langham to wait on the front steps for one particularly late guest.'

She nodded. 'I was fearfully late, wasn't I?'

His eyes twinkled. 'Fearfully so, my lady.'

'And were you aware of Lancelot's whereabouts all this time?'

He shook his head. 'For much of it, my lady, but not all. At the commencement of the ball, young master Lancelot stood behind his lord and ladyship to greet guests as normal. Then he hung around the doorway leading to the west wing. It appeared he was looking for someone.'

'Really?' She blushed slightly and hurried on. 'So once all the guests were holding champagne flutes and waiting to twirl the evening away, where were you stationed?'

'By the orchestra, my lady. From there I have a bird's-eye view of the ballroom… and any guests in need of assistance.' His eyes sparkled once more.

Eleanor shrugged. 'I did rather fall on my face, literally. I never thought Lady Fenwick-Langham would speak to me again.'

She suddenly remembered Lancelot's words: *The jewel thief does seem to pick parties we're at, though… I suppose, if you think about it, that does make them suspects.* She decided to find out all she could during the interviews about the movement of Lancelot's bright young things.

She resumed her questioning. 'Shortly after my arrival, when I asked after Lancelot's whereabouts, you kindly told me you'd seen him in the garden?'

Sandford rubbed a hand over his slicked-down hair. 'Yes, the young master's friends had taken to the garden to partake of a little tobacco. Once they had finished, they returned to the ballroom. It was then Prince Singh alerted me to his regrettable need to return to Oxford due to an emergency. I arranged for his car to be brought to the front steps, which caused a little consternation in her ladyship and the group of guests with her.'

'Why was that?'

'I believe there was a queue of ladies waiting to dance with him.'

She rolled her eyes. 'Yes, I suppose dancing with a prince is quite a draw. Do you know what time he left?'

Sandford thought for a moment. 'I believe it would have been around eight, my lady.'

She nodded to herself. That tallied with what Coco had told her at the ball.

'Thank you, Sandford. You've been most helpful, and I hope I've not been too terrifying an inquisitor.'

As Eleanor waited for him to send in the next of the staff, she closed her eyes and tried to relax. Any tension she exhibited would be picked up by those she was interviewing.

The door opened and Sandford announced, 'Mr Andrew Parsons, footman, my lady.' He left, leaving her alone with the extraordinarily tall servant.

'Ah, Parsons. Thank you for coming. Please do sit down.'

He perched like a giraffe on the edge of his seat.

'I wish to ask you a few questions, as I'm sure Sandford explained.'

'Indeed, my lady.'

'Please, tell me, what was your principal duty on the night of the ball?'

'I was charged with the serving of champagne in the ballroom. I remained at my post as instructed throughout the evening.'

'You weren't called away for any little hiccups that Lady Fenwick-Langham mentioned as having occurred during the ball?'

'No, my lady. Mr Bates is in charge of such things. I am part of the butler's pantry staff. As the first footman, I am Mr Sandford's second in command. There were no hiccups in the catering department.'

'Right-oh.' Eleanor continued, 'Were you aware of the colonel's whereabouts in the half hour leading up to his demise?'

'Yes, my lady, but only for a brief period. There were a great many influential guests to attend to. My only encounters with the gentleman were on his arrival in the ballroom and then later in the proceedings when he declined a second glass of champagne before he went upstairs.'

'Not a man for bubbles, then?'

'The gentleman was most vehement in his negative response, my lady. I fear it is not something I could repeat.'

'Gracious, how rude can one be about a sparkling wine?'

His face flushed. 'The gentleman's comment was not directed at the beverage, but at another guest.'

'What did he say?'

The footman blushed again. 'I cannot repeat exactly what the colonel said in your presence, my lady, but basically he said, "There goes the cad!"'

Eleanor kept her voice even. 'And did you happen to see to whom the colonel was referring?'

He nodded. 'To a guest dressed as a—'

'Pirate?' she finished for him.

He looked at her oddly. 'Yes, my lady.'

'And did you, by any chance, tell the police of this?'

'Of course. I told the Detective Chief Inspector himself. He congratulated me on the assistance I had given to the investigation.'

Eleanor groaned inwardly. 'And when do you think this was?'

The footman flushed. 'I believe it was shortly after you… fell, my lady. I think just after eight or so, I can't be sure.'

She frowned. She'd estimated that she'd fallen around eight fifteen, but it could have been a few minutes earlier. Either way, that meant the colonel would have been upstairs for ten minutes or so before he was killed. *What was he doing for that time?* Looking for her pirate, perhaps?

'Thank you so much, Mr Parsons, that will be all.'

*

As the door closed behind him, Eleanor flopped back on the settee. She sighed. Unless someone had seen the colonel upstairs, there was no way to find out his movements. She shivered. Obviously someone *had* seen him up there – his killer.

'Are you alright, my lady?' Sandford enquired from the doorway. She shot up and smoothed her hair. 'Quite alright, thank you.'

'A restorative coffee, perhaps? I can bring you up a pot.'

Eleanor smiled. 'Do you know, that would be just the ticket. Thank you, Sandford. In the meantime, do keep them coming.'

'Very good, my lady. Miss Lillian Glew, head housemaid,' Sandford announced.

The maid took a few tentative steps into the room and halted by the tallboy, her hands clasped in front of her. Her dark wavy hair, almost tamed by her white lace headband, set off the deepest blue eyes Eleanor had ever seen. She looked to be in her mid twenties.

'Miss Glew, please do not be anxious.' Eleanor gestured to the seat. 'I wish only to ask what you remember from the evening of the ball.'

'Yes, my lady,' the maid whispered.

'Excellent, then let's begin with Colonel Puddifoot-Barton. I assume you knew who he was since he was staying at the Manor?'

The girl bit her rosy bottom lip. 'I did, my lady. The gentleman didn't bring a gentleman's gentleman with him, so I was given to take care of his things somewhat.'

'I see and was the colonel stationed in one of the guest suites in the east wing?'

The maid shook her head. 'The colonel, God rest his soul, after his first night requested that he be put up in one of the rooms in the west wing.'

'Why the west wing?'

'On account of the birds, my lady.'

'What birds? I didn't know his lordship kept birds?'

'Oh no, my lady, he doesn't, well only the game birds, of course, for shooting. The birds the colonel argued with were the crows.'

Smiling inwardly at the idea that the belligerent colonel had even managed to pick a fight with nature's feathered friends, Eleanor nodded for the girl to continue. 'Crows?'

'Yes, my lady, huge great family of them living in the old oak tree. Cook says they've been there generations, longer than the Manor itself.'

'And what was the colonel's objection?'

The maid swallowed hard. 'The colonel got a terrible fright. 'Twas early in the morning. I met him rushing along the corridor just as I was going down the back stairs to check that Molly had lit the ranges in the kitchen.'

'Did the colonel say anything?'

'Yes, my lady, he kept mumbling, "Six, six of the blighters." Oh, pardon my language.'

Eleanor flapped a hand to dismiss the maid's concern. 'But six what?'

'Crows. Six crows. That put more than the wind up him, especially after one of them tapped on his window.' The girl shivered and crossed herself. At Eleanor's confused look, the maid explained, 'You know, my lady, 'tis a sign of… death. Naturally, the colonel marched into the breakfast room as soon as her ladyship was up and demanded to be moved.'

'So he took to a set of rooms in the west wing?'

'He did. The birds, they go mooching in the woods on the far side so he would have been fine. That is' – she crossed herself – 'if he hadn't already been jinxed. Can't believe some folk say 'tis a myth.'

'Quite.' Eleanor tried to think what else to ask. 'Moving on, Miss Glew, have you noticed anything amiss in the study since…

that night?' Apart from an empty safe and a missing candlestick, she thought.

The maid's hands flew to her mouth. 'I… I haven't been in there since the colonel was… you know. He mightn't have passed over yet. Only been a few days, could be that his spirit is still there. That policeman asked me to have a look on the night and I begged him not to make me go in there.'

Eleanor could see she had worried the girl. 'That's quite alright, my dear, forget I asked. Last question, do you remember anything else unusual about that night?'

'No, my lady.' She paused. 'Except that gentleman what's a prince left early. Oh, and I thought I was seeing double, like.'

'What do you mean? Seeing double?'

The girl blushed. 'Well, it was nothing really. Just I saw a guest dressed as some sort of pirate, I think it was supposed to be. And then later I sees another dressed identical, like.'

'So there were possibly two guests dressed as pirates?' Eleanor tried to keep her expression relaxed, but her heart was racing. Hadn't Sandford said a few of the guests had come dressed in the same costume?

The maid interrupted her thoughts. 'Actually, now I come to think of it, it could have been the same guest, couldn't it?'

'But something made you think it might have been two guests dressed identically, rather than the same guest twice?'

The girl looked as if she wished she'd never mentioned it. ''Cos I saw a pirate going up the stairs twice, but I didn't see no pirate come *down* the stairs, so I figured it must have been two pirates going up once each, if you get my drift?' She frowned. 'But he could easily have come back down one of the other stairs and then gone back up. There's a lot of stairs at the Manor.' She sighed. 'And all of them need cleaning.'

*

It was close to an hour and a pot of coffee later when Sandford announced the last of the staff.

'Mr Nathaniel Pickerton, second coachman.'

The man stood in front of her in his shined boots and grey fitted waistcoat. His boyish features and tufty blond hair made it hard to deduce his age.

'Pickerton, I would appreciate your help with anything you can remember of the night of the ball.'

'Of course, my lady. It'll be a pleasure if I can help the young master. What a terrible business.'

'Indeed.' She tried to stay focused. 'Now, on the night of the ball, you would have looked after the guests' cars, I imagine?'

'Yes. There were some absolute beauts. I don't think I've ever seen so many Rolls Royces, Alvises, Austins and even an Alfa Romeo.'

'So you were kept busy then?'

'Well, once everyone had arrived it quietened down, course.'

'But surely Jenkins, the chauffeur, was there to help you?' Eleanor realised he hadn't appeared in the line-up of staff Sandford had arranged.

'Mr Jenkins wasn't at the Manor on account of his mother passing. Her ladyship said the timing was awfully off what with the ball and everything but she supposed he'd better go and see to things. He's back now, of course.'

'Of course.' She thought for a moment. 'Sandford mentioned that one of the guests left early.'

The coachman blushed. 'Truth is, I left my station for just a moment, my lady, to answer…' He blushed again. 'I did tell Mr Sandford, as I was so sorry and all that. Wasn't expecting anyone to leave so early.' He stared at his boots.

'So you didn't actually see the guest leave?'

'No, my lady, but the Rolls that foreign prince came in was gone when I'd returned.'

CHAPTER 11

'My compliments to Cook if you will, Sandford, the pheasant pie was delicious. And please thank her for the most restoring pot of coffee I've ever had too.' Eleanor patted her stomach.

Sandford nodded. 'Cook is a strong advocate of the use of Madeira in such a dish for both its taste enhancing and medicinal purposes. Likewise, with the brandy in the rhubarb tartlets. Would you like more coffee before you begin your interviews again?'

She shook her head. 'No, thank you, Sandford.'

The splendid lunch had done nothing to boost her enthusiasm for more interviewing. The sunshine outside beckoned her. All she wanted was to drive back to Henley Hall, collect Gladstone and go for a soul-reviving tramp through the woods. Instead she followed Sandford as he led her down the steps to the edge of the lawn. 'There are jugs of iced lemonade, lime wedges and a sun hat for yourself in the Arabian tent, my lady.'

She consoled herself that at least the next round of interviews would be held outside. Her heart skipped at the sight of the ornate cream-and-gold striped marquee, its pointed roof and scalloped edging adding a magical hint of the Orient.

'What ho, Eleanor!' Lord Langham's voice boomed behind her.

'Afternoon, Harold. We're up for croquet, I see.'

He offered his elbow, which she took, nodding to Sandford as they walked towards the tent.

'Clever ruse of the old gal's, eh? This way you can interrogate the enemy without them knowing, what?' He winked and lowered his voice. 'Just between ourselves, croquet is a frightful game, my dear. Spending one's day hitting a small wooden ball at a stick should have one labelled as the village idiot. But, add some elegant ladies in posh frocks and gentlemen in blazers and bally heck, it's a British institution!'

She laughed out loud, causing Lady Langham to poke her head out of the tent. She gave them both a cheery wave and ducked back inside.

'That is a beautiful tent. Did it come from one of your previous travels?'

He stopped and patted her hand. 'Many years ago,' he said wistfully. 'I used to do the whole camping out thing.'

'With Lancelot?' she asked quietly.

He nodded. 'Got no sleep at all, of course. High jinks at night, you know. We had to sneak away from his mother in the afternoons and get some shut-eye. Something about a boy needing a routine or else he'd something or other. Didn't understand a word of it.'

He spotted his wife waving frantically from the tent entrance.

'Oops, the fire-breathing hostess is calling. Best look lively to avoid the full roasting.'

As Eleanor approached the tent, she groaned inwardly as she recognised the cranky Dowager Countess of Goldsworthy, her limp niece Cora Wynne and the pretentious Viscountess Delia Littleton, the self-titled American guru of Parisian fashion.

Turning to the group, Lady Langham spread her arms wide and announced, 'Three a side, dear friends. Let the game begin!' She called across to Sandford. 'Now, we will require an adjudicator. Sandford, if you will?'

He nodded and pulled a small notebook and pencil from his waistcoat pocket.

Eleanor smiled at the dowager countess. 'Are you a keen croquet player, Lady Goldsworthy?'

'Three times winner at Craiglockhart,' came the tart reply.

Cora sidled up to Eleanor. 'Aunt Daphne is very proud of her trophies from the oh-so-eminent championship in Edinburgh. Although,' she lowered her voice, 'it's best not to enquire exactly where she was placed in the finals.' She held up four fingers behind her back as she wandered over to rejoin her team members.

As Lady Langham declared the game underway, it struck Eleanor that she hadn't prepared for interviewing on the move. Suddenly, Viscountess Littleton appeared at her elbow.

'It was good of you to stay on... afterwards,' Eleanor said, thinking on her feet. 'It must have been quite the shock on the night of the murder.'

'Absolutely! That inspector fellow was too much! I'd like to see the likes of him trying the pompous act back where I grew up. Governor Coolidge stamped on the police getting uppity only last year. They won't try their shenanigans again. The other night, your English inspector seemed to be obsessed with the state of my and Cuthbert's marriage, the wretch!'

Eleanor tutted aloud, secretly smiling inside. 'Did you know the colonel well?'

Lady Langham interrupted their conversation, calling across to their group, 'Ladies, red and yellow balls for you. Black and blue for us. Do be first striker, Daphne dear.'

Viscountess Littleton rolled her eyes and turned back to Eleanor. 'Did I know the colonel well? Only through Lady Langham. That guy was one mean snake. He took every possible opportunity to insult Cuthbert.'

'But why would the colonel be so rude to your husband?'

Viscountess Littleton raised her eyebrows. 'You'd be better off asking who the colonel *wasn't* rude to!' She turned back to the other players. 'Oh, ducky shot, Lady Goldsworthy!'

A rousing round of applause followed. The dowager countess turned to the two women. 'Lady Swift! You'll learn more from my expertise if you adopt a position near to where the game is being played.'

Feeling like a scolded child, Eleanor hurried across the lawn, taking a spot near enough to Cora to continue her investigations. Looking down at the girl she noticed a thin, black lace ribbon poking out of her dress sleeve.

'A tribute to the colonel?' she asked softly.

'Gracious no, has it slipped down?' Cora hurried to tuck it back under the cuff. 'I know one shouldn't speak ill of the dead and all that but honestly, Lady Swift, he was… well, I shouldn't say.'

'Go on, I shan't say anything.'

Cora shook her head. 'Forgive me, that was terribly indiscreet. Look, Viscountess Littleton has missed the green altogether.'

Eleanor was itching to press the girl further, but the dowager countess called out to her, 'Lady Swift! Are you ready? Our team is sadly diminished in the skill set in one corner.' She glowered at Viscountess Littleton who was busy adjusting the ankle straps of her satin pumps.

'Right-oh! I'm rather rusty, I'm afraid, but best mallet forward and all that.'

As Lady Langham moved across to Cora, Eleanor stepped up to take her first shot.

'You're too leftwards of the hoop,' the dowager countess said.

Eleanor ignored her and whacked the ball through the first hoop, bumping Lady Langham's ball out of line as it powered on towards the next hoop.

Everyone applauded.

'Not too bad,' the dowager countess offered as she strode up to Eleanor. 'So you've played once afore, I see?'

'Really, a lucky shot, nothing more. I'm better versed in elephant polo.' Eleanor seized her opening. 'It must be a terrible strain, though, for Lord and Lady Fenwick-Langham, what with their son, you know, in prison.'

The dowager countess spun round to face her. 'Their son! Augusta's an old, old friend but what I say to you I've said to her many a time, and I told that policeman the other night. They've spoiled that boy rotten, and he's turned out the bad apple I always predicted.'

She threw her arms up. 'Cora! Don't be so feeble, girl! Hit it like you mean it.'

Eleanor felt a hot flush burn across her cheeks. Fearing she might take an irate swing with her mallet at this cantankerous old kilt, she held it behind her back.

The dowager countess turned back to Eleanor. 'Cora can scrape a passable tune on the violin and isn't intolerably stupid. She's not even got the face of a cow's behind. And she's the niece and ward of his mother's best friend. Any decent man would have taken her off ma hands afore now. And to think it was planned he'd take her as his bride.'

Eleanor gasped. *The dowager countess was trying to marry her niece off to… Lancelot!* This was the first she'd heard of it.

Unaware of Eleanor's shock, the dowager countess continued, 'And to think Cora would have been married to a murderer, that's a pretty result, if you please!'

Eleanor bit back her reply. *Hold your tongue, Ellie. You can have your say when Lancelot's out of prison.*

Lady Langham joined them. 'Daphne, dear. You're up again.'

Eleanor shot the dowager countess a black look as she strode across the lawn.

Lady Langham followed and took Eleanor's arm. 'Are you alright, dear girl? You're quite the colour you know.'

'Yes, thank you. It's just the heat…'

The hostess patted her hand. 'It was just an earful of spiteful hot air, I can imagine. Daphne determined a long time ago that Lancelot would rid her of the burden of Cora but he would have none of it. And I understand her anxiety. Daphne is in her late seventies and she is a caring aunt… underneath it all.'

She lowered her voice. 'Cora can't inherit a bean of the estate unless she has a husband to manage it for her. Those are the terms Daphne's husband wrote into his will. And Cora's mother left her practically nothing. If Cora is unmarried when Daphne passes away, she will be considered destitute.'

Eleanor gasped. 'But Cora doesn't act that way. Does she know?'

Lady Langham shook her head. 'The girl has always believed there is a trust fund in her name, left by her mother's brother. But during the war that disappeared… like so much else.'

'Hence the dowager countess' disparaging opinion of Lancelot?'

Lady Langham nodded. 'I know it seems odd, ridiculous even, that I'm entertaining someone who seems to be the epitome of a cantankerous old witch from the Highlands. However, she was very kind to my mother in the past. We have a history.'

'But surely you would take Cora in?'

'Well, of course. But she would be a kept charge, looking at a bleak future as a spinster.' Lady Langham sighed. 'Life is uncomfortably messy, my dear.'

The game continued with the dowager countess' constant complaining and Cora's angry looks as her aunt disparaged her every shot. It was a relief to the entire party when Lady Langham declared it half-time and herded them back to the Arabian tent.

Eleanor was as taken with the inside as the outside. Low sofa seats in matching cream and gold were arranged around a central rug, with floor lanterns acting as sentries at each corner. Lord Langham shuffled over to the drinks globe and clapped his hands together.

'Who's for a little spice in their afternoon tea?'

All hands, except Cora's, shot up.

'Good show! Hard work all this croquet lark. A small tipple will sharpen the eye.'

Eleanor took a seat next to Viscountess Littleton. 'Gracious, how rude of me not to ask before. Where is Cuthbert?'

'Called away to some business emergency the morning after the murder. Left me to fend for myself!'

As promised, Lady Langham changed the teams around for the second game. She partnered herself with Eleanor and Cora while Lord Langham was ordered to play alongside the dowager countess and Viscountess Littleton.

Eleanor looped her arm through Cora's, making sure no one else was within earshot. 'My dear girl, your mourning band I saw earlier isn't for the colonel, is it? It's for Lancelot.'

Cora searched in her dress pocket. 'Yes. I'm so worried, Lady Swift, that he will be…' Her words dried up as she produced a handkerchief and dabbed at two fat tears.

Eleanor looked at Cora intently. 'My dear, do you know anything about that dreadful night that might help Lancelot?'

Cora nodded hesitantly.

Eleanor's heart quickened. 'What is it?'

'It's too awful. How could it help Lancelot? It would likely send him to the gallows!'

'Cora, dear, without our help, he is already quite desperately alone, facing a most uncertain fate.'

'No. It's a certain fate. My aunt is trying to see to that. If she'd let him alone, he might have taken more interest in me. She's messed the whole thing up, but she's blaming him!'

Eleanor rubbed the girl's shoulder sympathetically. 'I'm so sorry to have brought all this up. But please tell me what you know, for Lancelot's sake.'

Cora dabbed her eyes and took a deep breath, 'I saw… oh, Lady Swift, I saw Lancelot in the garden in his pirate costume. He'd taken the mask and hat off and… and was having the most fearful row with the colonel. It was just before…'

Eleanor bit her lip. She didn't need to ask Cora just before what. This wasn't what she was hoping to hear. No wonder the girl had kept it to herself.

'Did you hear what they were arguing about?'

'Not really, only snippets. They seemed to be whispering at first but then things got really heated. The colonel shouted something about "aeroplanes" and Lancelot being a "disgraceful wastrel". Then he said something most peculiar about Lancelot being a "something beef". I've never seen Lancelot anything but laughing and joking but he looked as though…'

Eleanor was already dreading the reply as she asked, 'As though what?'

'As though he was going to strike the colonel!'

Lady Langham stood on the top step of the grand entrance to Langham Manor, her arm looped through Eleanor's. 'My dear, I haven't the words for how grateful Harold and I are for, well everything. Tell me, did you uncover anything at all helpful?'

Cora's words were still ringing in Eleanor's ears. 'Possibly. However, my head is whirling with all the information I've collected across the day. I need to go home and sift through it.'

'With Mr Clifford's input too, I do hope? You really are quite the unorthodox team.' Her hostess squeezed her elbow. 'Ah, the car has arrived. Jenkins!'

The chauffeur leapt from the gleaming Rolls and stood to attention on the bottom step. 'Yes, my lady.'

'Lady Swift is being taught to drive by Clifford. If she asks, let her have a go at the wheel.'

Eleanor gasped and stared first at the now white-faced chauffeur and then back to Lady Langham.

Jenkins stuttered, 'Beggin' your pardon, your ladyship, but his lordship…'

Lady Langham gave Eleanor a gentle hug and gestured down the steps. 'No buts, Jenkins. This is the nineteen hundreds, not the eighteen hundreds!' Winking at Eleanor, she strode into the house.

CHAPTER 12

The following morning Eleanor felt as though she had missed a week of sleep. She descended the stairs only to be bowled backwards by Gladstone's exuberant welcome at the bottom. After convincing him that jumping up wasn't good for a chap of his advanced age, she carried on down the hallway with the bulldog padding alongside her.

Polly was waiting halfway along. The young maid curtseyed, spilling cleaning polish on Eleanor's dress. 'S-s-sorry, your ladyship! Oh, I messed up your lovely dress. I'm such a dolt.' She slapped her forehead.

Eleanor swallowed her dismay at the stain on the front of her dress. It had been one of her mother's favourites. She took the crestfallen girl by the shoulders. 'The truth is, Polly, *I* owe *you* an apology.'

The maid's head jerked up. 'Apology, your ladyship? But... but that can't be right, can it? Meaning you're the mistress and I'm just the maid, not to be rude, of course.'

'No, I've been terribly remiss, Polly. I have entirely forgotten to tell you something very important.'

The young girl's eyes were the size of saucers.

'I have forgotten to tell you that you... are the best maid I've ever had.'

Polly's hand flew to her mouth, her eyes welling up. 'Me?'

'Yes, you. You are quite irreplaceable. So no more talk of you being a dolt or anything else uncomplimentary, do you hear me?'

The maid nodded. 'Yes, your ladyship. The best maid... Thank you. Golly, shall I ask for your breakfast, your ladyship?'

'Perfect. I'll have a light breakfast in the morning room today.' Her stomach was still full from the mountain of food they'd plied her with at Langham Manor the day before.

Polly skipped down the hallway towards the kitchen, failing to see Mrs Butters, feather duster in hand, peeping out from behind the bannisters.

The housekeeper grinned as she emerged.

'My lady, you are so kind. She means ever so well. It's those gangly arms and legs that make her so clumsy. And her so young. Keep thinking she'll have to grow into them one day, but I'm beginning to wonder.'

'I meant what I said, Mrs Butters.'

'I have no doubt about that. And neither me nor Mrs Trotman will stick a fork in her bubble by letting on she's the *only* maid you've ever had.' The housekeeper winked. 'Although, you never having a lady's maid before is quite, well, irregular, if you don't mind my saying, my lady.'

'Well, Mrs Butters, as you are aware, my parents were quite "irregular", as was my upbringing, until... they disappeared.'

'Of course, my lady, God bless their souls. I'll bring the breakfast things shortly. Cook's tried out a new pastry recipe, cinnamon and vanilla twists. Seeing as you wanted a light breakfast, they'll be perfect and soon put the spring back in your step. Though, they're not for sharing with Mr Greedy there.' She pointed at Gladstone now lying on his back on Eleanor's feet, his stumpy tail beating out a muffled rhythm on the deep-pile rug. 'And don't fret, that beautiful dress will come up good as new, I'll make sure.'

She left Eleanor to wonder for the thousandth time how this kindly woman was always able to lighten her mood.

*

When Clifford knocked and then entered the morning room, he found Eleanor changed into a new dress, waiting for him with her notebook at the ready.

'Now, Clifford I need to run over what I learned yesterday and come up with our next move.'

He placed her breakfast tray on the table and waited patiently. As she ate, she recounted all that she had learned the day before at Langham Manor. Occasionally he interrupted her to clarify a point, but otherwise listened silently and attentively until she had finished. As this coincided with her finishing her breakfast, he cleared her plate away and poured her another tea.

'First of all, I must congratulate you, my lady, on your efforts yesterday. As to our next move, I would say the information you obtained from Mr Sandford about the movements of young Lord Fenwick-Langham's gang, as you refer to them, particularly Prince Singh's early exit, suggests they are a group we should certainly find out more about. Miss Glews' assertion that she may have seen two guests dressed similarly as pirates going upstairs may or may not be a red herring, but we should follow it up nonetheless.' He paused and cleared his throat. 'As to the information you gleaned from the guests, I would suggest the most salient revelation was not that the dowager countess had intended her ward, Miss Wynne, to be young Lord Fenwick-Langham's wife, for that was fairly common knowledge—'

Eleanor snorted. 'Not to me, it wasn't, Clifford!'

Clifford mopped the tea off the tablecloth. 'Agreed, my lady. However, as I was saying, the most salient information was that young Lord Fenwick-Langham was heard by Miss Wynne arguing with the colonel shortly before the colonel was killed. The difficulty with following up that line of enquiry, of course, is that unless someone else overheard the argument we can't move forward with it, seeing as the two gentlemen involved cannot readily be questioned.'

Eleanor sighed deeply. 'I know. One is… dead and the other is incarcerated.' She shook her head. 'I'll just have to persuade the inspector to let me see Lancelot again, although I don't know how.'

A knock on the morning-room door interrupted them.

'Yes?'

Mrs Butters entered. 'Apologies for the interruption, my lady, you have a visitor.'

'Who is it?'

'It is Lady Coco Childs.'

Eleanor blinked. 'Really? What on earth can she want? Maybe she'll have some news that will help Lancelot. Please stick her up on the terrace, it's a beautiful morning.'

As the housekeeper left, she turned to Clifford. 'I'll have to swim through another pot of tea I suppose. You know I doubt that the Duchess of Bedford really thought through her invention of the oh-so-fashionable afternoon tea. She clearly gave no regard for the consequence of one having a host of unexpected guests.'

Clifford tutted. 'Most irresponsible of the duchess, my lady. Perhaps she never envisioned it being served in the morning?'

Eleanor ignored the quip. 'I say, how about you do your wonderful butler thing of hanging around unnoticed. You might pick up something I miss.'

'It will be a pleasure to' – he sniffed – 'hang around unnoticed, as you put it.'

'Good-oh!'

'Lady Childs!' Eleanor said as she stepped onto the balustraded terrace, which was bathed in the midday June sunlight. The intoxicating scent from the lilac and lavender borders rose up with that of the recently mown lawn, heralding this was summer proper. Dashes of tiger-orange lilies and montbretia brought the steady hum of bees busy about their business.

Her guest immediately leapt to her feet and kissed Eleanor on both cheeks. 'Good morning, shall we just go for Coco? All that other stuff is such a bind, don't you find?'

Eleanor was left with a smell of quite delightful perfume and an immediate sense of warmth towards her unexpected guest. 'Of course, Coco, call me Eleanor. To what do I owe the pleasure?'

'You are sweet. I would have understood entirely if you'd sent me away with a flea in my ear when I arrived unannounced. Frightfully rude, I know, but I really need to talk to you.'

'Fire away.' Eleanor pulled out a chair and adjusted the parasol to keep the sun from both their eyes. 'You'll take tea, of course?'

Coco nodded as Clifford set the tray down. Running her finger along the edge of her cream silk scarf, she sighed. 'It's this awful business with Lancelot. I can't believe he's been accused of…' She leaned forward and hissed, 'You know, murder. That's why I'm here. Because we… well, I, hoped you would be able to help. By the way, were you interviewed by that handsome detective fellow? Dreamy or what!'

'Interrogated would be a better description,' Eleanor said.

'Interro— you mean he accused you?' She put her hand over her mouth in shock. 'Of what? Stealing Lady Fenwick-Langham's necklace? Not of… murdering the colonel? The very idea!'

'Something of that sort, yes,' said Eleanor.

Lady Childs picked up her cup and took a shaky sip. 'I'm so sorry, my dear. I realise one mustn't speak ill of the dead and all that, but I would understand entirely if you had done the terrible deed. The colonel was rather bothersome to be around.'

'Did you know the colonel well?'

'Not so much knew him as kept running into him. Social circles in these parts are distressingly small in the main. We like to hang out elsewhere but have to put in an appearance at the right event every now and then, you know, to keep the… er, allowance rolling in.' A slight colour hit her cheeks. 'Lucas and Johnny used to get in a rage about the colonel always being there, pouring cold water on everyone's fun.'

'Oh yes, but did *Lancelot* ever row with the colonel?'

'Not exactly row, not like pistols at dawn, but they had plenty of heated exchanges.'

'What about?'

'Well, not to put too fine a point on it, the colonel thought Lancelot a wastrel and an embarrassment to his parents. He let Lancelot know his opinion of him in his usual untactful way and Lancelot, being Lancelot, told him in no uncertain terms what he thought about the colonel.' Coco paused. 'You know, Lancelot never stopped talking about you.'

'He didn't? How tiresome for you all.' Eleanor tried to shrug it off, but her face betrayed her. She hurriedly gestured to the iced finger fancies that Mrs Trotman had managed to magic up. Coco shook her head.

'Oh, Eleanor, come on, we're just girls together here. You're dying to find out what he said about you and don't pretend otherwise.' She accepted her refilled cup with a coy smile. 'Everyone likes a fun, handsome chap to be interested in them.'

Eleanor's face flushed. 'Coco, honestly, I've only been here a few months and I've already got caught up in things I never dreamed of.' She sighed. 'I really haven't got time for any other… complications.'

'Whatever you say, but that's exactly why I thought you could help. We all heard about how you solved that last murder.' She shuddered. 'I can't understand how another human being could actually take a life. What a monster you'd have to be!'

Eleanor peered at her elegant, slim guest, recalling one or two of the more unsavoury characters she'd encountered on her journeys who would have slit a stranger's throat for a shilling without a moment's regret.

Coco was still speaking, '... and it was Lancelot who told us about it all.'

The mention of his name pulled Eleanor out of her reverie. 'Coco, how long have you known Lancelot?'

'I'm not sure. Sometimes when he's being annoying, it feels like forever.' She giggled. 'He does go on with his jokes and his wheezes. Actually, we've known each other since we were kids. I say, that makes me sound frightfully old, doesn't it?' Before Eleanor could politely disagree, she hurried on. 'May I tell you something in total confidence?'

'Of course.' Eleanor had to fight to keep her eyes off Clifford as he stood just inside the door out to the terrace.

'Well, I came here... to help Millie really.'

Eleanor digested this piece of unexpected information. 'Go on.'

'Well, poor old stick, she'd kill me if she found out I'd told you. It's embarrassing really, but she's had a thing for Lancelot for simply yonks.' Coco's face fell. 'Golly, I'm probably treading on your toes, how insensitive of me.'

Eleanor pretended not to be jealous. 'Not a bit, do carry on.'

'Well, Millie has done everything to catch Lancelot's eye but no matter what she does, he just seems to think of her as a friend, a chum. It's awful. I've watched her break her heart over him for so long. Millie's gutted about him being arrested, as we all are. I thought if you could help, it might help her particularly.'

Eleanor set her cup down and sat back in her chair. 'Coco, I appreciate your honesty and for taking me into your confidence regarding your sister's feelings. I don't believe Lancelot is guilty and I intend to make sure justice is done by him.'

Coco sat back with a sigh of relief. 'Oh, Eleanor, thank you so much, I can't tell you how grateful I am. We're supposed to be Lancelot's oldest friends but the others are all just mooching about saying things like, "Would you believe it!" and "Who'd have thought!" We're pretty useless at the whole sleuthing thing.' She gave a weak smile. 'Good at partying though. At least that's what people say about us.'

'What do they say?'

'Oh, you must have heard. Someone like the colonel would surely have climbed aboard his hobby horse when you were within earshot. It's so tired, all the stiffs…' Coco clapped both her hands over her mouth. 'Oh no, no, I didn't mean "stiff" as in… no longer with us. Oh, I wish I was better with words.' She shook her head. 'The talk is that we're brash, frivolous, over-privileged and well, rather vacuous. But we do get invited to all the top society events, so there must be something people like about us.'

Lancelot's words came back to Eleanor again: *No one knows the identity of the jewel thief… but he does seem to pick parties we're at.*

Perhaps he was onto something? Perhaps one of his gang was the jewel thief? The few leads she'd picked up from interviewing the staff and guests at Langham Manor seemed tenuous at best, so she was willing to grasp at any straw, and Clifford had said they should follow up on Lancelot's gang.

Her guest was staring at her, a puzzled look on her face. Eleanor shook her head.

'Sorry, Coco, maybe I can help. And perhaps the best way would be to chat to Lancelot's friends who were at the ball. You could arrange that, couldn't you?'

'Lovely idea!' she said quickly but then hesitated. She turned her cup back and forth on its saucer. 'You know we're pretty select about who we invite to hang out with us. There's been so many desperately awful hangers-on who want to be seen with the "In Set".' She shrugged and then leaned forward. 'Hang on! I say, why don't you come along tonight? We're partying at the Blind Pig, it's a fabulous club on the outskirts of Oxford. It really is the bee's knees. I'll tell the others I've invited you.'

'Sounds great.'

'Wonderful. And thanks again for offering to help out.'

'No problem, we'll do everything we can.'

'We?' Coco glanced at Clifford, seemingly seeing him for the first time. 'Gracious, I had forgotten that you worked with your butler on the other case. You really are quite the unconventional cat! See you tonight.'

'I look forward to it,' said Eleanor, kissing Coco goodbye.

'Thank you, darling, you're a lifesaver.' She left with a wave.

Once they were alone, Eleanor turned to Clifford. 'Well, what do you think, Clifford? Millie Childs is in love with Lancelot. Who'd have thought?'

'Who indeed?' said Clifford. He looked a little amused.

She hurried on. 'You see, I remembered something Lancelot said in jail, that the bright young things gang were at most of the society events at which the jewel thief struck. So I thought if I met up with them again, I could do a bit of digging.'

Clifford nodded. 'A fine idea, my lady. However, their presence at those events is interesting, but not necessarily that incriminating. The social set at that level is quite limited here, compared to, say, London. The guest list for most high-end social gatherings tends to be distressingly similar.'

Eleanor shook her head. 'That may be, Clifford, but at the moment it's the best we've got apart from following up on the few leads I ferreted out from my interviews earlier.'

She glanced at Clifford when he didn't reply.

'What?' She made a face at him. 'Okay, maybe I also want to find out if Millie and Lancelot had a fling, and if it really is all over. Mind you, I don't care much for the sound of this nightclub. What was it? The Bloated Pig? Sounds charming!'

'The Blind Pig, my lady. It really is quite the place to be seen if you want to be one of the "in" crowd.'

'Well, I definitely don't, but I'd better pretend I do. Oh blast that Lancelot, the things he's got me doing are ridiculous!'

CHAPTER 13

'If you remember, my lady, Lord and Lady Fenwick-Langham are due in ten minutes to discuss our progress.'

It was just after midday, and Eleanor had indeed remembered. In truth, she was glad of the distraction. She wiggled out from under Gladstone's bulky form and brushed down her dress.

Out in the bright sunshine she settled on a bench, while Gladstone, who to her surprise had woken up and followed her out, collapsed at her feet and promptly started snoring. 'Great help you're going to be, old chum,' she said softly as she ran her hand over his warm round belly.

She looked across the perfect lawn at the exquisitely decorated table Clifford and the ladies had prepared. Below individual ivory parasols, four white wicker wingback chairs sat precisely spaced, the cushion on each matching the silk embroidered tablecloth of delicate pink and crimson roses. Their cheerful ambience was echoed in the bright, fine-china tea service of exquisitely painted birds, each bearing a different flower in their beak.

Mrs Butters appeared on the terrace and waved to Clifford.

'Ah, I believe your guests are just arriving, my lady.'

'Eleanor, my dear. It is so good to see you.' The corners of Lady Langham's deep-blue eyes crinkled as she held both of Eleanor's hands and smiled fondly at her. Two rebellious grey curls fluttered against her pale and drawn cheeks.

Eleanor smiled back. 'Likewise. I confess I've been worried about how you are holding up. And Harold too, of course.' She turned to him and was relieved to see a glimmer in his deep-set grey eyes. His handlebar moustache quivered as he grinned.

'Keeping up appearances, what. Frightfully proud of the mem-sahib though, backbone of steel my wife has.'

Eleanor looped her arm through Lady Langham's. 'I think you're both doing an incredible job. Please, come and sit down.' She steered them to the table. Eleanor sat opposite Lady Langham and Lord Langham plopped down beside his wife. Gladstone sprawled by Eleanor's feet with a contented huff.

'Clifford, I believe we are ready for refreshments. And if you would join us, please.'

'Very good.' Clifford gave a discreet semaphore with three gloved fingers to Mrs Butters who was poised at the top of the terrace steps. He stood beside the last chair, hands clasped in front of him.

Lord Langham flapped his napkin at him. 'That's not joining us, Clifford. You're a major part of this bally detective enterprise.'

Eleanor patted the arm of the chair. With a deep breath, Clifford allowed himself to perch rigidly on the edge of it.

The tea and several silver stands of savoury pastries arrived with a smiling Mrs Butters and an anxiously jiggling Polly. Much to Eleanor's delight, there was an impressive array of different options. At her feet, Gladstone's nose began to twitch.

Lord Langham rubbed his hands. 'Spiffing show, my dear Eleanor. Advance compliments to Cook.' Mrs Butters curtsied and gently pushing Polly in front of her, disappeared up the steps.

Eleanor nodded to Clifford to pour the tea, which he dutifully did, adding a generous measure of brandy to Lord Langham's. Lady Langham indicated that a soupçon should be added to hers as well.

'No pressure, Eleanor my dear, you know how grateful we are that you are trying to help our son, but do you have any good news for us?'

Knowing she couldn't put off the inevitable, Eleanor nevertheless tried to ease into the conversation gently. 'Possibly, but I must congratulate you, Augusta, on your ingenious idea of the croquet match.'

Lord Langham smacked his lips after his glug of tea. 'Marvellous creature, eh? So inventive and resourceful. Could have done with her out in the woolly wilds of the subcontinent on occasions.'

Clifford coughed. 'Lady Swift told me all about it. Most ingenious. She and I were just going over the facts of the case before you arrived. There were a great number of guests at the ball.'

At the 'b' word, Gladstone jumped up, tail wagging. Eleanor shook her head until he flopped back onto the grass with a heavy sigh that made his jowls flutter.

Clifford continued. 'How to narrow them down? Well, we know that the notorious Oxfordshire jewel thief was present, so we're likely looking for someone at your ball who was present at the other parties where the robberies took place.'

'Indeed,' said Eleanor. 'We've come up with a list of the other parties and the dates on which they were held. It doesn't seem that the colonel was at many of the other parties where jewels were taken, so it is unlikely that he was intimately acquainted with the jewel thief.'

'Therefore with your permission,' said Clifford, 'might I offer the suggestion that the colonel's demise may have come as the result of being in the wrong place at the wrong time. Regrettably, he disturbed the jewel thief and paid the terrible consequences.'

'Of course,' Lady Langham said quietly. 'Maybe you're right, although he ruffled some feathers over the years. He could certainly poke his nose in when it wasn't wanted.'

Eleanor noted her cool tone and hastened on. 'An alternative possibility is this. Your head housemaid, Miss Glew, mentioned that the colonel had asked to move from his original rooms. Perhaps he left the ball for a moment to retrieve something and happened into the study on his way past?'

Lady Langham pursed her lips. 'He did rather take it upon himself to wander around as he wished. But he had no business being in the study at that time. He should have been downstairs, playing second host with Harold.'

Lord Langham stroked his chin. 'Something made him toddle off up there, though. Perhaps one of the staff knew why. They seem to have a better bally hold on who comes and goes in my house than I do.'

'That, my dear Harold, is because unless it looks like a pheasant and you're up to the top of your favourite hunting boots in mud, it rarely registers with you.' Lady Langham's stern tone was undermined by the affectionate smile she gave her husband. She turned to Eleanor. 'Did any of the staff see the colonel just before the fateful moment?'

Eleanor nodded. 'Parsons, Sandford's second in command. He said he saw the colonel going upstairs just after I landed on my face in the ballroom.' Clifford raised a questioning eyebrow. She waved a hand. 'Long story. Anyway, he mentioned seeing the colonel go on up muttering something about "there goes the cad!"'

'The bounder!' Lord Langham spluttered. 'I'll put the fellow in his place, what!'

'Those weren't Parsons' words, Harold. Eleanor was quoting the colonel.' Lady Langham sighed and patted his hand. 'Do keep up, dear.'

Lord Langham looked suitably contrite. 'Right-oh, old thing. Sounds like something Pudders would say, though. But who was he referring to?'

'I was rather hoping you might be able to help us there.' Eleanor mentally crossed her fingers.

''Fraid not, my dear. Haven't a bally clue,' said Lord Langham. 'Clue! I'm starting to sound like a real detective, what!' he said, sounding delighted.

'Ah well, never mind. Clifford and I shall return to the attack after lunch,' said Eleanor.

'All credit to you, my dear Eleanor.' Lady Langham shivered. 'Discussing murder on a full stomach would surely bring on my dyspepsia, I fear.'

'Perhaps a strong stomach is another of my blessings.'

'And a hearty, country appetite.' Lord Langham laughed, pointing at the multitude of pastries Eleanor had been munching through.

'Harold!' his wife chided. 'Sorry, my dear. I do hope Lancelot is more courteous than his reprobate of a father.'

Eleanor smiled at them both. 'Shall I give you the short version of what I learned at the croquet match?'

Lord Langham held his hands up. 'My dear girl, tell us the pertinent facts while we lay waste to more of these delicious pastry fellows. Have you tried this mushroom concoction, Augusta? Sublime little beast.' Gladstone's stare intently followed Lord Langham's hand as he waved the pastry. 'Carry on, old thing.'

Eleanor took this as her cue. 'The only unfortunate revelation was that the delightful Miss Wynne said she witnessed Lancelot having something of a tiff with the colonel in the garden. No one else saw, so hopefully that will not reach the ears of the police.' She fiddled with her teaspoon. 'Cora did also discreetly mention that perhaps Lancelot had been, erm…'

'Lined up by Daphne to be her saviour?' Lady Langham said. 'It's alright, my dear, we can be candid here amongst ourselves.'

'Thank you, but I'm sure Cora wouldn't do anything that might get Lancelot into trouble, even if she were miffed that he hadn't ridden in on his white charger and swept her up.'

Lady Langham shuddered. 'He'd have been more likely to roar in on that wretched motorbike he insists on keeping.'

Eleanor hoped they wouldn't get on to the subject of the dowager countess and her motive for wanting revenge on Lancelot. The dowager countess, after all, was one of the Fenwick-Langhams' oldest friends and the idea was preposterous anyway. Which didn't mean that she and Clifford had ruled out the possibility, just that she had no idea how to broach it with Lady Langham.

Clifford seemed to sense her embarrassment. He rose and refilled each of the teacups and offered the pastries round again. 'Perhaps we should move on to Viscount and Viscountess Littleton?'

Eleanor smiled in relief. 'Good idea, Clifford. I believe Viscountess Littleton said that her husband had been called away the morning after the poor colonel's passing?'

Clifford coughed discreetly. 'It did strike me as most odd that Viscount Littleton would leave his wife in such a situation, whether the murderer had apparently been caught or not.'

Eleanor turned to Lady Langham. 'Have you known them long?'

Lady Langham set her cup back on its saucer. 'To answer your question, Eleanor dear, we've known Cuthbert for about six... no, seven years now. Obviously, his wife for less long. He came to advise Harold on some difficult legal aspect when we had a dreadfully tiresome matter hanging over us and he has somehow become part of our regular guest list ever since.' Lady Langham looked thoughtful. 'I confess he suffered at the colonel's waspish tongue all too often.'

'Over anything in particular?' Eleanor asked.

'It seemed to be a long-standing dispute that the colonel refused to drop. I believe it was regarding some legal advice Cuthbert gave which the colonel felt had disadvantaged him considerably. Isn't that right, Harold?'

''Fraid so. Pudders was never one to let go of an old argument. Total terrier when he thought he had reason to be aggrieved. Dashedly vocal about it too, silly fool.'

Eleanor noted the tinge of sadness in his voice and racked her brain for a new direction to steer the conversation in. She clicked her fingers. 'One of the most important things we needed to do was account for everyone's movements over the course of the evening, notably around the time that the... er, unpleasant event brought a finale to your wonderful ball. Your staff were very diligent in their duties and consequently were able to assure me of most people's movements throughout.'

'Sandford is a gem, keeps the staff in good order,' Lord Langham agreed. 'Like you, Clifford, a quiet force to be reckoned with.'

'Thank you, sir. It is fortuitous that all of your guests were well known to you, although of course, it was a masked ball, I understand.'

'And some were in full costume,' Eleanor added, waving for the bulldog to sit. 'Like Lancelot and his friends.'

'And his young lordship was dressed as a pirate?' asked Clifford.

Eleanor frowned. 'But he might not have been the only pirate.'

'I didn't see any others,' Lord Langham offered. 'But apparently I only spot game birds.' He gestured towards his wife. He took his napkin from his lap and shook it over the grass, smiling as Gladstone pounced on every last morsel of the flaky pastry crumbs.

Eleanor smiled at the greedy bulldog. 'Augusta, did you see anyone else dressed as a pirate?'

She tapped her chin thoughtfully. 'No, but I wouldn't have been surprised.' Then she peered at Eleanor. 'What is it, my dear? You look quite perplexed.'

'Oh, it was just something else Miss Glew said about Lancelot's costume.'

Clifford tilted his head. 'Which was, my lady?'

'That she thought she saw Lancelot go up the stairs, but then saw him go up again shortly after. That's why I wondered if someone else had come as a pirate.'

Lady Langham tutted again. 'Probably one of his pranks. He likely went up the stairs normally, and then slid down the servants' staircase so that he could magically reappear and be seen going up again.'

'But why would he do that?'

'My dear girl, why does Lancelot do anything that he does? I love him with all my heart, but I rarely understand an ounce of what is going on in his head.'

Eleanor mentally agreed. 'Aside from Miss Glew mentioning a pair of pirate legs going up the stairs, the only other person who reported seeing more than one pirate was Sandford.'

'Was there a common theme among the costumes of his young lordship and friends, perhaps?' Clifford asked.

Eleanor ticked them off on her fingers. 'Not that I could detect. Pirate, Cleopatra, a bird of paradise, a Raphael painting and a harlequin.'

'Hmm…' Lady Langham stared at Clifford over the rim of her teacup. 'But perhaps I interrupted your thoughts, Clifford?'

'Not at all, my lady. I was merely wondering what his Royal Highness Prince Singh sported as a costume? Perhaps he came as a pirate too?'

Eleanor shrugged. 'I missed Lucas' effort. He'd already left before I arrived.'

Lady Langham huffed. 'Young people these days. Whatever are standards and manners coming to, Clifford?'

'I really couldn't comment, my lady,' Clifford replied.

Eleanor tapped the table. 'But we didn't find out what Lucas was wearing.'

This made Lord Langham chuckle again. 'I know. And it wasn't a pirate. Saw the fellow when he arrived. Thought it was quite striking. A highwayman costume, the full Dick Turpin with black cape, black hat and mask.'

'If his costume was so singularly themed in black,' Clifford said, 'it might explain why no one saw him leave the premises. After making his way to his car, he would have been quite the invisible man in the dark.'

CHAPTER 14

Eleanor stared out of the Rolls' window at the blackness beyond. 'I'm all up for partying but, honestly, starting at eleven o'clock in the evening is a bit of a jolt for the old body clock. I am seriously out of practice at this.'

'It is all part of the rebellion against authority and social propriety I believe, my lady,' Clifford said.

'Well, I should fit right in then.'

Clifford pulled up at the steps to the club. 'Perhaps, my lady. However, if you will forgive me repeating my earlier concern, if one of young Lord Fenwick-Langham's friends did commit the crimes, you could be in significant peril.'

Eleanor turned to face him. 'Honestly, it's going to be so horribly crowded in there, no one will have the chance to do anything untoward, trust me.'

He nodded to the glass-fronted entrance. 'I believe that is Lady Coco and Lady Millicent Childs arriving now.'

Eleanor watched the two sisters step out of the car, Millie marching up the steps, leaving her sister scrabbling with the strap of her elegant grey dance shoe.

'There's my cue then.' She battled with the folds of her emerald-green beaded dress, the gold tassels along the drop sash waistband threatening to create an impossible tangle. 'Hang on though, Clifford, you can't sit out here all night waiting for me, it'll probably be something horrible like dawn when we leave.'

'No problem, my lady. There is a club I am a member of on Abingdon Street, The Carlton Club. It is behind the spires you can see just to the right.'

'Marvellous, then settle yourself in there and I shall appear when we're done.'

'With apologies, my lady, I fear it would be most unwise of you to walk there…'

'When will you realise that I am eminently capable of looking after myself? Dash it, I made it around the world on my own for long enough. I think Oxford is unlikely to be a match for the dangers of Bombay or Isfahan.'

'Granted, one is always mindful of your adventurous exploits, my lady. However, how many times were you possibly in the company of a murderer?'

She started counting on her fingers and then grinned at his frown. 'I shall be just fine. See you later.'

Eleanor noted that Clifford waited until she had walked up the steps before easing the Rolls out of the swing-through driveway. The two doormen flanking the glass doors opened them simultaneously on her arrival. Suddenly feeling like the gawky new girl, she straightened the pearl studded headband of her gold lace fascinator and slapped on a smile.

The oval-shaped lobby shouted opulence with its heavy use of gold drapes and red velvet flock wallpaper. Glittering chandeliers hung low, adding to an atmosphere that whispered entry beyond this point demanded a large wallet and a penchant for the illicit. The cloakroom attendant stood behind a long counter, the front panel inlaid with black-and-white tiles in a bold geometric pattern.

'Good evening, miss. First time here?' The petite girl's blonde curls bobbed against her highly rouged cheeks.

'I'm meeting my friends, Lady Millicent and Lady Coco Childs,' she said, handing over her shawl.

'Ah, they'll be down in the swing room, in one of the purple velvet booths near the stage. Lady Coco is a very generous tipper, she's super kind.'

'And Lady Millicent?' Eleanor asked.

The girl smiled weakly. 'Lady Millicent is... very generous too. Take the left-hand staircase and have fun.'

'Thank you, you too.'

'Good evening, sir, shall I take your coat?' The girl's voice faded as Eleanor made her way down the sweeping, red plush carpeted stairs. She paused as the swing room came into view, searching for Coco. Spotting her at the far end, she waved and Coco beckoned her over.

She rose as Eleanor arrived at the table, which, as predicted, was only a short distance from the stage where a seven-piece band was setting up.

'Hey, welcome.' Coco smiled. 'You made it.'

'Of course. Howdy!' Eleanor gave a general wave to the table.

'Hi there.' Lucas waved his glass. 'Great to finally meet you.'

Eleanor smiled at him. 'And you too. I hope you sorted your emergency out the night of the ball.'

He looked confused for a moment and then laughed. 'Oh, yes, that. All fine now, thanks. An aunt was having a "fit of the vapours", as I believe you call it? Our family loves a spot of drama.'

'Good evening.' Albert half rose from his rather low seat, pulled up to the table.

'Are you planning to entertain the assembled crowd once again with your flailing frog on the floor impression, Lady Swift?' Millie's face lit up with a smile that didn't reach her eyes.

'Millie, please!' Coco hissed.

'Oh, rather.' Eleanor grinned. 'I intend to make an absolute spectacle of myself on the dance floor. Nothing like notoriety I always find.'

The others laughed heartily, except Millie, who rolled her eyes. 'Johnny's late, as always!' Coco tutted.

'He really is a shocker for timekeeping,' Albert said.

'Actually.' Eleanor slid in next to Lucas. 'I'm pretty shocking at arriving on time, too.'

Albert snorted. 'But Mister So-Special-Seaton does it on purpose. He's a total blockhead about needing to make an entrance every time we meet, always has to be the centre of attention.'

'Who?' Eleanor frowned.

Coco raised her voice over the noise of the band tuning up. 'He means Johnny, his surname is Seaton. Albie's jealous because Johnny tends to turn lots of heads whenever he finally deigns to arrive.'

'And dear old Albie doesn't.' Lucas slapped his friend on the shoulder.

Albert glared at him. 'We can't all be born princes.'

'Johnny's not titled, is he?' Eleanor asked Coco, who laughed at the question.

'No, but he certainly acts the part! His father's a banker. But we don't care about all that stuff, anyway. The whole class system is so antiquated. Times are moving.'

Millie scowled. 'Well, I'm not giving up my title for anyone. If you think I'm going to marry a commoner, you're dumber than a slapped maid.' She turned her stare on Eleanor. 'What about you, *Lady* Swift, what do you say?'

Eleanor smiled sweetly. 'Oh, I'd say marriage needs to be for love, regardless of titles. Not much point in having all the trappings if you're not happy.'

'Hear, hear!' Albert said.

Millie snorted. 'Of course you'd agree, Albie, you simple pimple, you haven't got anything to give up.'

Albert banged the table. 'I jolly well have. I've got the best degree of the lot of you. And ideas. And… connections.'

'Yes, but only with us, you chump.' Lucas laughed and stood up. 'Round three, my turn, same again all?'

Millie banged her glass on the table. 'About time, mine's been empty for ages. An Aviator Fizz for me this time, a large one.'

'If it's not too lowly for you to buy a commoner a drink?' Albert held his glass out.

Coco clapped her hands. 'Make mine one of those fabulous looking things in the tulip-shaped glass. The one with a lemon twist wound round the stem.'

Millie shook her head. 'It's called a Hanky Panky. You could try and be a bit more cool, you know. Lucas, don't forget about Eleanor, the poor thing hasn't even had one yet. We don't want her to feel she's lagging behind now, do we?'

Lucas ignored the snipe and grinned at Eleanor. 'Sorry, new chum of ours, how rude of me. I should have run to the bar when you arrived. What'll it be?'

Eleanor couldn't see a drinks menu anywhere. 'What's the signature cocktail here? Oh, though given the name of the club, it's probably some hideous concoction made from beech nuts with bacon bits floating on the top.'

The table roared with laughter at this, except Millie who crossed her arms. 'Lucas, I know the perfect cocktail for Eleanor.'

He cocked an eyebrow.

'Get her an Angel Face.'

'You know, Millie, you're really mean sometimes.' Coco threw Eleanor an apologetic smile.

'What?' Millie said innocently. 'She looks like an angel with her gold organza halo.'

Eleanor shrugged at Lucas. 'That sounds wonderful, thank you.'

'Back in a jif.'

He crossed the dance floor to the ivory-and-turquoise bar that ran the full length of one wall. Eleanor looked about, taking in the elaborately tiled faux renaissance pillars and artful silhouettes of dancing couples covering the other walls.

She caught sight of Johnny as he came down the stairs. Effortlessly debonair, he paused and bowed to the many heads he knew he'd turned, before skipping down the last steps as lightly as a dancer. He headed over to the bar where he slapped Lucas on the back. The women at the tables nearest the bar tried to hide their obvious interest in this suave new arrival. She watched Johnny waltz an imaginary partner over to their table.

'What ho! What round are we on?' He leaned across and kissed Millie and Coco on both cheeks.

'Well, it should be your round by now,' Albert said.

'Nonsense, old bean. It must be yours, simply because it's been your round since 1819.'

'Tommy rot! I pay my way.' Albert's face coloured.

'No one's saying you don't, Albie.' Coco's tone was soft. 'Johnny, let him be.'

'Anything for the ladies,' Johnny said. 'Ah, but I see we have another Lady in our midst.' He nodded at Eleanor.

Millie leaned her elbows on the table. 'Yes, she is a Lady but she's prepared to give it all up for love. Such a noble attitude.'

Eleanor glanced at Millie. 'Apparently my outlook on marriage is somewhat amusing.'

'But you're not married.' Coco frowned.

Eleanor shrugged. 'Not any more.'

Coco gasped as Millie whispered to her, 'Ha! Divorced. Lady Fenwick-Langham won't accept that, not for all the roses in England.'

Eleanor decided not to enlighten her. In fact, she was a widow. She'd married in South Africa six years previously after losing her head to a dashing officer. He turned out not to be an officer at all, and vanished shortly afterwards pursued by the South African authorities. For what, she never found out. Then the war started and she heard nothing more for several months until a government official informed her he'd been shot for selling arms to the enemy.

At that moment, Lucas came back, deftly balancing a large tray of drinks and, to Eleanor's delight, a silver tiered stand of savoury finger nibbles.

'Good show.' Johnny took the drinks off the tray two at a time and handed them round. 'What the heck is that?' He peered at the highball glass stacked with ice, a lethal-looking amber liquid and orange slices hanging from the rim. 'Wait, Eleanor, you didn't let Millie order for you, did you?'

At her nod, he laughed. 'Silly girl, you'll soon learn.' He placed her drink in front of her. 'Good luck and God bless your head tomorrow! Now, a toast to our absent friend!'

Everyone raised their glasses. 'To dear old Lance, may he soon be back among us!'

Millie took a long sip of her Aviatior Fizz, then turned the champagne saucer in her diamond covered wrist. 'Lucas, the band are in full swing now. I want to dance.'

'Then I'd better oblige, dear lady.' Lucas took a swig from his glass and looked at Eleanor. 'I've got to make the most of this. I'll be back in India in two years when father believes I will have' – he mimed quotation marks with his fingers – '"finished my education". And that'll be the end of twirling about with outrageous women.'

'I'm not outrageous.' Millie was obviously delighted with the accusation.

'Yes you are!' the others chorused.

Millie cocked an eyebrow at Eleanor. 'Don't worry though, Lucas, at least I won't embarrass you by falling on my face.'

Lucas took her hand and they disappeared across to the centre of the dance floor. Eleanor noted Millie's gold satin heels were ridiculously high for dance shoes and wondered how on earth she'd stay upright.

Johnny tapped a cigarette on the silver case he'd pulled from his inside pocket and stopped with it halfway to his mouth. He waved at someone across the room. 'Excuse me, an old chum.' He rose and strode towards the bar calling, 'Jeffers, long time, no see, old man.'

'I'm going to powder my nose.' Coco rose and left Eleanor alone with Albert, who sat glumly staring at his drink.

She tried to think of something to break the silence. 'Do you dance, Albie?'

'No, I write poetry. You can't write poetry *and* dance.'

'Well, not at the same time, I suppose.' She searched for another topic. 'Do you all come here often?'

He nodded. 'Yes. Lancelot thinks it's the bee's knees and the cat's pyjamas and other ridiculous expressions he picked up from his American friends. He's been dragging us here for ages.'

'How did you meet Lancelot?'

'I'm a private tutor. I have several clients.' He straightened his jacket collar. 'One of whom is Coco and Millie's younger brother. Coco invited me along with the gang.'

'And now you're good friends with them all?'

'Hmm, some of them have a funny way of being friendly, but what goes round, comes round.' He turned his glass in his hand. 'Do you know William Blake's poem, "Poison Tree"?' Without waiting for her reply he began to recite:

'I was angry with my friend
'I told my wrath, my wrath did end

'I was angry with my foe

'I told it not, my wrath did grow.'

While he was reciting the poem, Albert's eyes had filled with a strange glow. Eleanor had seen that look in men before. That dark brooding stare, alarmingly hawkish, with the pain of a wounded animal behind those intense eyes. She mentally made a note to find out as much as she could about Mr Appleby. As at last the poem finished, she said, 'That's… er, beautiful and… poignant.' Unable to shift the frown that pulled across her forehead, she stood up. 'Would you excuse me just a moment?'

She made a quick escape and found the ladies' powder room at the top of the stairs. As she entered she caught a low voice.

'Just do it, you little beast. Don't ask any questions or I'll have you fired!'

She instinctively stepped into a stall and pushed the door almost to. The voice had sounded familiar. She stood frozen behind the door. The footsteps paused at the basin.

'I'll be waiting,' the same voice hissed.

Eleanor looked down and saw two ridiculously high gold satin heels.

CHAPTER 15

Back in the swing room Lucas and Millie were returning to their table, with Johnny close behind. Once seated, Johnny picked up his drink and turned to Millie.

'I'm parched, just let me have a swig and I'll dance your feet off, seeing as you've begged so plaintively.'

'Begged! You arrogant fathead.' She slapped him on the shoulder, looking pleased.

He downed his glass and slid her arm through his. 'Come on, twinkle toes, let's show this place how to swing properly.'

Lucas clapped Johnny's retreating back. 'Thanks, old man, she's a wildcat. I'm bushed!'

He plumped down next to Eleanor, much to Albert's annoyance as he had half risen to slide into that very seat.

'Too slow, Albie. Honestly, you wouldn't last a minute in India, a tiger would have you in a blink. You've got to be watchful, fast, the hunter not the hunted.' He looked at Eleanor, his dark eyes glinting.

'Which part of India are you from?' she asked.

'The largest part,' Albert muttered loud enough for both of them to catch.

'Sour fruit, Albie my friend. My father is, as you well know, the maharaja of the demurely sized province of Malwar. It's not all fun and playboy living. That's why I'm making the most of being here. It'll be a very different life back at the palace. I'll have no choice but to… behave.'

Albert huffed at the word 'palace' and stared at Eleanor. She tried to divert his attention. 'Ah, now you see I was disappointed to have missed out on seeing Malwar while following the Ganges and earlier, the Silk Road.'

'Well, in that case you've missed the most beautiful part of India.' Lucas frowned. 'Hang on, the Silk Road? Ladies don't just happen to follow Signore Marco Polo's epic route.'

'Oh, it was when I was travelling and working.'

'Working?'

'Yes, I was scouting out routes for Thomas Walker's travel company. He rather fancied setting up some tours from Tibet and India that would deposit adventurous tour goers at the Bengal basin where they would take the steamer around the coast and up to Bombay.'

He looked at her with new respect. 'Or *Mumbai*. That's its Indian name. I'm awfully grateful for my English schooling, but underneath I'm an Indian Nationalist, I'm afraid. I wish for her to be returned to her own people.'

Eleanor nodded. 'I understand. I often felt the people that were so hospitable to me while I was travelling in India had lost a big part of their identity, whatever they may, or may not, have gained in exchange.'

Lucas waved his drink. 'Exactly!' He stared at her for a moment. 'You know, you're a lot like your uncle, I imagine. Not the conventional British aristocratic lady at all.'

Eleanor gasped. 'You knew Lord Henley?'

'No, but my father did. He talked about him and the... help he gave to my father.'

Lucas paused and seemed to decide that he'd said enough. Eleanor tried to think of something to keep him talking. 'I bet Colonel Puddifoot-Barton didn't agree with your views on home rule. Did you ever talk to him about them?'

Suddenly his mood darkened. 'Your uncle was the opposite of that blasted Barton oaf. Banging on about British rule, divide and conquer. I'd have divided him in half with a talwar if I'd had one!'

Eleanor caught her breath. As if he could read her mind, he looked abashed. 'Seems someone beat me to it, though. And anyway, I shouldn't speak ill of the deceased.' He smiled and drained his drink. 'Perhaps I haven't quite mastered the English art of thinking one thing and saying another?'

Eleanor laughed uneasily. Up to then, she'd just assumed that the colonel had disturbed the jewel thief, and the thief had killed the colonel on the spur of the moment. She hadn't really given any other theory credence. But suppose it was the other way around? Suppose the colonel *had* been the target all along and the jewel theft just a blind to throw the police? She needed to talk this over with Clifford as soon as possible. Until then, she needed to find out as much as she could about those who were becoming her two chief suspects: Lucas and Albert. She tried to draw Albert into the conversation.

'Albie, tell me about your latest poem. I'll bet you're working on something meaningful.'

Albert rose and finished his drink with a shaking hand. 'Indeed, I am. It's a tragedy about a man who was entirely unappreciated and constantly put down by his so-called friends, but who finally got his revenge! Please excuse me.' Slamming his glass down on the table, he pushed past Coco without a word.

'Crikey, what's got into Albie?' Coco settled next to Eleanor.

'The truth.' Lucas placed his hands palms down on the table.

'Oh, Lucas! You know what he's like,' Coco said. She bit her lip. 'Honestly, without Lancelot here Albie was hoping for some respite from all the jibes.'

Eleanor was confused. 'Does Lancelot rib him especially?'

Coco nodded. 'Yes, but he's worst when Johnny's around. They're like a pair of jackals forever circling poor old Albie, waiting to pounce with a comment or a dig, usually about his terrible poems. Or the fact that his father is' – she grimaced – 'a miner.'

Eleanor took a sip of her drink, mulling this new information over in her mind.

Millie arrived back at the table, leading Johnny by the hand. 'You boys are pathetic, you have absolutely no stamina.'

'Whatever you say, Millie old gal.' He flopped into the seat opposite Eleanor.

Millie looked at the glasses, all empty except Eleanor's. 'Lucas, it seems no one has bothered to follow up on your round.' She stared pointedly at Johnny, then back to Lucas. 'Come and whizz Coco and I round the floor together. We'll do that one, two, three move, it's hilarious.'

Lucas groaned but rose.

Coco grinned. 'It is rather fun actually.'

'Well, just watch my toes,' Millie said. 'I nearly lost half of them last time.' The three disappeared.

Johnny smiled at Eleanor. 'Would you like another drink?'

She stared at her glass. It seemed two thirds full, yet she was sure she'd finished it. Had someone bought her another? 'I'm okay for a while, thanks. What about you?'

He winked and pulled a hip flask from his pocket. 'I'm more of a fine cognac man than these made-up cocktails.' He tipped a hearty measure into his glass and held the base with both hands, swirling the golden liquid in delicate circles. 'Bad business about Lancelot, what?'

She stiffened, struck by the fact that none of the others had mentioned the matter.

'It's far from ideal,' she replied, more tersely than intended.

'I hope he's being a good boy and cooperating.'

'Why do you say that?' She leaned across the table.

Johnny relaxed back in his seat. 'Because he's an impossible, fat-headed clown.' He grinned at her. 'You must have noticed that, what with all the chasing you've been doing?' At her huff, he held up a hand. 'I'm just pulling your leg. I assumed you'd be missing his relentless gags.'

More than I can tell you.

He lit a cigarette, inhaling slowly and letting out an impressive smoke ring. 'Millie told me that you and your… butler fellow were going to get him out of jail.'

'Millie said that? But I haven't spoken to her about it. Actually, she hasn't really spoken to me at all.' Eleanor made a face.

Johnny grinned. 'Don't worry about her, she's a mean cat but her claws aren't as sharp as her tongue.'

'What are you spouting on about, Johnny?' Millie appeared behind him. 'I came for a cigarette. Give me one of yours.'

He waved his cigarette case at her. 'Here you are, old chimney pot.'

'This is your last ciggie, better get yourself some more.' She threw the empty pack on the table and sashayed back over to the others on the far side of the dance floor.

Johnny watched her go and turned back to Eleanor. 'So is Lancelot playing ball with the boys in blue down at the police station then?'

Eleanor sighed. 'No, he isn't. He's his own worst enemy.'

Johnny took another long drag from his cigarette. 'Of course, there are a few things that don't look good for poor old Lance, besides being found with the body and the murder weapon, that is.'

She stared at him. 'Like what?'

He leaned across to her and said with a serious tone, 'Just between you and me, right?'

She nodded, her pulse quickening.

'Thing is, it's his plane.'

'What about it?'

'The question should really be, what about them? This current one…'

'Florence.' Eleanor smiled at the memory of the day she had met Lancelot and found out that he called his plane 'Florence'.

'Precisely.' Johnny waved his cigarette at her. 'Well, he's had two others. Delores and... Daria, I think it was before her. The man's a terrible pilot, you know. Amazing he's still here, keeps crashing. Anyway, after he totalled Delores his mater pulled the plug on funding any more of his "circus antics" as she called them.'

'So how did Lancelot afford to buy his third plane, Florence, then?'

'No idea. It's probably completely legitimate, but it does look suspicious, what with all the jewel thefts that have happened at so many of the parties he's been at. I hope he ends up with the best lawyer in the land because I think otherwise...' Johnny ended with a low whistle.

Lucas' arrival with Millie draped around his neck and Coco with her arm through Albie's interrupted Eleanor's musings.

'I'm sorry,' Johnny said. 'I have to go. Some obscure old relative has turned up at the family pile and I need to dutifully welcome her. Catch you later.'

Once he'd left the table, Eleanor checked her fob watch. Two forty-five. A little late for seeing a relative, old or not.

'Bored, bored, BORED!' Millie seemed strangely more animated than before.

'Me too.' Coco looked at her sister and giggled. 'Come on, it's time for some proper fun.'

Albert blew his nose repeatedly and stared at Eleanor until she felt decidedly uncomfortable. Even Lucas appeared to have lost some of his composure.

'We're going to quit this dump and P.A.R.T.Y.' Millie's eyes flashed as she pouted at Eleanor. '*Do* come along, you've been such great company tonight.'

'Oh, thanks.' Eleanor rose. 'But I've got a whole heap on tomorrow. I'm going to head off.'

'I do believe, Eleanor, that you are a lightweight,' Coco said.

Eleanor smoothed out her waistband beads. 'Another time I'll show you all what I'm really made of.'

Lucas took her hand. 'I'm sure you will. And I'm sure we'll all be in awe. Come on, rabble, let's go!'

Albert hung back. 'Will you get home safely?'

Eleanor smiled at this awkward square peg. 'Thank you, Albie, you are a gentleman. I will indeed.'

He scuttled after the others and held his arm out stiffly for Coco, who pushed him jokingly and ran on ahead, looking back over her shoulder at him.

'Right!' Eleanor said to the empty table. 'Time to find my ride, as the Americans would say.'

In the lobby, the blonde-curled coat-check girl passed her her shawl. 'Had fun, miss?'

'Honestly, I'm not sure.'

'Shame, another time perhaps? There's no car waiting for you outside. Would you like me to call you a taxi?'

Eleanor called over her shoulder. 'No, thanks, I'm hoping the air will help me think.' She stopped. *That voice!* She quickly checked no one else was in the lobby and crossed back to the desk.

'Have you forgotten something, miss?'

There was no time for a subtle approach, someone could come at any moment. She was sure she was right. Eleanor leaned on the counter, uncharacteristically serious, her face only inches from the young girl. 'Listen, I know about you providing certain guests, particularly Lady Millicent Childs, with, shall we say, substances. If I were to tell the manager, or even... the police...'

The girl turned pale. She furtively glanced around the reception area. 'I-I-don't know what—'

Eleanor stood upright. 'Okay, the police it is.' She turned to go.
'Please, miss!'

Eleanor turned back. The young girl looked close to tears. 'Please
don't tell anyone. I don't have a choice. Lady Childs says she'll get
me sacked if I don't. I need this job, my mum's not well and I have
to pay for her doctor's appointments and medicine. Please, miss!'

Eleanor felt for her, but Lancelot's liberty – and possibly life –
was at stake. 'So, as long as you pass Lady Childs certain... drugs,
she doesn't make up some tale and get you sacked?'

The girl nodded.

'Does Lady Millicent ever ask you to get her anything else...
illegal?'

The girl shook her head. 'No, never.'

Eleanor took the girl gently by the shoulders. 'Go to your
manager and hand in your notice.' The girl opened her mouth,
but closed it again at Eleanor's look. Eleanor let go of the young
girl's shoulders and fished in her bag for a card. 'Then ring this
number tomorrow. Either I, or my butler, will answer. We'll have
you a better job in a few days where you don't have to get mixed
up in that sort of thing.' Lady Fenwick-Langham had mentioned
that they were short of a maid when they'd visited. She hoped they
still were. If not, she'd employ the girl herself.

Before the girl could respond, the doorman admitted a couple,
who strolled up to the desk, chatting animatedly. Eleanor smiled
at the girl and left her with the new arrivals.

At the top of the steps, she looked about for the spires Clifford
had pointed out. *Ah, there they were!* Somewhere a bell tolled three
a.m. Pulling her shawl tighter round her bare shoulders, she set
off thinking about what she'd learned. So many questions, but no
real answers. Why was Millie so mean to her? Was it really just
because of Lancelot, or was there more to it than that? And Albie's
grudge against his fellow gang members, how deep did that really

run? And how far was Lucas really willing to go to break the rules while he could? And, most disturbingly, where did Lancelot get the money for Florence, his plane?

The clip of her feet slowed as her thoughts drew her up short. She looked around. She was in a small park. She felt more than tired... woozy. How much had she drunk? Surely not enough to feel so light-headed. Had one of them spiked her drink, or were the cocktails that lethal?

A flash of movement to the left caught her eye. She peered into the darkness. That hunched shape wasn't a bush, it was a person, wasn't it? Or was it the effects of the Angel Face? No, they were definitely eyes staring back at her!

In different circumstances she might have stood her ground, but with her head befuddled and the streets deserted, she retreated. Cursing the dancing shoes she hadn't needed all evening, she ripped them off and ran to the streetlight. Scanning the empty road in front of her, she raced unsteadily across it and swung left past the wide stone bridge over the river. The mist swirled in, obscuring her vision. Where was Clifford's dratted club? The tap of muffled footsteps behind drove her forward, her stockinged feet smarting.

Abingdon Street? Yes, there was the sign! She stumbled right and ran along the smart, three-storey terrace. The club, what was it called?

There! The hurried footsteps behind again!

On she sprinted. A bowler hat disappeared down a side alley. Bingo! That had to be it. She followed. On the door a brass sign read 'The Carlton Club, exclusively for Butlers and Gentlemen's Gentlemen'.

She pushed the door. Tripping over the step, she fell into the tiled reception. Jumping up, she spun round. No one. Then footsteps came from behind. She whirled round, knee raised and kicked out instinctively.

The man doubled over, wheezing horribly. Before she could lash out again, her eyes adjusted to the light. 'Gracious, I'm so sorry. Are you the night porter?'

'Yes… ma… dam.' The man leant against the desk, eyes watering.

'As I said, I really am most dreadfully sorry. I was being chased… gosh, that doesn't matter. I'll fetch someone to help you.' She reached for the door that led into the club.

Wincing, the porter stumbled in front of her, keeping himself more than a kick away. 'Madam… you cannot go in… there. It is strictly… against club rules.'

'Next time I'll come dressed as a man, then,' she replied tartly, and then felt bad. 'Look, I am most awfully sorry. Can I do anything for you?'

'It's alright, madam,' he said, coughing. 'I've had worse. Who are you here to see?'

'I'm looking for Mr Clifford. He's expecting me.'

The porter stopped wheezing and straightened up as much as he could. 'Ah… apologies, you must be Lady Swift. I wasn't expecting…' He looked down at her ripped stockings and blackened feet. 'Please… take a seat.'

A moment later, Clifford appeared. He gave his customary half bow, looking her up and down. 'How delightful, my lady, you've enjoyed a wonderful evening, I see. Shall I take you home?'

She gave the porter a large tip and hurried out into the night.

CHAPTER 16

Oh dash it, you're late already, Ellie! She hurried through the lobby of the village hall. The wooden floor wore the scuffs of a thousand boots beneath a patchy layer of polish. Mismatched sashes hung from the hooks either side of the thick, red velvet stage curtains and the walls were clearly awaiting a paintbrush. The heat of the afternoon sun hadn't penetrated the hall and she shivered at the change in temperature.

In a moment of weakness ('madness', Clifford had called it) she'd joined the local amateur dramatic society, or am-dram as they abbreviated it. It met on a Thursday night, which happened to be Clifford's night off, which meant the Hall was horribly quiet, but, she insisted to herself, that had nothing to do with her decision. As she was now the lady of the manor in the pretty little Buckinghamshire village of Little Buckford, she simply wanted to do the job properly and immerse herself more in local life.

'I say, where is everyone?' she called.

The stage curtains parted and Elizabeth Shackley's soft brown curls piled in a topknot poked out. The wife of the local baker, she smiled warmly at seeing Eleanor.

'Welcome, welcome, Lady Swift. We're so delighted you've come to join our little amateur dramatics group.'

'Thank you for the invitation,' Eleanor said. 'I do have to warn you though, I haven't been in anything like this, well, not since the enforced drama production at my hideous girls' school.'

She climbed up on stage where a semicircle of wooden chairs had been arranged around a large table on which balanced a precarious pile of scripts.

'Good afternoon, everyone.' Eleanor smiled at the ring of expectant faces.

'Welcome, Lady Swift,' Morace Shackley beamed, his shoes leaving a telltale trail of baker's flour as he stepped forward and offered her a chair.

'Always happy for a new recruit,' said Dylan Penry, the butcher, with his singsong Welsh lilt.

Thomas Cartwright nodded curtly. 'Lady Swift.'

Eleanor and Cartwright, a local farmer, had met, and instantly fallen out, during the recent quarry murder affair she had found herself caught up in.

'Delighted to have you aboard.' John Brenchley doffed an invisible cap, then absentmindedly tried to slide his hands into the shopkeeper's overcoat he'd left back at his general store.

Elizabeth gestured to a greying, bespectacled man wearing a dog collar under a garishly striped shirt.

'I'm sure you know Reverend Gaskell, Lady Swift?'

'Regrettably not,' Eleanor said. 'I fear I have been the most dreadful new girl in the village, Reverend. Each time you called I had unfortunately been anywhere but at home.'

The reverend pumped her hand exuberantly. 'No matter, Lady Swift, no matter. How fortuitous that our first meeting should be here as we prepare to tread the boards in this fine little theatre of ours.'

'Absolutely.' She turned to the heavily lined face on her left. 'And you are?'

'Pearl Brody.' The woman smiled thinly. 'But everyone calls me Pearly.'

Elizabeth turned so only Eleanor could see the face she pulled. 'Pearly runs the Reading Room in Chipstone. She joined us when she used to live in the village.'

'Ah!' the reverend exclaimed. '"Happy is the man who finds wisdom, and the man who gains understanding." Proverbs Chapter three, verse thirteen.'

'Adversity brings knowledge and knowledge wisdom,' Penry added.

'Lady Swift,' another female voice piped up, 'so nice to see you again. Who knew that we share a love of the theatrical? Imagine that.' Mable Green, the sub-postmistress in the local village of West Radington, smiled at her.

'Indeed, Miss Green,' Eleanor said. 'Tell me, how is your mother? Keeping well, I hope?'

Elizabeth shuffled her chair next to Eleanor's and whispered, 'She's over there. She can't be left for a moment. The poor old coot is as mad as a bucket of frogs.'

Eleanor managed to turn her chuckle into a cough. Shackley stood and clapped his chubby hands together.

'Now then, we should make a start, seeing that our full cast is here.'

'Starting the work is two-thirds of it.' Penry moved to the pile of scripts.

Cartwright scratched his head. 'Don't see as how that works. Being at the start can't be anywhere but the start.'

Shackley hastily intervened before Cartwright and Penry started one of their regular arguments. 'Ladies and gentlemen, I propose we each have two minutes to put forward our suggested play, offering both the merits and the deficits for balance and fair judgement by all.'

'Splendid!' the reverend beamed.

The mid-meeting tea stop couldn't have arrived at a better moment. Eleanor was amazed at the ferocity with which the am-dram members had each defended their preferred play. She was finding it great entertainment, but the vicar had stepped in and declared it, 'High time for tea and a truce, dear folk.'

Elizabeth and Mabel appeared at the top of the stairs each bearing a large tray.

'Let me help.' Eleanor pulled the chairs out of their way and made space on the table among the scripts. 'I say, those fruit buns look absolutely delicious. Mr Shackley, are they of your fair hands?'

The baker nodded proudly. 'Extra fruit and extra honey glaze for the hardworking entertainers of our local community.'

The reverend picked up a small wooden box from under his seat. 'Perhaps, this is as good a time as any to pop our subs in?' Pockets and purses were opened and coinage dropped into the slot.

Eleanor fumbled in her bag hoping to have the right change, but having no idea what that was, scooped out a random amount.

Elizabeth set down the tray. 'We agreed on four shillings each to cover the tea and refreshments, but we get it back from the ticket proceeds.'

'Of course, of course.' Eleanor dropped her dues into the box.

Pearly took her cup with a sniff. 'I still can't comprehend why you all don't see what I see! We've got the opportunity to do the village the service of educating them on women's rights and—'

Elizabeth folded her arms. 'Honestly, Pearly, Little Buckford isn't ready for more suffragette shenanigans. Some women have got the vote now after all, though why they want it, I shall never know. I leave all that sort of thing to Morace and I'm happy to.'

Pearly crossed her arms. '*He and She* is a modern play highlighting the inequalities—'

Cartwright glared at her. 'Next time you're out cantering your feminist hobbyhorse up and down the byways, Mrs Brody, be sure to stop by the farmhouse and discuss it with my good lady wife. She'll put you straight.'

Eleanor shot a glance at Shackley, who shifted uncomfortably in his chair. He cleared his throat. 'I say again that we need to do another comedy, like last year. That *Baby Mine* farce went down a storm.' He glanced around the group.

Elizabeth nodded and patted her topknot. 'It was so fun to do something silly. I don't often get to let my hair down.'

Brenchley waved the script in his hand. 'But what about my choice? *The Bad Man* has got everything going for it. A dash of drama with a slice of comedy. And easy sets to build too. With Thomas' help, I could easily recreate a cattle ranch here in the hall.'

The reverend smiled round the group. 'Personally, I do like the sound of a comedy. Not sure I'd make much of a cowboy though. Never so much as set foot on a horse.'

'None of you have said 'owt about my choice,' Cartwright said. '*Ladies' Night* was a smash hit in the West End.' At everyone's silence, he added, 'Come on, give me one good reason why not?'

'Because I'd rather dress as a Mexican bandit than parade around the stage in a bathing suit, you animal!' Pearly cried.

'Shh, you'll wake mother,' Mabel hissed. 'You know she's easier when she's asleep.'

'If you want to see ladies' legs, Mr Cartwright, I suggest you go to the penny movies!' Pearly choked.

'Oh lighten up, Mrs Brody. You and your so-called progress, you'd have us all shackled in the prim and proper eighteen hundreds.' Cartwright rose and moved towards her, seeming to delight in her squeal of fright. 'Ooh, do cover up, my dear lady. The very idea of the glimpse of an ankle is making me come over all giddy.'

Eleanor jumped in. 'Leaving aside Mr Cartwright's choice for the moment, can you tell us about your suggestion, Mr Penry? I think I may have missed it.'

Penry grinned. 'It's called *The Bat* and, well, I think it'd be perfect. It's a comedy with suspense thrown in. It's still running up in London. I'm happy to direct.'

Elizabeth frowned. 'And is there a good part for each of us?'

Penry nodded. 'It's set in a country house. There's a maid, a devious niece, a no-good doctor, a policeman, a country lady…'

All eyes turned to Eleanor who shrugged. Penry continued, 'There's the villain, obviously, a love-struck fiancé, a lawyer, even a Japanese butler which the crowd will love.'

'Oh, it's perfect!' Elizabeth cheered.

'I'd rather like the part of the no-good doctor, he sounds a right rascal.' The reverend grinned at the shocked faces. 'Just think of the extra impact my Sunday sermons will have after the villagers have seen me playing a baddie.'

Penry pulled out a piece of paper. 'No problem, Reverend.'

Elizabeth gave a light cough. 'Please can I be the maid? I bet she has less to say and I'm not that good at remembering too many lines.'

'Of course, my dear. I pencilled you in as just that.'

He ran down the list of parts and called out his suggested colleagues' names.

'So I'd be the gardener and the fiancé, right you are.' Brenchley nodded.

'Oh, the devious niece for me. That sounds quite a large part. I will, of course, rise to the challenge, Mr Penry.' Mabel patted her hair.

'And I'll play a great dead body.' Shackley laughed. 'That's right up my street. You say he's not on stage that much so I can do the curtains and be the prompter as well, how's that?'

'Well done, luv,' his wife said.

'And if Lady Swift is happy to play Miss Cornelia Van Gorder?' Penry cocked an eyebrow. 'She is quite… elderly.' He blushed.

Eleanor laughed. 'Somehow I fear that learning and perfecting my part might age me considerably so we should be fine.'

'So, two male roles left, I see.' The tone was icy.

'Now, Pearly, don't get your women's rights flag all in a tangle. I thought you played a man most convincingly last time. You'd do the lawyer chap equally well, I'm sure of it.'

The others nodded in agreement.

'So Mr Penry, what have you saved for me?' said Cartwright.

Penry smiled. 'The villain, naturally.'

'You know, Clifford, the play we've chosen has the perfect role for you. How well can you do a Japanese accent?'

He walked round to the driver's side and opened the door. 'Japanese? A butler role, perhaps? And is Mr Cartwright to play the bat?'

Once again, Eleanor marvelled at Clifford's perception. *Maybe he really is a wizard?*

'Well, what about it?'

'I think not, my lady. To be frank, I would rather lie in a frozen ditch and be trampled by pigs. Would you care to drive?'

Eleanor settled into the driver's seat as quickly as possible.

'This is going to be great. The sooner I can drive, the sooner you won't need to interrupt your precious Thursday evenings. I am awfully grateful at you coming out tonight, by the way.'

Clifford nodded and then pointed to the ignition. 'Perhaps we'll arrive home more swiftly with the engine running, my lady.'

Eleanor had never heard a motorcar make those kinds of graunching noises before. 'I believe it's time to send the old beast off to the mechanic, Clifford. Sounds shocking.'

'Indeed, but I'm sure Johnson's the coachbuilders will have a shrewd idea what the cause is. The shearing of metal teeth tends to lessen when the left pedal is depressed when changing gear.'

She shot him a look and put her foot down.

His gloved hand reached out and pushed the steering to the right. 'The road itself is so much easier to drive on than the steep roadside banks, I often find.'

At the top of the lane, the village hall was still clearly visible in the rear-view mirror. She threw the indicator switch with gusto and heaved the wheel right. 'Homeward driver... ouch!' She clutched her forehead where it had smacked against the windscreen as the Rolls lurched to a stall halfway across the junction.

'Are you alright, my lady?' Clifford offered her a clean handkerchief from his waistcoat pocket.

'Quite fine, thank you. No damage done.'

She pressed the ignition button and yanked her hand back as the car seemed to bite her.

'The engine is already running, my lady. One press usually suffices.'

'There's quite a bit to master here, Clifford,' she admitted as the engine stalled again.

'No rush. There is only the one steam truck approaching at speed.'

More by luck than anything else, Eleanor cleared the crossing just in time to avoid the truck as it passed in the opposite direction.

'Congratulations, my lady, the Little Buckford Amateur Dramatics Society will not have to find another leading lady this year after all.'

Back at the Hall, the housekeeper was waiting.

'There is a message for you, my lady.'

'From whom?'

'Chief Detective Inspector Belton... wait, that's not right.'

'You mean Detective Chief Inspector Seldon? What did he want?'

'For you to call him back. He told me to say that there's been a...' The housekeeper scratched her nose. 'Ah, that's it, a development in the case, my lady. He left his home number as I said you would be back late.'

After only two rings, the exchange connected her.

'Abingdon three-two-five-five.'

'Inspector, it's Lady Swift. I do hope it's not too inconvenient a time for me to call.'

'Not at all, Lady Swift. I felt you ought to know. Lady Fenwick-Langham's jewels have been recovered.'

'Fantastic!'

'Lady Swift. This is in strict confidence, this information won't be released to the public until the trial.'

She let out a frustrated sigh. 'I won't tell a soul, I promise. Now, where did you find them?'

'They were found… in Lord Lancelot Fenwick-Langham's plane.'

She closed her eyes.

CHAPTER 17

'Oh, look at that unusual duck!'

'It is a cormorant, my lady. They are not uncommon here on the River Thames.'

'They're all ducks to me, Clifford.'

It was a perfect summer's day with not a cloud in the sky. A light, cooling breeze wafted scents of honeysuckle across the water as the rowboat seemed to slide effortlessly along. She smiled at Gladstone's legs dangling over the bow, his stare fixed firmly on the waterfowl gliding past and placed a protective hand on his collar.

'Gladstone's certainly enjoying the birdwatching element of our jaunt. Though I doubt he'd be up to a swim.' She watched Clifford give another expert pull on the oars. 'Come on, it really is my turn now. My ribs are fine after that last murder case business. I need to regain some strength and I've been so mind-numbingly good about being careful for two whole months.'

'It is fortunate that you did not sustain more serious injuries.'

'It was fortunate I wasn't shot by the killer sitting next to me, Clifford. A few minor… scratches are hardly—'

'I do not think the injuries you sustained could be called "minor", my lady.'

'Well, I'm fine now, that's what counts.' She grabbed the oars and peered over the side. 'You know, I don't much like the look of that weed. What if we fell in? I'm not convinced Gladstone would dash to my rescue, or that he'd be much good if he did.' She shivered. 'Goodness only knows how many dead corpses are caught in that.'

'I believe *all* corpses are dead.' Clifford adjusted his cuffs. 'Are you sure that taking part in a murder play whilst investigating an actual murder is a good idea, my lady?'

Eleanor groaned. 'Possibly not, I'm not doing very well at learning my lines either.' She threw him her battered copy of *The Bat* script. 'Start me off from where we stopped, please.'

He picked up the script and cleared his throat. 'Cornelia Van Gorder arises from her chair as the lights flicker and threaten to go out.'

Eleanor imagined herself an elderly lady and croaked, 'Lizzie! Lizzie! Where are the candles, girl? We'll be plunged into darkness in a breath.'

Clifford frowned trying to get into character as Lizzie, Van Gorder's maid. 'Oh my lady, I is terrified those icy fingers will be upon us if the lights go out.'

'Lizzie, I will hear no more! There is no ghost of Mr Fleming floating about the corridors.'

'Drifting, my lady.'

'Oh, okay, there is no ghost of Mr Fleming *drifting* about the corridors.'

Clifford tightened his grip on one side of the boat and grabbed hold of Gladstone with his free hand. 'No, my lady, our boat actually *is* drifting towards that rather elegant slipper launch to your right. I fear a collision would put a fearful dent into those painstakingly varnished teak boards and likely deposit us both in those corpse-filled weeds you mentioned.'

'Crikey!' Eleanor grabbed the oars lying slack in her lap and rowed with all her strength. 'Ha! You see, ribs are fine.'

'But not the gentleman's jacket, I fear.' Clifford doffed his bowler hat at the man standing up in the launch waving his fist.

'What a fuss!' She called over, 'Water's beautifully clear, won't leave a mark at all!' With an extra heave she sped off down the river. 'Maybe a break from the script for a moment, Clifford, you know, to concentrate on rowing.'

'As you choose, my lady. There is, of course, the matter of Mrs Trotman's picnic. Perhaps, given the amount of water sloshing about our bilges, it might be prudent to partake before her kind efforts are floating about inside the basket?'

'Rather! All this rowing gives one quite an appetite.'

With the boat secured and Clifford having shaken the worst of the water from his trouser turn ups, they set up on the bank with Gladstone seeming to do everything he could think of to get in the way. She gasped as Clifford unveiled the picnic. He unfurled a striped parasol and erected it over the picnic rug providing much-needed shade.

'That really is an incredible spread. Mini pork pies, sandwiches, baby tomatoes, breaded ham, fresh rolls… ooh, have we got some of that amazing red stuff Mrs Trotman conjures up?'

'Port and red onion chutney? Of course, my lady. And a half of sherry, same of ginger wine, plus mignon cinnamon and vanilla pastries with coffee to finish. Master Gladstone has his own version, a serving of dog food and a knuckle bone for afters.' He set the offerings in front of the bulldog who instantly leapt on the bowl.

Eleanor turned her plate in her hand. 'It does feel a bit wrong, you know, Clifford. I mean, messing about in boats, picnic lunch, even going to that ridiculous Blind Pig Club while Lancelot is locked up. Not sure what I'm thinking of.'

'I believe you are keeping your thoughts fresh and in sufficiently good order to be able to work through the facts and uncover the truth. Whatever that turns out to be,' he muttered.

'Yes, whatever that is.'

Clifford passed her a plate. 'Perhaps we should abandon the play altogether and go over the facts of the case as we have them so far.'

She nodded, her mouth full of beef and mustard sandwich. After a sip of ginger wine, she sighed. 'You know, I can't believe we're back here again, investigating another murder. I've only been here a few months. It really is incredible. Except of course the stakes feel much higher.'

'Rather than dwell on that, my lady, perhaps we should establish a few basic details and then you could divulge what you gleaned from your sleuthing at the club?'

Reaching for a mini pork pie, she pulled off snippets of the crust and nodded.

'Here goes. Each of Lancelot's friends seem… innocent enough on the surface. But…' She rubbed her forehead. 'There's something I can't put my finger on with each of them. Take Lucas, for instance.'

'Is that Prince Lucas Singh, son of the Maharaja of Malwar?' Clifford asked while topping up their glasses.

'That's him. While he's here, he's determined to have all the fun and ignore all the rules he can. And what better game than to be a jewel thief?'

'If I might add to your theory, my lady? His father, the maharaja, is something of an expert on gems. Not surprising as the family's main business interests have lain in the mines of Golconda and Subramaniam for centuries.'

'How on earth do you know that?' asked Eleanor, never failing to be astonished by the breadth of Clifford's omniscience.

'Your uncle,' he said, not batting an eyelid.

'Ah, now you come to mention it, Lucas did say they were acquainted. Diamonds?'

'As well as sapphires and rubies.'

'So it's likely that Lucas would be able to recognise a real jewel. Could our serial jewel thief be a prince?'

'It is also possible that he may have picked up some expensive habits here, ones he could not justify to his father in asking for an increased allowance.'

'Absolutely. And he left the ball early. *And* on top of that he argued with the colonel over self-rule for India. He said he'd cheerfully have cut the colonel in two if he'd had, what was it? Oh, yes, a *talwar*.'

'Strange, my lady.'

'Not really, Clifford, the colonel could test the patience of Buddha.'

'I meant a strange choice of weapon. A khanda would have been more suitable for the intended purpose. A talwar is largely a cavalry sword, whereas the khanda is a much heavier blade, designed—'

'Clifford, we don't need a dissertation on Indian swords and their suitability as a murder weapon. We do, however, need to add him as a suspect.'

'As you wish, my lady.'

She reached for her notebook and opened it. On her suspect page she wrote Prince Lucas Singh and drew a curved sword next to his name.

'Now, on to Albie. Albert Appleby to you, Clifford. He's a peculiar chap, in truth. The problem for our investigation is that his beef actually seems to be with the other members of the group, rather than with the colonel. The others tease him rotten, including it seems Lancelot.'

Clifford offered her a fresh roll from the picnic basket. 'So, even if we were to go with the theory that the jewel theft was merely a ploy to cover up the colonel's murder, Mr Appleby would seemingly be without a motive.'

'Mmm, yes. Unless his motive is revenge, and the actual target was Lancelot.' She frowned. 'We briefly touched on that idea when we discussed the dowager countess and her ward, Cora. And, again,

I just can't see it. Albie's real problem, in a nutshell, is that he's way out of his league socially, being the son of a miner.'

'Forgive my ignorance, but I thought one of the main tenets of the "modern set", as they call themselves, is that the class system is antiquated and reprehensible?'

'Well, that's what they say. However, they behave like the wildest bunch of hooligans you've ever seen.' She smiled at Gladstone now holding his bone as an otter would as he munched on it.

'At the risk of being indiscreet, it would seem safe to assume that Mr Appleby has no allowance?'

'Exactly, he earns his own money tutoring.' She stopped mid drink. 'Golly, I hadn't thought about it like that. A private tutor's wage wouldn't last a moment at the rate they party. Especially,' she said, leaning in closer, 'with the drugs.'

Clifford straightened his tie and uncorked the sherry. 'Indeed, the street price has more than doubled in the last two years since the introduction of the Dangerous Drugs Act.'

'How on earth do you know things like that?'

'All butlers and gentlemen's gentlemen are required to keep a handle on their master or mistress' day-to-day accounts. Some of my colleagues have had a much harder time doing so in recent years.'

'Enough said. But where does that leave us? That the son of a prince and the son of a coal miner could be equally short enough of the readies to be our jewel thief? And possibly our murderer? Sounds rather far-fetched, wouldn't you say?'

'With apologies, my lady, in the case of murder, no theory is too far-fetched. I have never met a man, or woman, and instantly classified them as a killer. It has always come as something of a surprise.'

She laughed. 'Fair point.' She added Albert Appleby's name to her suspect list with a sketch of an apple. 'Well, that makes four, so now for the Childs sisters.' She took another bite of her pork pie.

'Unless I missed something, the sisters don't seem to be wanting in the financial stakes. I've no idea who or what their father is.'

'Lord Childs, Earl of Wendover, is a financier of high repute. He is a member of the prestigious board at Coutts of London.'

She gave a long, low whistle. 'So unless the girls are too worried to ask for an increased allowance, they can't have any money worries, no matter how wild their antics become.' She frowned. 'If we are going to take the idea seriously that the whole thing might be an act of revenge that got horribly out of hand, perhaps Millie simply snapped and decided to get revenge on Lancelot after he'd rebuffed her? "Hell has no fury as a woman scorned" and all that.'

'"Nor hell a fury."'

'What?'

'That is actually a common misquote, my lady. The line comes from William Congreve's poem "The Mourning Bride": "Nor hell a fury like a woman scorned."'

'Really? I wonder if this Congreve fellow knew Millie, it sounds just like her.'

'He died in 1729, my lady, so it seems unlikely.'

'Well, she's so unspeakable I can easily see her biffing the colonel on the head and then whingeing she'd broken a nail doing it. I also overheard her threatening to have someone fired at the club.'

'Interesting.'

'But not terribly incriminating. It just turned out she was bullying the poor coat-check girl to supply her with drugs.' Eleanor sighed. 'Uncharitably, I wish I could say I had a whole heap of evidence against Millie, but I simply don't. However, I feel she needs to go on my list as a suspect as she does have a possible motive.' She added Millie's name and swiftly drew a cat with its claws out next to it.

'And Lady Coco?'

'She's a hard fish to pin down, you know. When she came here asking for help, she seemed genuine.'

'But has Lady Childs the capability of being a notorious jewel thief? The thief who, despite a concentrated police effort, has remained at liberty.'

'Seems unlikely, doesn't it? Unless she has an accomplice.' She frowned again. 'I think we'll add her just in case.' She wrote 'Coco' and next to it added a cocktail glass.

'Which leaves?'

'Mr Seaton, alias Johnny.' Eleanor shook the crumbs from her dress, much to Gladstone's delight, as he briefly paused in trying to bury the remains of his bone in a molehill to lick them up. 'Of them all, Johnny seems the most together. He has that same unshakable confidence Lancelot has, only he's super cool with it.' She sighed. 'At present, I haven't really got anything on him but he should go on the list...'

Next to his name she drew a pair of dancing shoes. 'And that's it on new suspects at the moment, I think.' She glanced up. 'Clifford, are you alright? You look unusually pensive?'

He nodded distractedly. Eleanor waited. After a moment he cleared his throat. 'I do apologise, my lady. A thought struck me that might put a very different "spin" on events as it were.'

Eleanor was intrigued. 'Do go on.'

'Well, suppose just for a moment that we are wrong and Colonel Puddifoot-Barton's death wasn't a spur of the moment attack? Suppose the murder had been meticulously planned and the jewel robbery was merely a blind?'

Eleanor nodded slowly. 'That crossed my mind too, but that's quite a big change of direction.' She thought for a moment. 'But that would mean there is another source of suspects we should also consider investigating. There would have been quite a handful at the ball, ignoring Lancelot's bright young things, who knew the colonel through the Fenwick-Langhams or through other connections, I would think.'

'And murders are largely committed by those who know the victim.'

'Yes, unless he enraged a stranger so acutely on their first meeting that it resulted in the stranger finding himself with the murder instrument in one hand and the colonel's head in the other.'

'Very possible, my lady. However, to avoid speaking ill of the deceased, shall we assume otherwise?'

Eleanor grimaced. 'So maybe the colonel did know his attacker.' She shook her head. 'I confess, it makes me feel we're even further from solving all of this.'

'My lady, there are two of us. If you can continue your investigation of Lancelot's friends, I can tackle the investigation from another angle.'

She scratched her head. 'I can get a list of guests who knew the colonel and I didn't interview from Lady Langham, but, forgive my bluntness, Clifford, are the colonel's other acquaintances likely to be very forthcoming?'

'Forthcoming, my lady?'

'Yes, you know, when interrogated by…'

'By a butler, my lady?'

'Yes. Won't they send you off with a flea in your impudent ear for nosing about?'

He raised a hand. 'No problem, my lady. Like the mole I shall work underground.'

She looked him up and down in amusement. 'You don't seem the type of man who likes to get his hands, or frock coat, dirty.'

He rolled his eyes. 'I meant it figuratively, my lady. "Yet digg'd the mole, and lest his ways be found, work'd underground." Henry Vaughan, "The World",' he added by way of explanation.

'By which you mean?'

'If I may say so, behind every titled man and woman is an untitled but all-seeing servant.'

'Ah! Now I know what you do at that Butlers Club of yours. You make and break lords and prime ministers.'

'Not exactly, my lady. However, if all that was known by the members of such organisations as the Carlton Club were made public, many illustrious gentlemen would no doubt find their situation precarious.'

She gasped. 'I do believe you're a socialist on the quiet, Clifford.'

'It might surprise you to learn that despite being titled himself, your uncle was something of a socialist.'

'So the two of you were secretly plotting the downfall of the titled classes? How wonderful! And did this conspiracy of yours extend to royalty?'

Clifford uncharacteristically raised both eyebrows. 'I think you may be over-exaggerating my and your uncle's political stance. We weren't about to become the next Guy Fawkes.'

She grinned. 'Pity. I can picture you two laying kegs of gunpowder under Parliament.'

Clifford started clearing up the debris from the picnic while Eleanor finished her sherry. 'A focused approach, yes. I'll get hold of Coco and sort out another date with her and the others. You beetle, sorry, mole off to your Butlers Club and see what dirt you can uncover.' She winked at him.

Clifford loaded the picnic items into the boat, extracted Gladstone and his muddy nose from the crater he was digging, and then offered Eleanor a hand to step in.

'And we both need to be careful, my lady. If the killer is in any of these groups he, or she, will not take kindly to our investigations.'

She stopped halfway into the boat.

He looked at her curiously. 'Is something the matter?'

'I wasn't going to mention it, but when I left the nightclub I… I thought I was followed.'

CHAPTER 18

The church bells rang down in the village, their chimes filtering up to Eleanor on the terrace of Henley Hall. Despite wearing a sunhat, she shaded her eyes with her hand as she waved to Joseph, the gardener, pushing his wheelbarrow between the beds of bergamot and ornamental grasses. He didn't see her as he was chatting animatedly to Gladstone, who was trotting by his side. They were both soon hidden from sight by the high box hedging.

'Your coffee, my lady.' Clifford put the tray on the scrollwork table.

'Perfect, thank you. I say though, it's already Sunday. For our meeting with the Langhams this morning we need to be as sharp as… as sharp as…' She waved. 'Do you see? I can't even finish an analogy. Quick, coffee! And strong!'

'Certainly. In the meantime perhaps as sharp as *obsidian* would do? And I believe "as sharp as" is a simile, not an analogy, my lady.'

'Actually, I believe it is a metaphor.'

He coughed. 'A simile is a type of metaphor.'

She dismissed the matter with a wave of her hand. 'Whatever. What is *obsidiwhatsit*, anyway?'

'Obsidian. It is a type of volcanic glass, first used by the Malaysian Indians two and a half thousand years ago. It has a theoretical sharpness five hundred times that of any steel blade.'

'Really? You know, Clifford, I have never met anyone who has such a wealth of information I neither need nor want.'

He passed her the coffee cup. 'Thank you, my lady.'

She failed to hide a smile. 'And actually, I was picturing the woman who runs the Reading Room in Chipstone, Pearly Brody. Her tongue, it's so sharp it's incredible she doesn't cut her own throat just by swallowing. Golly, you should have heard her at the am-dram rehearsal. I mean, I'm all for women's rights, but there's a time and a place. And the Little Buckford am-dram rehearsal is neither the time nor the place.'

Clifford's eyes twinkled. 'I rather imagined it might be Miss Green, the postmistress, who harbours the most dangerous of forked tongues.'

Eleanor laughed. 'She's certainly close.'

'Indeed, choosing a play each season could be deemed a significant waste of their time.' At her confused look, he continued. 'It is merely an observation that one could simply place the am-dram members together in the village hall and open the doors to the public. The audience would be treated to as much intense drama, colourful discourse and unending conflict as any scripted play.'

She snorted and promptly spilt her coffee. 'Oops! But also, the audience would likely even witness a murder!'

Clifford finished mopping up Eleanor's coffee and refilled her cup. 'Might one enquire how you fared with your own performance, my lady?'

She groaned. 'Terribly, if I'm honest. Learning all those lines is really quite taxing. However, I shall persevere. I refuse. To. Be. Beaten!' Each of the last three words were accompanied by a rap on the table which sent more coffee flying. 'Sorry, Clifford, you've just cleared that up.'

He set to mopping up the second spillage. 'Most dogged, if one might say so. Your determination is to be applauded.'

She frowned. 'Well, that might be all the audience feel they can applaud if I don't learn my lines. Awful timing though, coinciding with this murder business.'

'Most inconvenient indeed.' He adjusted his perfectly aligned starched white cuffs. 'You might feel similarly about our need to set off now for your breakfast meeting with Lord and Lady Fenwick-Langham?'

'Yes, but remember, it's *our* meeting, Clifford. Lady Langham was formidably clear you are to be a guest as much as I. So, chin up. You'll have to tell them what you found out while I was at the am-dram rehearsal all day yesterday.' She frowned. 'Do you think the Langham Manor cook will do anything even close to Mrs Trotman's fabulous paprika relish? Maybe you could sneak some in for me.'

'Augusta is out with her beloved roses, my dear Eleanor. Clifford, good morning to you too.' Lord Langham waved to his own butler. 'Sandford, better give us a woman's half hour before sounding the breakfast gong if you will.'

'Very good, your lordship.' Sandford set off down the hallway towards the butler's pantry.

Eleanor accepted Lord Langham's offered arm. 'A woman's half hour? Might I enquire how that differs from a man's half hour?'

'Oh certainly. I'd say by a minimum of sixty or seventy minutes to our thirty. A fair assessment, wouldn't you say, Clifford?' He steered Eleanor forward.

From behind, Clifford replied, 'I really couldn't comment, my lord.'

Eleanor looked towards him just in time to see him nodding, his eyes twinkling with amusement.

'How is Augusta today?' she asked Lord Langham.

'Right now, she's content enough, pottering about with secateurs and her favourite little flower basket, but…'

Eleanor patted his arm. 'But as soon as we arrive and talk of suspects and clues, her composure will begin to wobble.'

'Kid gloves, Messrs Sleuthing Inc, what?' Lord Langham said softly as they emerged on the terrace.

Just as she did every time, Eleanor caught her breath at the sight of the exquisite rose garden before her. Each bed was separated by geometric lines of knee-high box hedging, a gently flowing stone path winding in intricate swirls between them. From underneath one of the many rose arches, Lady Langham appeared, seemingly busy selecting a few specimens from among those in her basket.

Lord Langham put a thumb and forefinger either side of his tongue and gave an astonishingly loud whistle. Lady Langham jerked up and waved for them all to join her.

'Morning, Eleanor, my dear. And welcome, Clifford. Harold, you could have sent Sandford ahead to tell me our guests had arrived instead of whistling as if I was one of the spaniels.'

'But you're my favourite leader of the pack. Loyal, shiny nose, wilfully disobedient.'

Eleanor couldn't help joining in with his chuckle. 'Have we a few moments to enjoy your roses, Augusta? It's such a treat to take a tour of the blooms.'

'Ooh, yes. Let's start with the epitome of all roses.' She led Eleanor along several twists of the stone path to the central, circular bed, which was filled with translucent, single pink blooms inter-twined with strikingly deeper pink, almost scarlet bushes. '"The Celestial",' Lady Langham said reverently. 'This is my world, the one where I can create, celebrate and matchmake precisely as I see fit. I have "Cardinal Richelieu" rubbing velvet shoulders with the quivering "Queen of Denmark", or "Koningen von Danemark" as she is known to us rose enthusiasts. Over there the "Marchioness of Lorne" is surrounded by "Gyspy Boys", proclaiming to all that she renounces her royal connection. My little couplings, transcend centuries, propriety and religious boundaries to boot.' She smiled. 'I can play out any story I fancy.' She looked away. 'And be at peace.'

They strolled on to one of three, pentagon-shaped beds grouped by an ornate rose arch spanning the cluster. Sinking onto the nearby scrollwork bench, she patted the seat next to her. The bench was hot from the sun and Eleanor had to arrange her dress carefully to make sure her bare legs didn't come into contact with the metal.

'This is… Lancelot's bed.'

Eleanor sat. 'He doesn't strike me as the gardening sort?'

Lady Langham laughed gently. 'Silly boy, he'd probably plant everything upside down. No, my dear child is definitely not the gardening sort.' She looked up at Eleanor, her eyes very bright. 'Sorry, my dear, I meant there is a rose bush planted in this bed to mark all the major events in Lancelot's life. In truth, I've been sitting here most mornings, staring at the rose Harold planted for me the day Lancelot was born, the "General Jack".' She pointed to a tall bush of vibrant cerise covered in chaotically sprouting, flamboyant blooms. 'Every petal that has fallen since he was taken away has torn another hole in my heart.' She dabbed at her nose with a handkerchief. 'And refute it all you like, but he adores you in his own, fatuous way.'

Eleanor could think of nothing to say. Instead, acutely aware of the two quiet tears that ran down her face, she ran her sleeve across her cheeks.

Lady Langham rolled her shoulders back and sat poker straight. 'Now, to business. What, if anything, might I know that could be of help?'

Eleanor composed herself. 'Can you tell me more about Lancelot's friends?'

Lady Langham thought for a moment. 'I have never witnessed anything particularly suspicious in any of them, if that's what you mean. Plenty of silliness and capers, intense and deliberate disregard for propriety but never property. In truth, I would be fairly surprised to hear that any of them had actually *stolen* anything. I mean, they all have so much. And Lancelot can't be that stupid, can he?'

Eleanor hoped her face didn't give away her thoughts.

Lady Langham continued. 'There is an odd one out, though: Mr Appleby, I think it is. Most peculiar fish out of water, batting way above his average financially Harold always says, but then my dear husband can only reference things in terms of cricket or hunting. Mr Appleby is the son of a miner, don't you know? You must have noticed his homespun costume at the ball; stood out a country mile. How on earth can he keep up with the likes of the Lady Childs sisters and the prince?' She shrugged. 'Ironically, however, Mr Appleby has always seemed the most well-mannered and respectful.'

'Have you any idea how Mr Appleby affords to hang around with them?'

'Absolutely no idea.'

'Did you ever witness Mr Appleby having an altercation with the colonel?'

'Honestly, not wishing to speak ill of the dead, but whenever I saw the colonel it appeared that he was deep in an altercation with whomever was unlucky enough to be standing in front of him.' She appeared momentarily lost in thought. 'Whether one of them retorted in kind though, you ask? Hmm, gracious yes! I had quite put it from my mind, so scandalous it was. You'd think he of all people would know better than to argue with an elder and a better.'

'Who was it?'

'The prince.'

'Lucas!' Eleanor breathed.

'My dear, it was shameful. It was at a musical soirée affair, just before you arrived at Henley Hall actually, otherwise we'd have invited you. I couldn't hear the words because the orchestra were rather enthusiastic. The prince though squared up to the colonel, gesticulating wildly, his face flushed as what I can only describe as a tirade erupted from him.'

Eleanor grimaced, thinking back to Lucas' version at the Blind Pig Club of what she assumed was the same heated discussion over British rule in India. 'How did the, erm, argument end?'

'Shockingly, as I said! On both sides, I might add. The prince poked the colonel in the chest, right in the middle of his medals.'

'The colonel wouldn't have taken kindly to that at all.'

'Quite. Hence him cuffing the prince smartly across the ear.'

'Bad show all round, that. Not the only time either,' Lord Langham said, joining them with Clifford.

Eleanor turned to him. 'Did you ever see any of the others in Lancelot's gang row with the colonel?'

Lord Langham hesitated, then glanced at his wife. 'No secrets you commanded, old thing?'

She shook her head wearily. 'No secrets.'

He sighed. 'Only Lancelot.'

Eleanor looked hopelessly at Clifford. He adjusted his meticulously aligned cuffs. 'Might I enquire if your lord or ladyship ever observed any particularly… odd behaviour amongst his young lordship's friends, aside from what I respectfully refer to as hijinks?'

'We did indeed. The elder of the Childs sisters, Lady Millicent, behaved disgracefully at the Worthingtons' Ruby Anniversary ball last year!' said Lady Langham.

Lord Langham let out a low whistle. 'She was definitely more than several sheets to the wind. Danced like a crazy thing for about forty minutes and then simply slid down the wall like someone had let all her air out. Went from chin chin to bottoms up in a blink. Caused the lady of the house a fierce blushing.'

Lady Langham tutted. 'Harold dear, I am quite convinced alcohol was not to blame. I fear it may have been something… *stronger* than champagne.' She turned to Eleanor. 'Children, my dear, they cause nothing but worry.'

Lord Langham snorted. 'Nonsense! Our boy has brought us years of laughter and happy days.'

'And a head of grey hairs!'

He stifled a chuckle. 'Perhaps, but they set off a tiara beautifully. And speaking of sparkly bits and Lancelot's friends, what about Prince Whatnot always being so complimentary about your necklaces and other twinkling trinkets?'

'What about it?' his wife replied. 'It's to be expected. His father owns half the gem mines in their region of India. I always took it as a safe topic he felt he could make polite conversation about with Lancelot's rather fusty mother. I'm under no illusion that's how they all view me, dear, hence Lancelot's less than becoming expression for us.'

'Fusty, eh?' Lord Langham grinned. 'Not from where I'm sitting. But back to the prince. Strikes a fellow as dash rummy now though, given the turn of events, his being so interested in talking to you about your jewels.'

Eleanor and Clifford shared a look.

'I think, Harold dear, that our pair of sleuths have already had that thought.'

Eleanor nodded. 'Yes, but we didn't realise he'd been so bold as to highlight his interest to you directly, or to scrutinise your jewellery up close.'

Their conversation was interrupted by the clamour of a gong reverberating from the terrace.

Lady Langham held up a finger. 'Ah! Breakfast.'

Lord Langham offered each of the ladies an arm. 'Food ahoy, I'm positively starved!'

'Me too. I think I prefer the man's half hour as a prelude to eating,' Eleanor whispered to him.

He chortled and called behind him. 'Fall in, Clifford. No dallying at the back, you're off duty, remember.'

'Very good, your lordship.' Clifford took up the right flank beside Eleanor, but still managed to arrive a step behind as they reached the house.

CHAPTER 19

Sandford waited until the rose garden party rounded the top of the wide balustraded steps to the terrace and then led the way into the grand drawing room with its lavish blue drapes and floor-to-ceiling portraits in gilded frames, and on into the adjoining, smaller dining room.

Lady Langham took Eleanor's arm and led her to the table set at one end with four place settings.

'I hope you don't mind my choosing the family room, rather than the main dining room. It feels more conducive for our discussion. Sandford, we will serve ourselves. Thank you for laying everything out so beautifully.'

With a bow, Sandford left.

Lord Langham waved at the five silver serving dishes in the centre of the table. 'Dig in, what.'

He then led the charge in unveiling the first offering. The waft of griddled bacon and herby sausages made Eleanor cry out. She cleared her throat.

'Sorry, they're my favourite.'

Lady Langham smiled. 'I believe Cook has undertaken a departure from our usual accompaniments this morning. This I believe' – she held up a decorative gravy boat – 'is paprika relish. A new recipe, apparently.'

Eleanor flashed Clifford a 'thank you' smile. He was, however, busying himself arranging the starched linen napkin on his lap.

Lady Langham clapped her hands. 'At the risk of being so gauche as to talk business, and murky business at that, over food, I am anxious to continue our conversation. If that is alright with you Eleanor, and with Clifford?'

'Absolutely!'

'Without reservation, your ladyship.'

'Good. Where shall we pick up from?'

'Actually,' Eleanor said with a sideways glance at Clifford. At his nod, she continued, 'We do have a question but it might seem frightfully impertinent.'

Lord Langham rapped the table with his knife. 'Nonsense! The walls don't have ears in here. Fire away, dear girl, only pass the eggs first, there's a sport.'

She did so. 'Ah yes, how well do you know Lord Hurd, the renowned textile tycoon?'

'He was at the ball,' Lord Langham said. 'Had to invite him, of course, one of the great and the good and all that.'

His wife peered at him over the rim of her coffee cup. 'I didn't find much good to report in the man. Why do you ask?'

Eleanor gestured to Clifford to elaborate.

'If I may explain, my lady. I was investigating the possibility we touched on briefly before, that Colonel Puddifoot-Barton's death was premeditated, and the theft of her ladyship's jewels a blind. Therefore I travelled to London yesterday to meet with Mr Leonard Burkett.'

'The colonel's valet?'

'One and the same, my lord. Mr Burkett was most forthcoming in his conversation with me, with impeccable regard for propriety, of course. I was rather surprised, however, to learn that Colonel Puddifoot-Barton had underwritten Mr Burkett a comfortable pension into his will.'

Lord Langham threw Eleanor a mischievous look. 'Bet you were surprised too, Eleanor old thing. To hear that Pudders had set up a generous pension for his manservant?'

'Initially yes, forgive me,' Eleanor said.

Lord Langham waved his sausage filled fork at her. 'No need, old fruit. Pudders was a peculiar mix, alright. The whole world found him damnably hard work, but the real Pudders, the one underneath his uniform, was hewn from good clay.'

'I wish I had realised earlier,' Eleanor said truthfully.

Lord Langham shrugged. 'Burkett is a good example, you see. He was injured while under Pudders' command at Tanganyika during the final throes of the Abushiri Revolt in 1891. Dashed bad business all round, senseless waste for both sides. Afterwards Pudders took Burkett in and made him his valet.'

Clifford nodded. 'Particularly generous, my lord, given that Mr Burkett's injury meant he was no longer able to negotiate stairs or move at speed.'

'Now I understand,' Eleanor said. 'Miss Glew told me the colonel came without his valet.'

'Absolutely.' Lord Langham nodded. 'Burkett rarely left the colonel's London digs, too difficult for the poor blighter.'

'Which means,' Clifford said, 'that Mr Burkett had a possible motive for killing his employer, id est to access his pension early, as it were. However, my lord, as we have already mentioned, he was not at the ball the night of the theft and murder. He was back in London spending the evening at his valet club, which I confirmed.'

Lady Langham stared at Clifford. 'So Mr Burkett is ruled out as a suspect. But what has all this to do with Lord Hurd?'

'Mr Burkett mentioned Lord Hurd to me. It seems his lordship and Colonel Puddifoot-Barton had been engaged in an ongoing battle over their divergent views on how to restore the economy.

Mr Burkett was privy to clashes between Lord Hurd and Colonel Puddifoot-Barton over this issue.'

Lord Langham nodded. 'Pudders had a holding in Hurd's company.'

'A substantial one, my lord?'

'Substantial enough, I imagine, to derail Hurd's plans if Pudders disagreed with him.'

Eleanor whistled. 'Okay, so we can be certain Lord Hurd and the colonel had a long-standing dispute. And if the real crime was not to steal the jewels but to... er, remove the colonel, then Lord Hurd is a definite contender. We need to trace his movements the night of the ball.'

Lady Langham put down her fork. 'I remember Lord Hurd was one of the last to arrive. Excluding you, Eleanor, of course. It must have been around seven thirty when he put in an appearance.'

'Clifford,' Lord Langham said, 'check with Sandford after breakfast, would you? I recall him saying Hurd was indisposed part way through the festivities, said he was resting up in the drawing room for a bit. Suffers from gout. Maybe he'd had one of his flare-ups. Don't remember seeing him again until the blasted police herded us all back into the bally ballroom last thing.'

His wife placed her hands on the table. 'Clifford, I detect that you learned something more from Mr Burkett, but hesitate to relay this in our company. However time is against us, as you are aware.'

'Very good, my lady. Putting Lord Hurd aside for a moment, my investigation then led me to the colonel's gentlemen's club where I was able to call in a small favour. Let us say that the doorman confided that I might better enquire at number twenty-three Dawson Street.'

Lady Langham shrugged. 'What's at twenty-three Dawson Street?'

'A different sort of club altogether.'

Lady Langham gasped. 'A brothel!'

'That is indeed the reputation of the establishment, my lady, although it is one considerably removed from the facts.'

'I'm confused. Is it a house of ill repute, or not?'

'Not, my lady. You see, it is not against the law to pay a lady for the service of sharing an afternoon tea or an innocent game of mahjong, although two-hand mahjong does require a slight deviation from the classic form. Instead of...' Clifford caught Eleanor's eye. 'Apologies. In essence, the ladies at twenty-three Dawson Street offer a companionship service only.'

Lady Langham shook her head. 'If I've understood correctly, the colonel would rather have it assumed that he frequented a house of... of prostitution than one of congenial companionship?'

Lord Langham nodded sagely. 'Makes perfect sense, my dear. Pudders never found his life's love, like I did. And you know the pressures on a fellow in his position to secure a wife. Chaps of the colonel's age, if they've remained single, well there is a tendency in some circles for certain allegations to be made against the gentleman's... proficiency in certain areas.'

Clifford nodded. 'Or indeed his... leanings, my lady.'

Lady Langham tutted loudly. 'And they say children are cruel! Clifford, did the colonel have a favourite companion perhaps, who might have known something of import?'

'Yes, my lady, a pleasant woman of middle to late years who was genuinely mystified that anyone would wish to harm the colonel. She divulged his particular fondness for lemon tea cakes and rounds of the card game Old Maid at each of his weekly visits.'

Lady Langham seemed to be trying to hide a wry smile and Lord Langham busied himself offering another salver to Eleanor.

Clifford waited a moment, and then continued. 'The lady also informed me that Colonel Puddifoot-Barton had been boasting that he was close to unmasking the notorious jewel thief who had been plaguing London and the Home Counties. She thought he was just "talking out of his pipe" as she put it. But given the events that followed…'

Eleanor looked sharply at him. 'You didn't mention this before, Clifford?'

'I'm sorry, my lady, but I left the Hall's number and asked the lady to ring me if she remembered anything more that might be of use. She rang this morning just before we left and furnished me with this piece of information.'

Eleanor raised her hand. 'I'm sorry, Clifford, I didn't mean to suggest you'd been withholding the information, it's just that this might be the breakthrough we're looking for.'

Lord Langham waved his fork. 'Hurrah!'

Clifford turned towards him. 'If I might request Lady Swift and myself visit the scene of the crimes, your lordship? It is possible it might jog her ladyship's memory as to the events of that night.'

Lord Langham nodded. 'Splendid idea! Help yourselves. I'll stay here with Augusta. She hasn't been in the room since that dreadful night.'

Upstairs, Sandford unlocked the door and left Eleanor and Clifford alone in the study where the colonel had been murdered.

Apart from the absence of a corpse, and a pirate, the room looked the same as it had the night she'd heard a noise and walked in and discovered… She ran her hands down her arms to try and quell her goosebumps.

'Feels horribly cold, Clifford. And… creepy.'

He nodded. 'Death does tend to leave its signature, my lady. But if you can keep your head—'

She cut him short. 'It's not my head I'm worried about, it's Lancelot's neck! Small consolation that beheading was banned some years back.'

'A great many back, my lady. In 1757, in fact.'

'Wonderful!' she said sardonically. 'Anyhow, let's re-enact the events of that night. That's what they always do in those police novels.'

She hunched over by the door, then tiptoed into the middle of the study. 'Right, I'm Lancelot creeping in, focused on stealing the jewels.' She paused mid creep and peered over at Clifford. 'First question, then. When I see the safe already open, why don't I turn and fast tail it out of there?'

'Because you see the unfortunate Colonel Puddifoot-Barton lying on the floor?'

'Of course. So despite not that long ago having had a fierce row with the old duffer in the garden, according to Cora, I slide over to see if he needs help. I realise he's dead, or at least seriously injured. Before I can go for help, I hear a noise. Is it the attacker returning? In a panic I seize the first thing that comes to hand to defend myself—'

'The candlestick.'

'Exactly.' She straightened up. 'You know, Clifford, most of the evidence now points to the colonel being onto the thief and following him into the study. But if that's what actually happened, why didn't the colonel go to the police or the Langhams rather than tackling the criminal himself?'

He tapped his nose. 'One last hurrah, perhaps?'

'Gracious, yes! Military pride and all that.' She puffed out her chest and snatched up a long tapered candle, swinging it under her arm like a military baton. '"I say, Pudders," he says to himself, "there's the bounder sneaking up the stairs. Let's go give him what for!" And the colonel then follows and is bashed on the back of the head by the thief.'

She re-enacted the colonel's final moments.

Clifford applauded. 'If you give as good a performance at the am-dram, my lady, you will bring the house down.'

'Thank you, Clifford, but there's something bothering me… and I can't think what.'

'It will doubtless come to you in time, my lady.'

From the doorway, Lady Langham's voice made them both jump. 'Maybe, but time is the one thing we don't have.'

Eleanor jumped up and brushed her skirt. 'Lady Langham, who else knew your jewel safe was located in here? Aside from Lancelot, of course.'

Lady Fenwick-Langham stared into the room, not crossing the threshold. 'Only him and Daphne. What looks like the main safe is located in Harold's study, but it's a dummy. This is the main safe. This room is set up to look like a small study for writing odd correspondence and such like. But Daphne will be seventy at her next birthday. She can wield a croquet mallet for a few minutes at a time, but stairs affect her heart enormously. Had she made it up here, she would have needed to lie down for a good hour.'

'And Cora?'

'Fit as a fiddle. Why? Are you suggesting Daphne told Cora about the safe being in this room?'

Eleanor hesitated, but there was too much at stake to talk around the subject. 'Given Cora's feelings for Lancelot, which I witnessed first-hand at the croquet match…'

'And given young Lord Fenwick-Langham's refusal to marry her,' Clifford added.

'Exactly, Clifford. It's possible that she followed Lancelot up here to seek a few minutes alone with him.'

Lady Langham looked confused. 'But what has that got to do with the colonel's death?'

Eleanor sighed. 'It's very unlikely, but we have to examine every possibility if we are to save Lancelot. The dowager countess and Cora both had reason to… to want revenge on Lancelot. Cora, with the dowager countess' help, could have… killed the colonel and set Lancelot up in revenge for him refusing to marry her. Or—'

'Or Cora could have lain in wait and killed old Pudders, mistaking him for Lancelot.' Lord Langham stepped into the room.

Lady Langham put her face in her hands. 'Oh, Harold!'

CHAPTER 20

'Well, whereabouts in Oxford is he, Sergeant Brice? Do you suggest I wander around the entire city on the off chance of bumping into him?' She held the receiver away from her ear and waved at Clifford to bring her a pen and paper. 'Blue what? Bore! Oh, *boar*, like the pig. What a peculiar name. And where is that exactly?'

She held up her scribbled paper for Clifford to see. He nodded.

'Thank you, Sergeant Brice.' A snort escaped from the receiver as she hung it on its hook.

She tapped her fingers on the ornate walnut telephone table. 'So, you know where this Blue Boar Street place is then?'

'Yes, my lady. Did Sergeant Brice say why the Detective Chief Inspector had returned to Oxford?'

'Mmm, yes, he said something about a new case that needs his attention.'

Clifford nodded. 'I see, and you intend calling on Detective Chief Inspector Seldon unannounced?'

She nodded back. 'Of course. I have to talk to Lancelot again. I'm sure he holds the key to all this, even if he doesn't realise it. If I call the inspector on the phone and ask to see Lancelot, he'll simply say no, whereas if I'm standing in front of him…' A glint of steel came into her eyes.

Clifford nodded. 'It is indeed much harder to say no to someone in person than on the telephone. Especially if that person is somewhat—'

'Stubborn? Bloody-minded?'

He coughed. 'I was going to say strong-minded, my lady.'

Eleanor smiled. 'Right, a trip to Oxford it is. How long will that take us?'

'Most likely an hour and a quarter. As you know, the lanes are steep and narrow to begin with and the centre of Oxford itself can be surprisingly congested even when the university is on summer recess.'

'Marvellous! I can also ask the inspector whether they've found Lancelot's fingerprints on the stolen jewels. And he's gone far too quiet about me being an accessory. I need to find out what he's up to.'

Eleanor was first to the Rolls. She climbed in the driver's seat and patted the passenger seat. 'All aboard, look lively.'

Before Clifford had finished closing the door, she put her foot down hard on the accelerator. The back wheels spun on the gravel, sending a shower over Joseph, who lurched sideways, tipping his wheelbarrow into the stone pool at the base of the ornamental fountain.

She waved through the open window. 'Sorry, Joseph! The beds are looking lovely.'

He returned a wary waft of his cap and offered a sympathetic nod to Clifford. 'Good luck, Mr Clifford.'

The Rolls roared along the drive and jerked on to the road.

'Mind that horse, my lady!'

She waggled a finger, her hand still fast on the wheel. 'Don't try and persuade me to stop looking at the road. Gosh, what a thing for a driving instructor to encourage in his pupil, tsk, tsk.'

Clifford's lips pursed. 'A most laudable observation, my lady. Only the animal *was* on the road.' He indicated the line of horse spittle that ran diagonally along the previously spotless side window.

She shot him a look. 'Clifford! I am in no mood for horses that have scant regard for the rules of the road.'

'There are rules are there, my lady?'

'This is England, there are blasted rules for everything!'

'Indeed.' He cleared his throat. 'Forgive the suggestion, but you might wish to try changing down? That intense juddering can be an indication that the gear you have selected is perhaps unsuitable for the speed of the vehicle.'

Eleanor tutted and then grunted as she wrestled with the 'blasted gear stick!'

'Shall I?'

'Leave it!' She grasped the gear stick with both hands. 'Get. In! Yes, yes!'

Suddenly aware that Clifford was holding the wheel, she coughed. 'Thank you. And does the expert recommend returning to top gear on the way down the other side?'

'Only if your ladyship wishes to join the ducks in the river.'

Childishly she stuck her tongue out at him. 'Perhaps it would be better if you drove the rest of the way to Oxford. I'm not sure the inspector will still be there at this rate!'

Eleanor's brain was too full to enjoy the scenery en route to Oxford but as Clifford manoeuvred the Rolls up a particularly steep, winding hill, she looked out. 'That is quite the view, isn't it?' All around them rolling green hills dotted with cotton-wool sheep stretched to the horizon, where a broad blue sky dotted with cotton-wool clouds met them.

Clifford nodded. 'Indeed it is, my lady, it is the highest point in the county and the original site of the gibbet where they hanged highwaymen and mu—' He tailed off.

She closed her eyes but could only picture Lancelot swinging from a gibbet. 'I'm really feeling the pressure on this, Clifford. If we don't get the answer we're hoping for from the inspector, I've no idea where to turn next. What kind of a woman am I anyway, taking advantage of the inspector's apparent interest in me to obtain information to save another? That's the scandalous plot of a penny dreadful novel, surely?'

'Undoubtedly so.'

She spun in her seat and stared at him before noticing the twinkle in his eye.

'Very funny!'

The rest of the twenty-three-mile trip passed in a blur of green until the edge of Oxford itself elbowed out the hedgerows. Streets of terraced houses turned to ornate spires, which grew into rows of monolithic buildings festooned with gargoyles peering down from every corner.

'Good job you know your way around, Clifford. All these buildings look far too similar to me. They're enormous, any one of them could be the town hall.'

'Actually, at present we are passing the prestigious Magdalen College. The Great Tower is the site of the May Morning rituals. For over five hundred years the Magdalen Choir have made the precarious climb of one hundred and forty-four feet to the top of the tower and then performed "Hymnus Eucharisticus". And now on your right is Brasenose College, famous for its rebellious student door-knocker incident of 1333.'

'You know, Clifford, I really think you missed your vocation in life, you should have been a tour guide. Now where is this wretched Blue Boar Street?'

DCI Seldon greeted the news of Eleanor's arrival unenthusiastically. His voice penetrated the glass partition door like a bullet.

'Oh, for Pete's sake! Go and tell her I can't see her.'

A softer, country voice answered. 'I tried, Chief, honest, but she's one of them force of nature bird… ladies.'

'Oh, show her in. I'll deal with her myself.'

The saggy-middled sergeant who'd been on the reception desk waved to them. With a deep breath, she entered the inspector's office, followed by Clifford.

Eleanor smiled sweetly. 'I intended to make an appointment, Inspector, but—'

DCI Seldon raised a hand, silencing her. 'Lady Swift, whatever the reason is you came here, I suggest you stop wasting police time. Now kindly leave.'

Eleanor forced herself to keep smiling. 'Wasting police time? I simply came here to ask for one more short audience with Lancelot before... it's too late.'

Seldon was staring at her. She stared back and he held her gaze. 'Lady Swift, not only are you the accused's friend but you are also a suspect in this case, possibly his accomplice in these reprehensible crimes.'

Eleanor's eyes flashed. 'His accomplice? How dare you!'

DCI Seldon rose from his desk, his face flushed. 'Lady Swift, if you erroneously believe you can influence the outcome of this case, you are wrong. Do you think this is the first case I've dealt with involving over-privileged wastrels believing that wealth can set them above the law? That their status will protect them? Times have changed, the country is sick and tired of your blasted bright young things running amok and getting away with murder, while ordinary folk are striving to make ends meet and raise a decent, God-fearing family.'

Eleanor heard Clifford's discreet cough before she could respond. *Clifford's right, Ellie, stay calm for Lancelot's sake.* She stared at him coolly.

'I may be a privileged wastrel, but I'm the privileged wastrel who will find out the truth and see justice done!'

Seldon sat down wearily. 'Justice?' He laughed without humour. 'What does someone in your privileged position know about justice?'

Eleanor opened her mouth to reply, but before she could, DCI Seldon's words transported her back twenty years.

Her mother was leaning over her bed, her father waiting in the doorway. She could picture that loving smile and those piercing green eyes that always seemed to know what Eleanor was thinking. Her mother brushed a hand across her cheek and kissed her. 'Good night, God bless, sweet dreams.'

And then she was running into a police station. The building was filthy, with peeling paint and dirt floors. She ran from room to room shouting, 'Where are my parents?' Laughter followed her down the corridor until she reached the end and turned round. At every door men stood, guns on hips, staring at the funny little girl.

A calmness came over her. The laughter stopped. She slowly walked past the men back to the entrance, all eyes on her. One stepped forward to grab her, but she spun round, the look on her young face making him step back…

DCI Seldon was staring at her. She looked up and spoke quietly.

'It seems I misjudged you, Inspector. Everyone deserves justice, whether they are privileged or not. Good day.'

Picking up her bag, she walked out of the office.

The purr of the Rolls' engine had been the only sound on their return journey, save for Eleanor's fingers drumming the inlay wood of the car door. Now back in the drawing room at Henley Hall, Mrs Butters tiptoed in with a tea tray and left silently. When Clifford knocked fifty minutes later, the tray was untouched and the rug decidedly flatter in a singular path to and from the window.

She cleared her throat. 'Clifford, I know that wasn't my finest hour in the inspector's office. I… I let my emotions get in the way.' She turned to him. 'In consequence it was a wasted trip, we learned nothing and I came away without seeing Lancelot. My fault entirely, so let's not say any more about it and move on.'

Clifford bowed. 'Very good, my lady.' He held out the afternoon edition of the *County Herald*.

'Whatever it is, Clifford, I'm not interested.' She half smiled. 'Unless it says the inspector's head fell off and rolled under a bus.'

He continued to hold the newspaper out to her. 'Except on this occasion I fear you may be. Page seven, my lady. Bottom story.'

She scanned the article and gasped. 'Clifford!' She dropped to the chaise longue and slowly read back through the piece. 'Road accident... one fatality... local man.' She let the paper drop and stared at him. 'I can't believe it. I was partying with him just a few days ago!'

CHAPTER 21

'Good morning, m'lady,' a disembodied voice called.

Eleanor spun round. 'What? Who's that? Show yourself!'

The gardener appeared high above her in the tall box hedging. 'Sorry to make you jump like that, m'lady. I thought you must have seen my barrow below.'

'Oh, Joseph. My apologies for the drama. I slept very badly. How are you?'

'I'm grand, thank you, m' lady. Rushed off me boots though. Season's been so busy, having to trim the box hedge early it's put on such a spurt.'

'You know, I am sorry, Joseph. I've been so caught up since I arrived, I've been remiss in seeking you out to thank you for the extraordinary way you care for the gardens.'

She looked around, her hand shielding the fiercely bright sun from her eyes. Like the rest of the grounds, the view back to the house had clearly been crafted by a passionate master hand. On each side of the immaculate lawn, flower beds of meticulously selected shades blended as perfectly as a seamless quilt, looking every inch as soft and inviting. A balmy breeze ran through, making the whole scene dance a shimmering rainbow sway.

'It's simply beautiful, Joseph.'

''Tis a pleasure. Has been for nigh on twenty year. By the by, if you'd care for a tour sometime? Place is so big, seems a crime no one sees it half the time 'cept me, and Master Gladstone, of course.'

She chuckled. 'It's a date!'

'Consider it in me diary. Now, if you'll excuse me, I'll get on.'

They parted company, Eleanor letting herself back into the house via the kitchen to a rapturous welcome from Gladstone with the gift of a soggy leather slipper. Mrs Butters heaved a relieved sigh. 'Ah, there you are, my lady. Breakfast's been ready a fair while so as Mrs Trotman's stressing on it going cold.'

Eleanor held up her hands. 'My apologies. I have been horribly distracted and regrettably thrown the whole meal schedule out the window.'

'Tsk, 'tis no matter. Mrs Trotman is a whizz at dressing up late breakfast as elevenses with a fancy name.'

A cough from the doorway interrupted them.

Eleanor waved cheerily at Clifford. 'It's okay, I'm here. The search party can be called off now.'

'As I see.' He pulled out his pocket watch and peered at it. 'And do you still require breakfast at this un-breakfast-like late hour, my lady?'

She grinned. 'All I require is that I don't put you and these wonderful ladies to any more trouble. I'll eat whatever is already prepared. Will you join me in the morning room, please? I want to pick your enormous brain for any ideas on the way forward.'

Mrs Butters' voice trailed off as Eleanor and Clifford left. 'Mouth closed, Polly my girl. You look like a cow chewing the cud!'

Once in the sunlit morning room, Eleanor waited for Gladstone to finish turning in circles before settling on her feet, then pulled out her notebook and looked at her scribblings. 'Oh, Clifford! I laid awake all night, scratching about for an answer and all I managed was a headache and bags under my eyes. Where on earth do we go from here?' She stared at him as he poured the coffee.

He passed her a cup. 'I fear, my lady, that without insider information about yesterday's tragic death, we will be stumbling in the dark.'

'Was it tragic though, Clifford?'

He turned to her sharply. 'My lady?'

'I know that sounds terrible, doesn't it? But we had Albie on our list as a suspect. Honestly, I felt horribly uncomfortable during my last conversation with him. Suppose he was the colonel's killer and then couldn't live with himself and took the easy way out.'

'Drowning in one's car is perhaps not the easy way out.'

'But the newspaper made it clear the police are not treating it as suspicious. So if we suspect foul play, we're going to have a devil of a job getting any info out of the inspector. Or even Sergeant Brice.'

Clifford tilted his head. 'We do, of course, have a secret weapon in that regard, my lady.'

'Of course! Abigail, Sandford's wonderful niece who works at Chipstone Police Station. She didn't get into any trouble for helping us on the last case, then?'

'None whatsoever. And she was quite overcome with your ladyship's kindness in sending so generous a gift for her trouble.'

'I know, she sent me the sweetest note. Shall I leave it to you to make the enquiries through the usual channel?'

'I will call Mr Sandford presently and sow the seed.'

After a moment's silence punctuated only by the soft snores of a contented bulldog, Eleanor spoke. 'In truth, you know, Clifford, I can't see Albie actually biffing the colonel and then taking his own life. Unlike Lord Hurd, his real beef seemed to be with Lancelot and Johnny for persistently being mean to him. I know he had an artistic temperament and all that but he is... *was* the only one of all of Lancelot's friends with a sense of reality. Not surprising perhaps, growing up as a miner's son. Even with the obvious suspicion that he was desperately short of funds, I honestly don't think Albie was the murdering type.'

'Might one enquire in casting your eye over your suspect list who does strike you as being the murdering type?'

Eleanor grimaced. 'Fair point. That's the problem with murderers, isn't it? It's never the obvious one. You know, the one with an eye patch and a hook for an arm.'

Clifford smiled at the image. 'Actually, I have news of Lord Hurd, my lady, and was waiting for a suitable point to mention it.'

Eleanor laughed. 'Why? Has Lord Hurd an eye patch and a hook for an arm?'

'No, but he does have a prosthetic limb, having lost his left leg in the war.'

'That is news, Clifford.'

'Indeed, my lady, it is hard to believe that a man with such an impediment would be capable of being our cat burglar and jewel thief.'

'And unlikely that he could whip up the stairs, open the safe, dispatch the colonel and get back down and mingle in such a short window of time.'

'I would say almost impossible. I followed up on our conversation with Lord and Lady Fenwick-Langham and spoke to Lord Hurd's valet. He informed me that Lord Hurd doesn't mention his prosthetic limb, and in daily life one would hardly notice. However, his lordship is quite unable to hurry and his valet makes sure he has ample time to dress and get to any engagement he has.'

Eleanor found Lord Hurd's name and crossed it through. 'Well, that's one suspect we can cross off.'

'I would say, two, my lady.'

She looked at him sharply. 'How?'

'Even if Mr Appleby was murdered, and it might have been by a different hand from that that struck down Colonel Puddifoot-Barton, I feel it is a more likely scenario that it was one and the same.'

She nodded her head. 'So we can rule Albie out as the jewel thief and the colonel's killer as well.' She crossed his name through for thoroughness. 'So that is indeed two suspects down.' She sighed. 'Fancy poor Albie's parents having to endure the allegation that their son lost his life while being under the influence of alcohol, or worse, drugs.'

'Although without being uncharitable, my lady, he may not have lost his life to it, but there is likely a strong amount of truth in the reporting, given your experiences at the Blind Pig Club.'

She groaned. 'I know. I really need to talk to the rest of Lancelot's gang and find out what they were up to the night Albie died. Let's just hope the inspector doesn't find out and throw me in jail for sticking my nose into the case.'

'Indeed, my lady, we will have to tread doubly carefully. I'll make that call and put Abigail on the case immediately.'

'Thank you. And then I'll chance my arm in ringing the inspector. I don't suppose he would have taken too much offence when I stomped off yesterday, do you?'

Clifford shook his head. 'I'm sure not, my lady. After all, you only accused him of perverting the course of justice in order to convict an innocent man.'

As Clifford left the room Eleanor called after him. 'Well, I was angry, what did he expect?' She took a bite of cold toast, muttering, 'Some people are just looking to take offence, what can you do?'

After a replacement round of hot toast, kindly supplied by Mrs Butters and intently ogled by the now awake Gladstone, Eleanor was fortified enough to tackle her phone call.

'Inspector… sorry, Chief Inspector – *Start off on the right foot this time, Ellie!* – Seldon, please. This is Lady Swift.'

She tapped her notepad with her pencil while waiting for the call to be put through.

A shrill, weasely voice came down the receiver, making her wince and switch ears.

'This is Detective Chief Inspector Seldon's office. I have instructions, Lady Swift, from the Chief Inspector himself, not to connect your calls.'

Eleanor stabbed the jotter with her pen so hard it broke in two. 'Listen, I am ringing to further the course of justice, not engage in petty squabbling. I called Chief Inspector Seldon to report a possible crime, which, I fear, has so far escaped police attention. I believe a man's life may have been taken and the police are not investigating the matter.'

There was a pause, then the voice came back on. 'One moment.'

After what, to someone of Eleanor's impatient temperament, seemed an age, DCI Seldon's voice came down the line. 'Lady Swift?'

'Inspector, how wonderful to hear your voice.'

A grunt came down the line. 'I was told that a man's life has been taken. Which man, for Pete's sake?'

'Albert Appleby.'

'That name means nothing to me.'

'His car crashed into a canal yesterday in the early hours.'

'Oh, him! Now I understand. He was one of those bright young things, wasn't he? Car went off the road, too drunk to get out, subsequently drowned. Probably drugs involved too. The local police examined the car as a precaution, but there were no mechanical faults found, and no indication it had been tampered with, before you ask. The case is closed. And to be clear, wasting police time and perverting the course of justice can both be committed via telephone as well as in person. If—'

'Inspector,' Eleanor's tone was icy, 'are you threatening me?'

She heard a weary laugh at the other end. 'You know, Lady Swift, I should actually be grateful to those bright young things.'

'Grateful? What are you on about?'

'Well, if they carry on as they are, they'll either all have killed themselves or got themselves locked up by the end of the year. And without any police time and money being wasted. Good day.'

With that the line went dead.

Eleanor slowly replaced the receiver. 'Right!'

She doodled for a moment with a spare pen, then marched back to the morning room.

She was staring out of the window as Clifford appeared with a fresh pot of coffee.

'Not good then, my lady?'

'And why would you assume that, Clifford?'

He held up the broken pen and a sheet from the telephone-table notepad. An ink-blotted doodle showed a head rolling under the wheels of an oncoming bus. 'Detective Chief Inspector Seldon, perchance?'

She flopped in a chair. 'Okay, you got me. He shot me down at the first sentence and has banned me from talking to him. At all. About anything, even the blasted weather I gather. And if I so much as stroll past the police station, I am to be arrested on any spurious charge he can come up with. Agh!' She covered her eyes with her hands. 'I feel another murder coming on, Clifford, and this time it will be me holding the murder weapon.'

'Understandable, but far from advisable, my lady. Perhaps waiting for Miss Abigail to report is the best approach? There is, however, one bright point on the horizon neither of us has mentioned.'

She peeked through her fingers. 'And that is?'

'Young Lord Fenwick-Langham was still incarcerated at the time of Mr Appleby's demise. If it does transpire that Mr Appleby's death was neither suicide nor an accident, it is clear that young

Lord Fenwick-Langham could not have been the perpetrator of the crime.'

'That would be a good point, Clifford, if anyone *were* treating Albie's demise as a crime. I need to see Coco and try to get a few answers about Albie from her.' She sighed. 'You know though, Clifford, we haven't considered the biggest problem of all.'

'Which is, my lady?'

'Suppose we pursue the matter of Albie's death, assuming it *is* murder and connected to the colonel's death, or the jewel thefts, and then we find it *isn't*?'

'Then we shall remove the egg from our faces and continue investigating. You are indefatigable when you have the bit between your teeth, if you'll forgive me comparing you to a horse.'

Eleanor dropped her hands and laughed. 'Forgiven, Clifford. I've been compared to much less agreeable animals.'

'I'm sure you have, my lady. But if I can get back to our conversation, I am not following your train of thought it seems.'

Eleanor sighed. 'The biggest problem, Clifford, is if we investigate Albie's death and it turns out to have nothing to do with the case, it will have been time wasted. It will have delayed us in solving the colonel's murder... and Lancelot's trial is...?'

'Ah!' He nodded slowly. 'Next week.'

'And we will be...?'

He looked down at his hands. 'Too late!'

CHAPTER 22

If the speeding car didn't stop lurching Eleanor felt sure she would part company with the oysters and cocktails she had eaten only an hour before. She'd wanted a more substantial meal, but the others had pooh-poohed her suggestion, claiming there was no time for eating until they'd honoured Albie's memory by winning the treasure hunt.

'Albie loved treasure hunts,' Lucas explained. 'He almost always came up trumps with working out the clues. This is how he'd want us to remember him.'

Ellie appreciated the sentiment, but would have preferred Lucas to have kept his eyes on the road while telling her.

'So,' Millie said, 'you'd better concentrate, as in the absence of poor Albie you've been voted our clue master.'

'Voted? When?'

'By me, just then.'

Lucas laughed. 'Sorry, Eleanor, but that's a bagsy, alright. You're now officially our clue master.'

Eleanor groaned inwardly. She wanted to honour Albie's memory too, but felt a more conventional manner might have been a better, and safer, idea. However, having been brought up unconventionally herself, she understood that this was their way of coping with loss. The gang had told her tonight's treasure hunt involved working out clues set by a mysterious 'Mr X', who Eleanor figured was probably just another bright young thing who organised the whole affair. Apparently, there were teams from all over Buckinghamshire and Oxfordshire hunting these clues. What Lancelot's gang hadn't mentioned was that once you'd worked out what object a clue referred to, you then had to dash across the countryside and steal the wretched thing.

Clifford was right, Ellie, why did you ever think this was a good idea?

In front of her in the passenger seat, Millie was mixing cocktails. She slapped Lucas' arm as the car lurched violently again. 'Lucas, you imbecile, you've made me slop double the amount of cognac in the shaker!'

Lucas pushed her back. 'Excellent, my co-driver extraordinaire, then we'll have double the fun finding the next clue.'

Millie giggled as she screwed the shaker cap on. 'Right on cue, here comes Johnny.' She turned and waved out of the window as Johnny roared alongside with Coco in the front seat.

'What ho, slow coaches!' He lent over between the two speeding cars and ran a finger along Millie's silk-clad arm. Her diamond-and-pearl collar bracelet glinted in the late afternoon sun. 'Where are the drinks? I'm parched.'

Coco leaned forward in the passenger seat next to Johnny, and shouted across to Millie, 'You've got to shake it to make it!'

The rest of Lancelot's gang took up the chant: 'Shake! Shake! Shake!'

'Ready?' Millie said. 'Johnny!' and with that she threw the cocktail shaker through the window to the other car. Johnny steered with one hand and deftly caught it with the other. She cheered. 'Slick Seaton, as always!'

'Coco, you're it!' He threw the shaker to her. It landed at Coco's feet, who picked it up and took aim.

'Millie!'

Millie missed, but Lucas caught it, skilfully saving the shaker from crashing onto the road.

'Johnny!' Lucas said. Johnny nodded and stamped alternately on the brake and the accelerator making the gap harder for him to aim for.

'Seaton you're a rotter!' Lucas turned in his seat to get a better aim and then hurled the shaker past Millie. Everyone watched it sail through the window and into Johnny's lap, which earned Lucas a raucous round of applause.

Johnny gave the cocktail a good shake before hurling it through the rear window of Lucas' car. 'Eleanor! Oh, good catch… for a girl.'

Millie leaned out of the window. 'Beast! Keep it up, we love it.' She blew Johnny a kiss and reached down to grab a basket of cocktail glasses. 'Name your waitress!' she yelled to both drivers.

Lucas and Johnny shared a look and chorused: 'Coco!'

Eleanor threw the shaker back to Johnny with surprising accuracy, accepting his nod of praise with a smug grin. He grinned back.

Coco laughed. 'Hurrah! This is my favourite part.' Lucas and Johnny brought the speeding cars even closer together. Clambering past Johnny, shaker in hand, Coco lay across his lap. 'Glass, please, sis.'

Millie hung her arm out of the window, glass in hand.

'Here goes.' Coco began to pour the cocktail. Most of the drink streamed out behind the two speeding cars and splashed on the road.

'Bravo, what a barmaid you would make.' Johnny peered past her prostrate form to try to see the road. 'First glass goes to Prince Almighty, Lucas of India-Masala-Biryania.'

Millie handed Lucas the cocktail. He raised the glass. 'Here's to Albie! He loved fast cars and cocktails, despite all that poetry nonsense, so let's honour him that way!'

The others all chanted 'Albie!' except Millie, Eleanor noted, who kept silent, a look of faint disgust on her face. At Lucas' choking, Millie giggled. 'Obviously just right. Next glass is for our green guest!'

This time a good deal of the contents ended up over Coco and Millie and down the side of the cars, which the sisters found hilarious.

After toasting the departed Albie again, and reeling from the cognac burn of the first glug, Eleanor waited for a suitable moment and discreetly tipped the rest of hers into the ashtray.

After a brief stop where first the men, and then the girls disappeared into the trees, Eleanor took the opportunity to change cars. Once back on the road, from the back seat, she casually turned to her new driver. 'Speaking of poor old Albie, I can't really understand what happened. Were any of you with him the night he... died?'

Johnny shook his head. 'I wish we had been. Unfortunately I had to spend the day at the family pile, attending some dreadful affair. I managed to escape in the evening. I picked up Coco around nine and then met Lucas and Millie at that fabulous new club in Cowley, The Hole in the Wall, around ten. Millie said Albie was supposed to be coming along later in a car he'd borrowed for some reason, something distasteful like work in the morning.' He looked at her. 'We often party till dawn and beyond as you know.' He turned his eyes back on the road. 'Anyway, Albie never turned up. Next thing we hear is the silly fool's gone and got himself drunk and ditched himself and the car in the canal. Poor sod.'

Eleanor sat back and digested this information. 'Did you party? Until dawn, I mean?'

Johnny grinned. 'You bet. We left the Hole in the Wall around midnight and hit Madame Bella's and stayed until three and then went back to my place until dawn.' Eleanor knew she should follow this up, but in her heart she didn't believe anyone would make up such an easily checkable alibi.

Then again, she reminded herself, the police hadn't established a definite time of death and weren't treating it as suspicious. The newspaper had said around one in the morning, but where they'd got that piece of information from, she didn't know. Unless someone had seen the car going into the canal, and as far as she knew there were no witnesses. Albie could easily have died a couple of hours either side of that time.

She realised Johnny was talking to her.

'But let's not forget our incarcerated friend in all this. We're relying on you, Eleanor, to pull something out of the bag and get poor old Lance back here where he belongs.'

Eleanor didn't know what to say. At the moment she wasn't quite sure if Lancelot would be in any less peril than he already was, with the way Johnny was driving and knocking back cocktails.

Johnny turned part of his attention back to the road. 'Now, what's our last piece of treasure to hunt, clue master?'

Eleanor scrabbled for the paper on the seat next to her. 'Right, yes that's me, isn't it?'

Millie, who'd switched cars at the same time as Eleanor, rolled her eyes at Johnny, being sure Eleanor could see.

Eleanor ignored her and shouted out the next rhyme on the crumpled sheet.

'Take my hand, oh what a mass

'That sweet caress of a tuneful lass

'The only sound in old Sanctus land

'Will be the roar of Lawrence Peel, the slow win man.'

Johnny hit the steering wheel. 'Balderdash and beyond, that's a tricky one!'

Eleanor was feeling decidedly green now. She could hold her drink if she needed to, and she was no stranger to fast cars, but that last oyster had definitely been off.

'Maybe we should pull over and look at the map? We'll likely save more time than chasing along trying to work it out.'

'As long as you promise to hurl away from the rest of us,' Millie called behind her.

Eleanor leaned forward and cooed into Millie's ear, 'Where's the fun in that?'

For the first time Millie looked unsettled.

With the cars mounted on the verge, Eleanor spread on the bonnet the battered map Lucas handed her. She'd managed to discreetly down a bottle of water and was feeling quite restored. A cool evening breeze rustled the map. She looked up. 'You're the experts at this treasure hunt lark, and the area. What are the clues in this? Tuneful? Hand? Sanctus?'

Coco leaned in and took the paper from Eleanor. 'Who the heck was Lawrence Peel? Never heard of him.'

Eleanor rubbed her forehead. 'Are the clues usually this hard?'

A mixture of nods and shrugs came in reply. 'We usually call on the boffin. I mean, we used to,' Coco said quietly.

Eleanor frowned. 'The boffin?'

Millie rubbed a hand down her arm. 'Albie. He always worked out the stupidly hard clues.'

Johnny reached into his front seat and grabbed a bottle of Tanqueray gin. 'A juniper toast to our dear departed friend, who would have taught us so much, had we been inclined to listen.'

Taking a swig from the bottle, he wiped the top on his coat-tail and handed it to Coco who did the same before passing it to Millie. Lucas went last. He took a swig.

'To Albie, RIP old chum. We're sorry for everything.'

Eleanor wondered what this last remark meant. Had Lucas also been taunting Albie like Johnny and Lancelot did? Did he think Albie had driven into the canal on purpose because he couldn't take any more of their cruel jibes? Or was it something else altogether?

Johnny quickly broke the silence. 'Better crack on with this clue then. Come on, no slacking!' He cocked his head towards Eleanor.

'You know, Lancelot said you're quite the sleuthing ace so this should be right up your alley.' He leaned forward with a cheeky grin. 'Or has he been labouring under a gross misapprehension?'

Coco slapped his back. 'Shut up, Johnny!'

Millie folded her arms. 'No, come on. I'm dying to see how good she really is.'

The desire to slap Millie's spite back down her throat miraculously sharpened Eleanor's wits. 'Whatever we're looking for, it's in a church, for sure.'

Millie snorted. 'Brilliant! There can't be more than a couple of hundred in the area!'

Unabashed Eleanor continued. 'As I was saying, a *church* because the clues says, "Oh what a mass", not mess. "Tuneful lass", hmm, what makes a tune in a church?'

Coco shrugged. 'An organ?'

'The choir?' Lucas offered.

'We can't steal a whole choir, old man.' Johnny laughed. 'Damn good fun it would be though. I'm game and' – he looked at Lucas with a mixture of admiration and amusement – 'I know you are.'

Lucas shrugged and said nothing.

Eleanor snapped her fingers. 'The bells! And "take my hand" must mean steal the clapper. Now this "Lawrence Peel" character…'

Millie leaned in close to Eleanor's face. 'I do believe he was a Tory minister, son of the renowned Sir Robert Peel. How's that?'

Eleanor smiled. 'Impressive. I didn't know you were such a mine of information. Sadly, however, irrelevant.'

Millie looked daggers at her. 'Irrelevant?'

'Yes. "Peel" refers to the bell and "Lawrence" is the name of the well-known church that houses the bell with the clapper we're supposed to steal.' *Let's hope so, Ellie, or you'll look pretty foolish.*

Coco pushed Millie aside. 'How do you know it's well known?'

'Look "Sanctus" has a capital, it's a name. So I assume it's well known enough to find.'

Lucas took the paper from Coco. 'Okay, so if "Lawrence Peel" isn't a person we're looking for, who is the "slow win man" who's going to roar?'

Johnny stepped forward. 'The roar will be the vicar's rage at the theft of his precious clapper by the sound of it.'

Eleanor grinned. 'Absolutely right. Have you worked out the last part? Where do you think this church with its famous bell is?'

'No clue,' Millie muttered.

Eleanor chalked up another childish, but satisfactory point. 'It's an anagram, silly! Is there a place anywhere near here called Owlswin, Swinlow or Swinowl?'

'Owlswin!' Coco and Millie chorused.

Johnny clapped his hands. 'In the cars, chop chop! To St Lawrence's Church, Owlswin!'

Lucas sidled up to Eleanor as she opened the rear passenger door. 'Very impressive, Lady Swift. It seems everything Lancelot said about you was right. Someone needs to watch their step.'

Back at home later that evening, Eleanor lay on the chaise longue in her silk house pyjamas and Ryeland wool shawl, with Gladstone wedged against her side.

Clifford coughed. 'Perhaps, my lady, there might be another way to obtain the information we seek. One where you are less likely to be killed or arrested, per chance. Unless, of course, your plan is to create the opportunity to converse with young Lord Fenwick-Langham through the bars of an adjoining cell?'

Eleanor lifted her head just enough to offer a disapproving stare. 'No, that is not my plan, as you know all too well. If you have a sensible suggestion, let's hear it. Trust me, I don't want to fall to my death scaling a church tower to steal a blasted bell. Nor do I want to be crushed under a train while trying to break into a signal box to nick some blasted lever! And I definitely have no interest in going to jail for breaking into a cricket ground, Lord's if you will, to pinch their wretched stumps!'

Clifford drew a sharp breath at her last words.

'I know, all this stealing stuff really isn't cricket.'

'Actually, my lady, even though I obviously do not condone stealing of any kind, I was more concerned that you may have damaged the square. There is a very important match tomorrow between—'

'Clifford!' Eleanor's tone held a warning note. 'As I was saying, the only consolation is that I did find out some details about the night Albie was killed. Oh, and I observed something rather interesting.'

'Indeed, my lady, perhaps due to the late hour we should discuss Mr Appleby's last evening tomorrow. However, I am curious as to what you observed.'

'Well, I didn't actually climb the church tower to steal the bell. Lucas did. And he climbed it like one of those steeplejacks who do it for a living.'

Clifford raised an eyebrow. 'Or like a...'

Eleanor nodded. 'Cat burglar. Anyway, I convinced the others to store all the treasure hunt spoils here.'

'Here, my lady? Is that absolutely wise?'

'Yes, on two counts. First, I fully intend to return all the items to their rightful owners the minute this wretched business is over. And no, I haven't got a plan for how to do so, before you ask.'

'I'm sure when you have, my lady, it will be quite the thing. And second?'

Eleanor wasn't sure if Clifford was complimenting her or not, so she let it go. 'And on the second count, it worked just as I intended in currying favour with Lancelot's gang. They said they used to hide the stuff in a barn somewhere but the farmer was getting suspicious. The only thing that forces them to keep a vestige of morality, or at least an appearance of it, is the threat of their parents cutting off their allowances, so my offering to hide the spoils was much appreciated. Honestly, Clifford, they are great fun but also a terrible bunch of spoiled children who only get out of bed each day to see what mischief they can create on their pocket money.'

'Then their pockets must be considerably more voluminous than average to house the vast amounts of cash needed to keep up with such activities.'

'Quite so. And I hate to admit it, but with all that drinking and driving, it's no wonder Inspector Seldon has no sympathy for poor Albie. On paper, it looks like it was only a matter of time before one of them ended up dead.' Eleanor pulled her shawl closer round her shoulders. 'But there's something I'm struggling to put my finger on. Trouble is, I'm so tired, my brain isn't working properly. Let's catch up tomorrow.'

Clifford gave his customary half bow. 'Very good, my lady. Perhaps after your am-dram rehearsal? Ah! But as you are now a fully paid-up member of the bright young things, you then have dinner with the gang at the Criterion in Piccadilly. Perhaps after that? But, of course not, you are all then partying at the elegant residence of Beau Brennant. Until the morn I would imagine. Perhaps you will be more disposed to continue our conversation then?'

Eleanor flopped back on the chaise longue and whispered, 'Clifford, please kill me!'

CHAPTER 23

The following afternoon, Eleanor entered the village hall determined it would be a short rehearsal. Reverend Gaskell spied her immediately and skipped over.

'Lady Swift, how are you? What a blessing this delightful summer weather is.'

'Hello, Reverend. The weather, as you say, is so bright… unlike your attire. Have you lost someone dear to you?'

'Lost someone?' He frowned in confusion then laughed. 'No, no. I'm merely getting into character as the evil Doctor Wells. Respectable on the outside…' He gestured at his sombre grey suit and then opened the jacket to reveal a scarlet waistcoat. 'But devilish on the inside.'

She smiled and looped her arm through his. 'I can see your standing ovation already, Reverend.'

He giggled. 'This is such fun, don't you think? My delightful housekeeper, Mrs Appleton, has been most kind in helping me learn my lines.'

'Lines, ah yes…'

'Bravo, Mr Cartwright! What a splendid performance. You'll have the audience fooled for sure.'

He pretended not to be delighted by her praise. 'This won't be my first performance, Lady Swift.'

Reverend Gaskell skipped over, his red waistcoat flashing as his jacket lifted. 'A true veteran of the amateur boards, Mr Cartwright.'

'Most folks call me Thomas.'

The vicar waved to the far side of the stage. 'I say, Elizabeth, my dear. Did you hear Mr Cartwright's rendition?'

Shackley stepped forward in the wings. 'Come along, we need to crack on with the next scene after tea and buns.'

Elizabeth's cheeks coloured. 'Well, it's only Nelson cake but the fruit peel gives a good zing. Morace thought it would keep us all fresh as daisies while we rehearse.'

Eleanor took a large mouthful and swallowed. 'This is quite simply the best I've tasted.'

'A drop of brandy would liven it up a notch,' Cartwright said as he took his position for the next scene.

Penry sniffed. 'As we say in the valleys, "everything we have in this world is just borrowed for a time". And that includes health in my book. A glass of the strong stuff every now and then is all well and good, but when added to cake, that's the start of ruin.'

Cartwright threw his script onto the chair next to him and set his shoulders square. 'Are you starting, Penry?'

Penry smiled innocently. 'Starting?'

Cartwright strode across the stage towards him. 'You know full well what I mean.'

Reverend Gaskell tottered in between them waving the teapot. 'As we are reminded in Ecclesiastes chapter nine, verse seven: "Go, eat your bread with joy and drink your wine with a merry heart, for God has already approved what you do." So, top up time for all, then we'll be refreshed and cheered from within.'

The two men glowered at each other before both turning back to their scripts. Eleanor sighed in relief. If they wanted to strangle each other that was fine with her, but not when she was meeting Lancelot's gang in an hour or so. She took another slice of Nelson cake. *Better fill yourself up, Ellie, those fancy restaurants always leave you hungry.*

Four hours later she would have eaten her words if she wasn't already so full. The exquisite veal pappardelle entrée had seemed innocent enough, as had the main, a mouth-watering venison ragout with juniper berry garnish. Her mistake had been having extra parmesan arborio rice and the entire first half of the cocktail menu.

As she idled at the restaurant's famous Long Bar, she was dreaming of her bed, and another one alongside for her stomach.

'And for madam?' a thick Italian accent asked.

'Um, a huge glass of water, please, but served in a fancy flute and shove some fruit or mint in so it looks alcoholic, will you?' She checked that none of Lancelot's gang were within earshot.

The waiter smirked. 'Senor Giordano, our esteemed chef, has done his job this evening? Your senses are sated, I think.'

Eleanor leaned on the bar. 'That's one way to put it, I suppose.' She jumped as someone tapped her back.

She turned to see Johnny's seductive smile. 'Life never tastes any better than at the Criterion, I say,' he said.

Coco appeared at his side. 'I can't wait for dessert. I'm going for a triple helping of that, that... Johnny, what's that amazing chocolate dessert called again?'

'Torta Barozzi,' he replied with a flourish.

The waiter returned with Eleanor's drink. 'Sir is to be congratulated on his flawless accent.'

Coco waved at Eleanor. 'Love the look of your drink, might have to try one of those. Back in a tick, off to the powder room.'

Alone with Johnny, Eleanor was itching to ask what he knew about Albie's death but he spoke first.

'So, how is he?'

'Who?'

'Why Lancelot, silly. You must have seen him in the last few days, surely.'

She shook her head and took a large gulp of her drink, wondering where the conversation was going.

He shrugged and leaned on the bar, his shoulder nudging hers. 'Bit disloyal. Poor old chap, there he is languishing in the cells and his maiden in shining armour hasn't taken the time to canter in to pep him up.'

Eleanor turned sideways, leaning on one arm as she swirled the ice, orange slices and assorted greenery round in her glass. 'Maiden in shining armour? Why, Mr Seaton, that's a bit over-romantic, wouldn't you say? Something I would have expected poor Albie to have come out with.'

'Ah, yes poor, dear departed Albie. It seemed none of his muses could help him that last, fateful evening. I rather fancy he should have been wearing the tragic mask he so often trawled out for a masked ball.'

She frowned. 'I remember him coming as a Raphael painting at the Langham Ball.'

'Honestly for a young chap in the prime of his life, he was hideously intense.'

'How short the prime of life can be.' She stared in the mirrored tiles behind the bar to gauge Johnny's reaction to this.

However, if Johnny had a troubled conscience he hid it well. 'Waiter!' he waved at the bartender. 'Two corpse revivers, here.'

She scoured the cocktail menu. 'What on earth is that? I can't see it on the list.'

He pushed the folded card down onto the bar. 'A suitable tipple to toast a departed friend. Said to be strong enough to bring back the dead. You'll join me? In Lancelot's place, of course.'

She nodded slowly. 'Of course.'

The waiter coughed. 'Would sir like Number One or Number Two revivers?'

'Oh, twos, definitely.' Johnny mirrored Eleanor's stance, leaning on the bar. 'Fitting spot, what? The Long Bar, here at the Criterion.'

'Fitting for what?'

'For an expert sleuth like you, obviously.' At her blank look he grinned. 'Oh, come on! You mean to tell me you don't know that this is the very bar where Sherlock Holmes' friend arranged for him to room with Doctor Watson?' He leaned in close, his aftershave teasing her nostrils, '"Sherlock" is Lancelot's pet name for you too, isn't it?'

She held her reviver cocktail up to the light. 'Do you know, Mr Seaton, I believe the juniper garnish or the aged parmesan have clouded your mental faculties somewhat.' She whispered into his ear. 'Sherlock is a fictional character, a figment of an overactive imagination, as perhaps is the sleuthing persona you mistake me for. I say we leave all of this to the police and seriously start partying. I did want to ask you one thing, though.'

Johnny took a sip of his drink. 'And that would be?'

'Last night, at the church. Where did Lucas learn to climb like that?'

Johnny laughed. 'He is rather like a human fly, isn't he? Apparently he told me he learned to climb as a child. His father's palace has these enormous stone walls and his servant, cum bodyguard, came from some area of India where they are known for their climbing prowess, so he taught young Lucas how to scale the palace walls. And to defend himself.'

'Really?'

'Oh, yes.' Johnny waltzed off towards the booths holding his drink aloft. 'You wouldn't want to get in an argument with him.'

*

'Oh, Clifford, how do they do it? I mean I've partied from Cairo to Cape Town but this lot party as if they have a death wish.'

'Perhaps it is a matter of a stronger constitution, my lady?'

'Great! Where can I buy one of those?' From her favourite chaise longue, she warily eyed the sausage sandwich languishing beside her.

'I shall enquire of Harrods, my lady. I believe one can purchase anything there.'

'Oh, I wish you could. My head is thumping, my knees are throbbing and my stomach still thinks it is doing the Turkey Trot or the Monkey Hug or whatever the heck they were called.'

'I suspect it is the Monkey Glide and the Buzzard Lope, my lady. The Turkey Trot I'm told is a little passé nowadays. Perhaps I should fix you a restorative?'

'Oh no, not that Mongolian concoction my uncle used to swig that you fed me once before?'

'The same. However, I do recall it worked its magic and brought you back from somewhere you described as akin to Hades?'

'Hmm, maybe, but does it have to taste so revolting? It's not supposed to be a penance.'

Clifford moved towards the drinks cabinet. 'Actually, my lady, I believe it is. Incidentally, how was the party? Other than generously supplied with liquid refreshments, that is.'

'Wild. Long. Loud. Which is precisely why I intend to slouch back up to bed in exactly'– she glanced at the clock – 'five minutes.' She thought for a moment. 'Actually, that Beau Brennant chap was very charming, and he has a great many friends who reminded me of Albie. You know, arty types.'

Clifford was pouring various ingredients into a long glass. 'Despite his young years, Lord Brennant has cultivated something of a reputation as a patron of the arts. The society papers often feature new musicians, painters or indeed poets he has championed.'

'That would explain it. It was like he knew Albie well even though he said he'd only met him twice. It's really odd, Clifford. Albie's death appears to be as a direct result of the gang's non-stop partying and yet it hasn't held them back at all. It almost feels like they're stepping up the pace in response. It was the same with Lancelot's incarceration. I really can't work it out.'

Clifford removed the sandwich and replaced it with the long glass. 'Grief affects people differently, as you are... acutely aware, my lady. And yet one can't help but wonder about their ethos of *carpe diem*, seize the day, as the Roman poet Quintus Horace Flaccus called it. It seems, as you say, that these bright young things have taken young Lord Fenwick-Langham's incarceration and Mister Appleby's demise as a signal to rebel even harder. And, it would seem, seize even more of the day.'

'And most of the night!' She leaned up on one arm and eyed the contents of the glass suspiciously. 'So again, I owe the inspector an apology.'

Clifford looked at her quizzically.

'He reckoned that by the end of the year they would all either be dead or locked up, with no help from anyone else and I'm rapidly coming to the same conclusion.' She sighed. 'Perfect! What a great time for me to have become an honorary member.'

'My lady, at the risk of repeating myself...'

She glared at him. 'Isn't there another way for me to poke about and see what I can glean? That's what you were going to say, wasn't it? And, yes, you would be repeating yourself rather ad nauseam. And the answer's no, neither of us have come up with an effective alternative.'

'Very good, my lady, then I shall report on the phone call you received earlier.'

She sat up. 'Oh, was it the inspector?'

'Regrettably not. You have received another invitation from Lady Childs.'

'Coco? How come she's already up planning more outrageous outings and I'm still in pyjamas! Okay, what ridiculous thing have they asked me to this time?'

'Lady Childs didn't specify, but she did include a piece of advice in her message; bring an extra strong bottle of stamina.'

Eleanor downed the glass in one go. 'Oh help! Clifford, why didn't you kill me yesterday!'

CHAPTER 24

'Come on, my Friday night sprites, so bright, with a thirsty appetite,' Lucas sang tunelessly as he eased his car to a halt.

'How trite!' Coco giggled.

Eleanor joined in. 'Why thank you, kind knight.'

'Watch the snake doesn't bite,' Millie finished as she slammed the door shut and stomped up the steps to the gold-fronted nightclub.

Coco slipped her arm through Eleanor's and whispered, 'Take no notice. She'd never admit it, but all this business with Lancelot has got to her terribly.'

Eleanor peered at Coco. 'Has she tried to visit him?'

'Good heavens, no! And see him incarcerated like a rat in a trap?' She looked down at her hands. 'It makes no sense. I still can't fathom why he was there. I mean, it was all off.'

Eleanor stopped. 'What was off?'

'Oh, golly!' Coco clapped her hands over her mouth. 'Dash it, I've got so used to you being with us, I forgot you didn't know.' She seemed to struggle with her conscience. 'Thing is, it's a secret. None of us mentioned it to the police because, well, it would look terrible for Lancelot.' She glanced around but the others had gone on ahead. 'Lancelot's parentals are struggling for cash, it's hideously embarrassing. So he came up with a great wheeze to steal old Lady Fenwick-Langham's precious diamond-and-ruby necklace. But then the blasted police said they would be at the ball that night, so Lancelot called it off. He's perfectly innocent, Eleanor. We know

Lancelot and he wouldn't kill the colonel. But that bit about his plan to steal the necklace, it simply can't get out.'

Eleanor turned to face Coco. 'But why would he still have gone ahead with it if he knew the police were there?'

Coco stamped her foot. 'That's exactly it, he wouldn't! He's a complete joker but he's not an idiot. Now promise you'll keep this to yourself. It's just between us, the gang?'

Eleanor nodded, one hand behind her back, fingers crossed. She changed the subject as they were ushered past the reception desk. 'Where are we?'

Coco gasped. 'You don't know of the notorious Underground Club? Where on earth have you been hiding? Honestly, you are a peculiar fish.' She paused and looked Eleanor's face over. 'I can see why Lancelot finds you intriguing.'

'Intriguing?' Eleanor laughed. 'I'm not sure that's the most complimentary description a chap can give a girl.'

Coco sighed. 'It is when Lancelot says it the way he did. Oh look, there's Millie, propping up the bar already. And wow, I don't believe it, Johnny's arrived before us. That has never happened, ever! Beaten by Pant Seat Seaton, impossible!'

'Evening, oh sirens of silk, how are we all?' Johnny rose as they arrived at the bar.

Eleanor cocked her head and smirked. 'Pant Seat Seaton?'

Johnny made an aggrieved face and pulled out a stool for her. 'Lady Swift, this rabble malign me terribly. I wish you would speak to them. They repeatedly slander my reputation by suggesting that I am, on occasions, a little tardy.'

Millie dropped three cubes of ice into her drink from a great height. 'Tardy! You are, as our American cousin Ginny so aptly described you, "a constant, nightmarishly late arrival of unforgivable elegance".' She grinned at him and then frowned at Eleanor. 'It was Ginny who dubbed him "Pant Seat Seaton". He flies by the seat of his pants, which is what American's call trousers, in case you didn't realise.'

'Eleanor must have been to the States, surely?' Johnny gave her a questioning look.

Millie sniggered. 'What, on her bicycle? With water wings across the Atlantic?' The two sisters huddled together whispering and then broke apart as they roared with laughter.

'Come on, Sisters Grim, share the joke,' Lucas said.

Coco smiled at Eleanor. 'Sorry, we weren't being mean about you, well I wasn't. It was just the image of you cycling across the Atlantic on a specially made bicycle with a paddle wheel.' She broke off as her giggles bubbled up again. 'In a bathing suit and frilly swimming hat. And… and then arriving on shore in New York and calmly declaring yourself to be Lady Swift of Little Buckford. And no, I don't have a ticket from the steamer, you oaf!'

The other four collapsed with laughter at this, Johnny slapping Lucas' back as he choked on his cigarette smoke.

Eleanor joined in the laughter. 'Hilarious. Do you know that sounds a fine adventure? I'll add it to my list.'

Johnny held a drink out to Eleanor. 'You really have travelled, haven't you? We were beginning to think Lancelot was making up stories. Your exploits were getting more and more fantastical. He told us you'd cycled around the world on a bicycle.'

'And that you'd worked for Thomas Walker scouting out new routes for rich tourists.'

'In India, Persia and South Africa.'

'Well, how much of it is true?'

She stared at the four expectant faces in front of her.

'Well, it's all true.' She grinned. 'Except the lies.'

Millie sniffed. 'Well, one only needs to buy a steamer ticket to be able to claim they have travelled.'

'Quite so,' Eleanor agreed.

'What rot!' Lucas cried. 'I don't believe you took a mouldy old steamer to the so-called land of milk and honey. Tell us the truth.'

Eleanor winked at Millie. 'Actually, I sailed there from Peru with my parents. Well, they did the sailing, I was too young. That was before they… disappeared and I was sent to boarding school. I started my cycling adventures after that.'

'What were your parents doing in Peru?' Coco asked.

'They were consultants to the Union trying to restore the country after its years of troubles. My father implemented educational and social reforms on the ground as it were.'

'So, they built schools then?' Coco asked as she sipped her drink through a straw.

Eleanor nodded. 'Amongst other things.'

Millie picked an ice cube from her drink and crunched it loudly. Eleanor held her glass up. 'Anyway, cheers! It's fantastic to be seeing so much of you all.'

Lucas grinned. 'You too.'

Coco and Millie intertwined their arms, glass in hand and giggled as they sipped each other's drinks.

Johnny pulled out his cigarette case. 'So, my Prince, are you up for it tonight?'

Lucas took a large gulp of his drink. 'Bring it on!'

'Good man!' Johnny pinched both of Lucas' cheeks in mock affection. 'You're in England, not India after all. Make the most of it.'

Johnny's coat-tails flew behind him as he spun impressively on his heels. Eleanor noticed the admiring female glances. He banged the bar with his glass as he finished with a flourish. 'Gang, I call this evening to order.'

'Oh rather!' Coco said. 'What's on our busy agenda tonight?'

Millie's eyes sparkled. 'Come on, Seaton, I'm feeling particularly wicked. I bet you can't come up with anything new and exciting.'

'Oh, I do love a challenge. Watch and learn, dear friends. You ain't seen anything of the Seaton genius so far. You can bow down to my magnificence when we breakfast on the beach after tonight's quest.'

'Which beach? Brighton? Le Touquet? Blouberg?' Eleanor asked.

Johnny emptied his glass. 'Love the attitude, Eleanor. I bet you're a better map reader than Coco too. But that's for later, way later. I have another wheeze up my sleeve first.'

The range was roaring as the staff at Henley Hall bustled round the room, each intent on their duties. Only Gladstone let the industrious team down, snuggled as he was in his quilted blanket box with a selection of stolen slippers.

'You know that really is a beautiful ballet, ladies.' Eleanor smiled blearily over the rim of her teacup.

'Ballet, my lady? Us not banging into each other is about as much dancing as Mrs Trotman should be allowed to do. She only tried proper dancing the once at the vicar's evening garden party a few years back and broke her ankle!'

The cook glared at Mrs Butters for a moment and rubbed her foot.

'Golly, Mrs Trotman, whichever dance were you doing? Must have been an awfully vigorous one.' Eleanor said.

'It was the quickstep, my lady. The vicar asked all the ladies to do a turn once round the lawn for the festivities, you understand. Well, you think he'd know the vicarage garden better than to lead me straight onto the sloping grass. I slipped and twisted my ankle. I remember feeling it go.'

Eleanor grimaced. 'You poor thing! I assume Doctor Browning was on hand?' Mrs Butters' tittering confused Eleanor. 'What am I missing?'

The housekeeper stepped across to the table and topped up Eleanor's tea. 'Between us ladies only, the good doctor was a tad worse for wear, having heavily sampled the parsnip wine. Trotters, bless her, was even more undignified in the morning. It's a wonder she didn't turn the air as blue as her ankle.'

'Whatever was the problem in the morning?'

The cook and the housekeeper shared a look. Mrs Trotman nodded for Mrs Butters to continue with the story.

'He'd only bound her ankle up so tight as to make it bloat like a puffball mushroom overnight. Polly, what was it you said when you saw it?'

The maid shook her head.

'Come on, my girl, it's alright to speak up when the mistress is taking tea in the kitchen, so long as you mind your manners.'

Polly blurted out, 'I said Mrs Trotman must have swapped one leg with an elephant, looked like someone had stuck it on for a laugh, like.'

Eleanor grinned around the table and then winced. 'I have to confess my feet are agony after all that dancing the last few days.'

Mrs Butters shook her head. 'What we need is an Epsom bath for your feet, my lady. Polly, when the two big kettles have boiled, take them to her ladyship's room, my girl.'

She patted Eleanor's arm. 'Mind you, salts won't work their magic if you don't keep off punishing your feet for a while.'

Eleanor groaned. 'Trust me, I'm done with dancing, treasure hunts, partying and absolutely everything else I've been caught up in these last few days. This investigating a murder business is much tougher on the body than I realised.'

Mrs Butters tutted gently. 'Well, your late uncle will be sorry to be missing you and your gang's rebellious shenanigans, I'm sure.'

Eleanor laughed, then lapsed into a quiet reverie. 'I wish you had met my parents, Mrs Butters. You can't be a rebel if there aren't any rules. I'm afraid to many looking on, I must have appeared as if I was raised like a wild child of the woods. I believe the polite term now is "bohemian" although I remember the whispered gypsy remarks my parents forever shrugged off as we moved around with their work.'

The housekeeper collected Eleanor's tea things and laid them out on a tray. 'If it isn't impolite to say so, my lady, from where we're all standing it seems they raised you better than could ever be said. They obviously nurtured your kind heart and let you blossom into the good-hearted and resourceful lady you are today. Can't ask for more than that, I say.'

Before Eleanor could clear the lump in her throat, Clifford stepped into the kitchen. 'My lady, will you still be requiring the car at ten o'clock this evening?'

Eleanor rapped the table with her teacup, spilling most of it and making Gladstone wake up with a jerk. 'Absolutely not, Clifford, thank you. We need to find another way to get information. This undercover stuff with Lancelot's cronies is killing me. And, more importantly, as we discussed before, it's taking too long. We… he… hasn't got that much time.'

In the silence that followed, Mrs Butters exchanged a look with Mrs Trotters. 'Begging your pardon, my lady, your footbath is probably ready if Polly hasn't made a mess of it.'

Eleanor nodded. 'Only a short crawl up to my bedroom then, that sounds wonderful. Clifford, later will you help me sort out any clues I might have amassed among all these blisters and cuts? Those rocks were ridiculously sharp last night when we were swimming.' She groaned at the memory. 'And why is the Atlantic so blessedly cold!'

Clifford raised a finger. 'That is due to it being precisely one third less wide at the equator than the Pacific, my lady. The Atlantic current also often mixes with the significantly colder—'

At that moment, Polly burst through the door, as white as a ghost. 'Th-th-there's a… thing… in the bath!' And with that she fainted into Clifford's quick-thinking arms.

Eleanor looked round the bemused faces. 'Ah! Yes, of course, poor Polly. My bish there. Clifford, I wonder if you wouldn't mind returning the "thing" somehow. It's probably missing its friends. It's from Oxford Zoo.'

'Would it be rude to enquire what exactly *the thing* is, my lady?'

'Not at all, Clifford. It's a penguin, of course.'

CHAPTER 25

'Agh!' Eleanor sprung forward. 'What the—? Get off!' The bed sheet wrapped itself around her flailing arms as she thrashed about looking like an unravelled Egyptian mummy.

'Polly? Wha—? Is that you?'

'Oh, your ladyship. I am so sorry.' The maid sucked on the edge of her apron, the cup of tea in her hand wobbling on its saucer.

Eleanor flopped back on her pillow. 'I… I was having such a nightmare. Someone was looming over me, not saying anything, just… watching.' She peered at her maid. 'Polly, have you been in here long?'

The girl nodded. 'Ages and ages, your ladyship. I've been trying to wake you for yonks, only I didn't want to disturb you.'

'I see.' Eleanor rubbed her eyes and tried to get her brain to engage. She was never at her best in the morning.

Polly stopped sniffing and looked up hopefully. 'You're not cross with me waking you, your ladyship?'

Eleanor tried hard not to sound grouchy. 'Cross? No, not a bit!'

Her grump had failed to disperse despite the brilliant sunshine already pouring in through the window. She needed coffee, not tea. And quickly. 'Perhaps you would be good enough to pass my bedjacket? Pop the cup on the cabinet first, that's it. And then the little green silk thing, just there.'

Polly carried Eleanor's bedjacket to her as though it were a newborn kitten. Standing by the side of the bed she bit her lip and stared at the floor as a tear slid down her cheek.

Eleanor softened her voice and held out a handkerchief. 'Polly, whatever is the matter?'

''Tis nothing, your ladyship. I am so sorry.' She grabbed the handkerchief and loudly blew her nose making Eleanor wince. 'Oh, golly, Mrs Butters will have words with me again.' At this she sank into loud sobs.

Eleanor shoved her arms into her bedjacket and swung her legs out of bed.

'One minute.' She crossed to her dressing table and pulled over the chair, which she placed next to Polly. 'Sit.'

Polly's lip trembled. 'Sitting in front of the mistress is against the rules.'

Eleanor gently pressed down on the girl's shoulder and whispered, 'Sit, and I promise we won't tell your mistress.' She looked into the young girl's eyes. 'Polly, what are you worried about?'

At this, the maid let out a wail. 'You'll… you'll ask me to leave your service.'

Eleanor put her arm around the girl's shoulder. 'Dear Polly, I have no intention of asking you to leave. Why would you imagine such a thing?'

'Because I'm a terrible maid, and everyone knows it. Mrs Butters doesn't scold me harshly, nor Mrs Trotman, nor Mr Clifford, he just gives me that look that makes me want the floor to eat me up. But they're all disappointed with me, I know it.'

Eleanor tilted her head. 'How long have you been at the Hall, Polly?'

The girl thought for a moment. 'Well, your ladyship, my mum and dad couldn't afford to keep us all, not after my dad had the accident. So me and my sisters were sent into service.' She furrowed her brow even harder. 'My mum wanted us sisters to stay together but it was after the war and no one could find a big house that was looking for three maids. My mum managed to find places for my sisters but I was eleven and, no one wanted me. Then a friend of my dad who knew Mr Clifford said he'd see if he could help and… so I came here. This will be my fourth Christmas, your ladyship, when it comes round.'

'So you're fifteen now?'

'Yes, my lady.'

Eleanor thought for a moment. 'So, coming to the Hall must have been your first appointment as a maid, I guess?' At Polly's nod, she continued, 'Well… coming to the Hall is my first appointment at being a lady.'

The maid's jaw hung open. She looked over her shoulder and then whispered, 'You mean… you're being a lady for the… first time?'

Eleanor nodded, trying not to grin.

Her maid took an absent-minded swig of the tea, which Eleanor smiled at.

'Polly, I fear we both find ourselves in a new situation without knowing exactly how it is supposed to work. And the staff are too busy trying to make sure the house keeps running as smooth as clockwork. We wouldn't want a wheel to fall off, would we now?'

Polly giggled at this. 'Can you imagine a house on wheels? How amazing! Wow, I could light the stove and keep it lit and Mr Clifford could steer. The ladies could do the… the other bits, whatever they are. And you could stand on the balcony with a big colourful map and we could all go and see wonderful places, together,' she ended on a whisper.

Polly's child-like wonder choked Eleanor. She swallowed hard. 'Please, can you do two things for me? Actually, three things. But don't worry, they are easy to remember.'

'Anything, your ladyship. Anything at all.'

'Firstly, you need to stop being anxious that I shall ask you to leave. And you must remember if Mr Clifford or the ladies seem impatient with you, it's simply that they are trying to show you how to do better. Okay?'

'I'll think of them being caught up in keeping the wheels from falling off the house.'

'Perfect. Number two, do your best to keep your lips buttoned and say nothing about this conversation to the others at the moment. I want to think more about how we can help each other.'

Polly rolled her eyes to the back of her head. 'No worrying and no saying about... wheels and buttons.' She mimed closing a button on her lips.

'Brilliant, well done.' Eleanor patted the maid's shoulders. 'And thirdly, please can you bring me a cup of coffee? Strong? Now?'

Clifford looked up from the battered copy of *The Bat*. 'I rather fear, my lady, that the third act is perhaps the most significant part of your performance.'

Eleanor flopped back onto the sofa and then shuffled sideways as Gladstone pushed his front feet into her ribs. 'Well, that's no help at all. That's the part I'm struggling to remember most! I've got way too many lines.'

Clifford took off his pince-nez spectacles and placed them carefully on the chair beside him. 'In the words of the eminent Victor Hugo, my lady, "Intelligence is the wife, imagination is the mistress, memory is the servant."'

'Then I fear I have paid too much attention to my mistress of late and neglected my servant. He is clearly on strike. Honestly, I'm all done. Cornelia Van Gorder and Detective Anderson can go hang for a while. Although I must say it is a masterful twist that the good guy turns out to be the notorious villain. But in truth, Clifford, any time we're not trying to save Lancelot feels like a terrible waste.' She ran her hand along the bulldog's round tummy, taking comfort from the warm softness.

'That may be, my lady, but you need a distraction.'

'I suppose you're right.'

They discussed the case throughout the morning, Eleanor devouring Mrs Trotman's delicious cheese and chive twists for elevenses and moving onto lunch at one. Gladstone trotting after them as they moved to the dining room.

'More rosemary potatoes please… and leave the gravy jug to hand. There's an art to filling a Yorkshire pudding to just the right level, I find.' Eleanor's tongue crept out as she concentrated while pouring.

Clifford arranged the roast parsnips in their salver by her plate. 'Perhaps, my lady, we have found the perfect distraction for you after all?'

Eleanor was concentrating too hard to notice the dig. 'Yes, it's a delicate operation. Too little gravy in the Yorkshire and there's hardly enough to cover your first roast potato as you dunk. Too much and your plate is awash with a tidal wave.'

Clifford bowed. 'I had no idea it was such a precise science. My knowledge has been quite incomplete all these years.'

She speared a crispy parsnip. 'Scoff all you like, Clifford, but the British Empire was built on the Sunday roast. How fun it would be to serve Gladstone his dinner in a Yorkshire pudding – it would be like an edible dog bowl.' She subtly passed the dog a corner.

'Going back to the investigation, my lady, there is another peculiarity we have yet to resolve. Why did young Lord Fenwick-Langham apparently try to steal the jewels even though it seems he knew the police were there that night?'

'Exactly, Clifford. Coco mentioned that very thing recently. Apparently Lancelot told the gang what he was up to and they roundly told him to call it off. Coco was as confused as we are about why he would even consider going through with it once he knew the police were at Langham Manor.'

'Perhaps young Lord Fenwick-Langham changed his mind and believed he could outwit the police?'

Eleanor snorted over the rim of her glass. 'Clifford, Lancelot couldn't outwit a tadpole in a jam jar.'

'My thinking was running along those lines, only somewhat more respectfully. I imagine young Lord Fenwick-Langham might have seen it as a game.'

'Probably. And now we have a whole bunch of people who know he intended to steal the jewels. The only good point is their loyalty to Lancelot in keeping silent so far.'

'Although, my lady, isn't it rather odd that the police did not find the jewels about his young lordship's person at the time of arrest?'

'Tell that to Inspector Seldon! He seems to think Lancelot had an accomplice, possibly me, who somehow ferreted them out of the room and into his plane.' Eleanor sighed. 'Let's move on to Albie, shall we, before we both decide Lancelot *is* guilty! Millie said something about Albie.' She frowned. 'Drat it, not being able to write things down at the time is dashed awkward.'

'Perhaps, your ladyship might like to try penning a few notes on your return to the Hall?'

'Yes, you did suggest that before. Trouble is, I've never got back in a fit state to do anything except collapse into bed and wake up with my head throbbing. Let me think.' Eleanor banged her forehead with her fist, making Gladstone look up from where he was sprawled by her feet. 'It's in there somewhere... oh yes, that was it! It seems peculiar that everyone is just accepting Albie was drunk the night he died and that caused the accident. From what

I saw he drank less than the rest of them, even though one of them did say Albie had never got the hang of pacing himself.'

Clifford nodded. 'The cause of the accident was indeed attributed to an excess of alcohol. Though apparently the local police came to that verdict without a proper examination of the body, according to Miss Abigail.'

'And the newspaper report reckoned it occurred at around one in the morning, didn't it?'

'Indeed, my lady. Perhaps with what you've learned, we should reconstruct what happened that fateful night.'

'Good idea, Clifford.' She marshalled her thoughts. 'Johnny told me that he'd spent the day at his family pile. He then picked up Coco around nine, I think, and then met Lucas and Millie at some new club in Cowley, The Hole in the Wall, at ten. Millie said Albie was supposed to be coming along later in a car he'd borrowed, which he did sometimes, usually because he needed to get back to work in the morning. They often party till dawn and beyond, as you know.'

Clifford raised his eyebrows. Gladstone dropped his head between his paws and let out a long sigh as if the very idea was too much effort to contemplate.

Eleanor rushed on. 'Anyway, Albie never turned up, so they went to some place called Madame Bella's around midnight and stayed until three. They left there and went to Johnny's pad until dawn. Johnny told me the next thing they know is that Albie's gone and got drunk and ditched himself and the car in the canal.'

Clifford returned from the serving table with a dish of buttered beans and honey glazed carrots. She nodded absent-mindedly for him to top up her plate. She added a generous dollop of horseradish sauce and then pushed the food round distractedly.

'Poor Albie, I can't think of any obvious reason anyone would want to bump him off. His poems weren't that terrible.' She gave an involuntary laugh, which was instantly halted by Clifford's reproachful look.

'How was it Mr Appleby became a permanent member of the group, my lady?'

'Well, Coco introduced him to the others. She seemed genuinely unconcerned by his background and was actually quite sweet to him. However, she said something about Lancelot and Johnny forever circling poor Albie, like jackals waiting to pounce with a scathing comment. Johnny remarked to me that he found Albie hideously intense.'

Clifford nodded as though he could imagine the spiteful ribbing.

'And his Highness, Prince Singh?'

'Lucas? He was less vicious than the others but I think that's just him, or perhaps his background again.'

'It is most likely that the gentleman is a Hindu, my lady. As such he would have been instilled with the beliefs of duty, virtue and morality from a very young age.'

'Well, he's not proving much of an embodiment of any of those when I've seen him. He's partying as hard as the others and no mistake!'

'My thoughts entirely, my lady. I fear whoever is responsible for these crimes is an actor of the most masterful skill.'

'Shame we can't collar him to play my part in the am-dram then!'

All thought out, Eleanor sighed as she devoured some more mouthfuls of her lunch. Gladstone tilted his head, his eyes imploring her to drop some of the crispy roast potatoes his way, his jowls trembling with anticipation.

'Clifford, I should really telephone Lord and Lady Langham with an update. Not that I've got anything much to report.'

'I believe they will be comforted just to hear that you are still working on helping his young Lordship… although there might be something worth asking them.'

'Go on, what have you worked out?'

'Nothing more than a hunch at this juncture. Forgive my assumption, my lady, but from your descriptions of the group, it seems that Mr Seaton and his young lordship were the most rigorous in their teasing of Mr Appleby?'

She nodded.

On the telephone, Lord Langham's voice roared through the earpiece. 'What ho, Eleanor, old girl. You want me to go to covert ops and find out from Seaton Senior if his errant son was with them when he said he was the day that poor young fellow died?'

'If you can. It might be nothing, of course. I'm going to probe the Childs sisters. Clifford has an idea for checking up on Prince Lucas.'

'No trouble. Augusta finds the Seaton tribe a tad vulgar, being new money and all, but I will be the most discreet of bloodhounds, fret not.'

Eleanor heard Lady Langham's voice in the background. After a muffled exchange, she came on the line. 'Eleanor, my dear. Harold says you suspect more foul play, this time over Mr Appleby's demise. For the first time, I am actually relieved Lancelot is being detained. If you can prove the same person was responsible, the police will have to release him!'

Promising to keep her abreast of progress, Eleanor ended the call and turned to Clifford.

'Oh golly, Clifford. I might have given Lady Langham rather too much hope!'

CHAPTER 26

Eleanor hadn't slept well and being dragged out of bed early again hadn't improved her mood.

'Dash it, Sergeant Brice, it's… whatever it is in the morning.'

'As I've already explained, Lady Swift, I've been instructed to call you.'

'Call me? By whom? And why?'

There was a pause on the other end of the line as if someone was counting to ten. 'Chief Inspector Seldon instructed me to call you. He has granted you a meeting with Lord Fenwick-Langham at ten o'clock.'

'What!'

'That's what I said. Prisoners pending trial are not permitted visitors. But the Detective Chief Inspector…'

Eleanor let out a yell. 'Thank you, Sergeant Brice! I'll be there at ten sharp.' She went to replace the receiver, but picked it up again. 'And make sure Lord Fenwick-Langham gets a decent breakfast!'

Sergeant Brice made a point of recording the time on the station clock when signing Eleanor in. She waited for him to finish, her fingers drumming on the counter.

He laid down his pen. 'Lowe. Door.'

Lowe jumped to attention, then hesitated. 'But, Sarge, his lordship hasn't had breakfast yet.'

Brice's face coloured. 'What the blasted heck have you been doing all morning?'

'It's like this, Sarge, his Lordship asked specifically for breakfast not to arrive before ten. He's not used to rising early, you see.'

'Ten? This is a police station, not a blasted hotel, right?'

The constable scampered away and returned with a tray bearing a hot cup of tea and a bowl of steaming porridge. 'This way, your ladyship.'

Brice called after them. 'Ten minutes, Lowe. Not a minute more.'

Eleanor winked at him and trotted after the constable. At the steel door leading to the cells, Lowe fumbled for the key while precariously balancing the tray.

Eleanor peeked behind her, then whispered, 'Let me take that.'

Lowe reluctantly handed it over before shoving the heavy door open with a grunt. 'The sarge is trying to stick to procedure on account of Detective Chief Inspector Seldon catching us out on a few things.' He carefully locked the door behind them.

Eleanor grinned. 'I bet he did.'

As they approached Lancelot's cell, she held a finger to her lips.

'Perhaps I should check first that the gentleman is suitably dressed for your ladyship?' Lowe whispered.

'Not a bit,' she whispered back. 'We normally chat when he's dressed in just goggles or a pirate costume. Whatever he's got on will be quite sufficient.'

Lowe's eyebrows shot up his forehead.

She banged the bars with the spoon and deepened her voice. 'Wakey wakey, Goldilocks! Your porridge is hot and ready.'

The bundle under the blanket twitched and a wool-socked foot poked out. 'Too early, Lowe. I told you…'

'Lancelot! Get up. It's me, you fool.' She rattled the spoon again. 'We've only got…' She glanced at the constable. '… fifteen minutes.'

Lancelot shot upright. 'Sherlock, I can't believe you're here! And you've brought me breakfast, now that's service, I'd say. Although Constable Lowe here is a fine waitress.'

Lowe blushed at the mixed compliment and swung the door open.

Eleanor stepped in and hovered over Lancelot. 'Are you going to sit up at the table like a good boy?' She put the tray down and held her hand out to him.

He grinned up at her. 'You've got to be the best surprise ever.'

'Oh no, not at all. Prisoners are not allowed surprises, or visitors come to that matter.'

'So you've broken all the rules, naughty girl! Anyhow, I think you'd look stunning in a policeman's outfit. Those stubborn red curls sticking out of the helmet at all angles as you arrested some wretched beast for doing something fearfully juicy.'

She slapped his arm. 'Were you never taught manners, you oaf? You're supposed to stand when a lady enters the room, not lounge about in bed. Especially in your…' She gave a low whistle as he wrestled to untangle himself from the blanket. 'Those are quite the fetching striped bed wear.'

Lancelot bounced up onto his feet and gave her a twirl. 'Now my secret is out. I really am the cat's pyjamas, aren't I?'

She caught her breath as he took her hand. 'Sherlock, it is *so* good to see you. I've… missed you.'

She cleared her throat. 'Your… your breakfast is getting cold.'

'Let it rot. Who needs food when you're here? Come, sit.' He gestured to the iron bed frame and threw the tiny pillow against the wall to make space for two.

She sat and stared at him. 'You know, you're not looking as good as last time.'

He tutted and offered her the mug of tea. She shook her head. After a big swig, he smirked. 'Now, that's where you're wrong, because I always look irresistible.' He tilted his head. 'And the blush that's just run up your neck and set your face on fire means there's no point pretending otherwise.'

She slapped his arm. 'Lancelot, we can play at teasing when you are out of here. Until then we need to work at making sure that day actually arrives.'

'Well, I never did. Fancy a lady swearing like that in front of a gentleman? Gracious, what is the world coming to!'

'What swearing?'

'My dear Lady Swift, I distinctly heard you use the "w" word.'

'What "work"?'

He clapped his hands over his ears and groaned. 'Sherlock, I thought you were more fun than that. Honestly, I let you out of my sight for a moment and you get corrupted by some frightful bunch of earnest dullards.'

She slapped his arm. 'You monkey, the only bunch I've been hanging out with are your blasted so-called gang.'

'What? You've been out with Johnny and the others? I see.' He rose and placed the mug back on the tray, fiddling with the handle.

Eleanor's confusion showed. 'But what was wrong with me going out with them? They're your best friends.'

'Oh yah, quite. Nothing's wrong, no nothing.'

She joined him at the table. 'Lancelot Benjamin Gerald Fenwick-Langham, I do believe you're jealous.'

He ruffled his already dishevelled hair. 'It's Lancelot Germaine Benedict actually, but it's good to see you've been keeping notes. Have you got a cute little scrapbook with my photo on the front?'

'Yes, and it's full of lines about what an infuriating dunderhead you are. Look, I didn't come here to bat my lashes at you.'

He stepped to the bed and flopped backwards on to it, staring at the damp patch of plaster on the ceiling. 'Shame! A dashedly, blasted, criminal bloody shame!'

'I thought I'd do that once you got out,' she whispered. 'So help me to help you! For the first time in your life, Lancelot, there's something that actually matters. Stop playing the privileged son of a lord and lady, will you? There must be something else you can tell me about the night of the murder.'

He slumped against the wall. 'You know, I've been racking my brains going over the evening of the ball, trying to work out who the jewel thief, and murderer, might be. I haven't got your, or Mr Clifford's, brain for this type of thing, but I've had a bash.' He straightened up. 'Right, to be clear I don't know enough about any suspects you and Clifford might have dug up outside of the gang, so I'll stick to them.'

'Fine by me,' she replied.

'First of all, Brice told me about Albie, so he's obviously out, poor blighter, so that leaves Lucas and Johnny in the trouser department. Of the two I wouldn't know who to choose. They both had arguments with the colonel, but then again, so did I. Lucas is quite fiery so I could see him knocking the old coot on the head in a moment of rage, but then again Johnny's certainly cool enough to be a jewel thief.'

He looked at Eleanor out of the corner of his eye. 'Moving on to the skirts, I'm not being all Victorian, but I can't see Coco having the strength to bash the colonel on the bonce hard enough to kill him. I assume you've seen her when you've been shifting some stolen goody or other on a treasure hunt, her arms are designed to lift cocktails, and that's about it. Millie's the same, but when she's riled, well, that's another matter. But really, I can't see either of them being the jewel thief, though they'd both look jolly good in one of those catsuits.'

Eleanor slapped his arm.

'Ow!'

Constable Lowe peeped round.

Lancelot grimaced and whispered to Eleanor, 'Totally forgot about him.'

Constable Lowe called through the bars. 'Lady Swift, apologies but I believe the sarge said I wasn't to allow you any extra minutes?'

'No need to apologise. I shall be sure to come to the door in exactly…' She tugged out her uncle's fob watch. '…six minutes.' She threw him a winning smile.

The young constable rubbed the back of his neck. 'Another six minutes? Are you sure?'

'Quite sure.' Eleanor and Lancelot chorused.

'Very good.' Constable Lowe retired back to his post.

Eleanor grabbed Lancelot's arm and steered him to the back of the cell. 'Listen, I need a breakthrough or I'll… I'll fail you.'

For the first time, she saw a flash of fear in his eyes. 'Darling fruit, you could never fail me. You've already done more than any chap could ask. I never intended for you to get caught up in this. I should have guessed that you wouldn't be able to keep your fabulous sleuthing trunk out of it though.'

His words were drowned out by a thunderous banging on the steel door out in the corridor.

'Lowe! Lowe, you idiot! Let me in.' Sergeant Brice bellowed through the peep hatch. 'Get Lady Swift out! Chief Inspector Seldon will have our guts! What have you done with the key, man?'

'I had it a moment ago, Sarge.'

A second later, Eleanor jumped at Brice's hand on her shoulder. 'Lady Swift. If you say another word, I will be forced to arrest you for—'

Lancelot stepped forward, his face contorted in rage, but she pushed him back.

'Coming, Sergeant.' She grinned. 'That was fun, thanks so much for having me.'

The cell door slammed behind her. She spun round, grabbing the bars and blew Lancelot a kiss. 'Au revoir, Goggles.'

Lancelot grasped the bars and whispered, 'But not adieu, Sherlock.'

*

Clifford was waiting for her by the Rolls. He held the door open and then walked round to the driver's seat.

'I took the liberty of topping up the brandy in the glovebox, my lady.'

She wrenched the flap open and took a long glug. Her voice was emotionless. 'Home, Clifford.'

Mrs Butters ran out to meet them as Clifford swung the car up to the front steps.

'Sorry to run straight out to you, my lady, but she said it was important you got the message the minute you were home.'

Eleanor glanced at the paper in the housekeeper's hand disinterestedly. 'I've had enough of messages today, Mrs Butters. It can wait until tomorrow.'

The housekeeper peered back at the house. 'Yes, my lady, but the lady's still on the telephone. She's hanging on because I heard the car.'

'Well, I'm really not in the mood.'

'The lady was most insistent. Sounded really agitated, she did. Frightened even. Said it had something to do with young Lord Fenwick-Langham.'

Eleanor's eye twitched.

Clifford took the paper the housekeeper held out and scanned it quickly. 'I think, my lady, you should take the call.' He handed her the paper.

Eleanor read the message and groaned. 'Oh, what did I do in a former life that was so bad, Clifford?'

'I do not know, my lady. However, I fear it was indeed most heinous.'

CHAPTER 27

The first of the sun's rays peeping between the hills were a welcome relief after the restless night Eleanor had spent fighting with the covers and battling the dark thoughts in her mind. It was barely past five o'clock when she tiptoed down the stairs trying not to wake the house. As she reached the bottom stair, she screamed.

'Agh! What are you doing here?'

Clifford bowed, perfectly turned out in his morning suit and slicked-back hair. 'I work here, my lady. Can I get you something?'

'Very funny. I meant what on earth are you doing here at this hour, like that?'

'It is a butler's duty to always be ready and presentable should the lady or gentleman of the house require anything.'

She looked at his immaculately pressed uniform. 'Have you been there all night, Clifford?'

'Of course not, my lady.'

'I, I think I'll have a few more hours' sleep.'

'Very good.'

As she reached the landing at the top of the stairs leading to her bedroom, she glanced back over the balustrade. Clifford had vanished.

She drifted off to sleep wondering how on earth the staff knew when she had woken up. Were there secret peepholes in the bedrooms?

*

Polly's head poked round the door. 'Good morning, your ladyship.'

'Good morning, Polly.' She struggled up, smiling at the sight of Gladstone barging past her maid, his favourite leather slipper hanging from his jowls. 'Please tell Mrs Trotman I am ravenous this morning.'

Her maid nodded and then whispered, 'I've been thinking wheels and buttons and it's worked. Thank you, your ladyship.' With a skip, she was gone.

Eleanor was still smiling when Clifford entered the sunlit morning room where Gladstone had sprawled on the deep-pile rug in a particularly long shaft of warm sunshine.

'Good morning, again, my lady. Might I make an enquiry before you breakfast?'

'Fire away.'

'Mrs Trotman is unsure how to prepare the rebellious fayre you have requested via your maid?'

'What? I... ah! I told Polly I was *ravenous*, not *rebellious*. Oh bless her, Clifford, she is a treasure. And you know, I have such a good feeling about today. Amazing really, everything seemed so bleak when I first woke this morning, but one or two extra hours' sleep...'

'Four.'

'Whatever. The thing is, to start I couldn't get past the idea of Lancelot's trial being so close and us seemingly no nearer to solving the case. He looked quite dreadful yesterday.'

'Lord Fenwick-Langham will have been dining very differently since his incarceration and likely exercising very little.'

'Hmm, yes, fair point. But listen, nothing is going to mar my mood today, so let's review the clues we've found so far. Ah, thank you, always one step ahead, Clifford.' She picked up the notebook on the tray next to her tea. 'I tell you, Clifford, nobody can upset me today.'

'An excellent attitude for your meeting with Lady Millicent Childs.'

Eleanor groaned. 'Blast! I'd completely forgotten. I take it all back. Quick, find a box of bullets engraved with my name and shoot me.'

'I seem to recall you insisted Lady Childs sounded genuine last night.'

'Y-e-s, but that was last night. Although, I do admit I'm fairly sure she wasn't faking the fear in her voice.'

Clifford coughed. 'Uncomfortable though it is, I confess to still having one leg straddling the fence, my lady. Lady Childs has proven herself to be somewhat—'

'Merciless? Malicious?'

'Neither are the word I was searching for.'

'Evil?'

Gladstone let out a whimper in his sleep.

Clifford tutted. 'More like—'

'A total witch?'

He peered at her as though she were a small child requiring a carbolic mouthwash. 'Emotional, my lady.'

'Emotional? You see Millie as a crier? Cripes, I can't see how you could ever wring tears out of stone.'

'I was referring more to Lady Childs' tendency to wear her heart, however cold, on her sleeve. Unless, of course, she is merely a very accomplished actress.'

'I really don't see that we have a choice, do you?'

'Indeed. If Lady Millicent Childs is on the level, she may well lead us to a vital clue.'

'Or a bullet, fresh from the engravers.'

Eleanor's words were still with them later that evening as they arrived at the Pike and Perch, the agreed meeting point. An inn on the busy road that led to Oxford, it had seemed safe enough, normally being open until ten, an hour later than their rendezvous with Millie. The weather had started to close in during the afternoon and the air was charged with electricity. An occasional whispered rumble warned of an approaching storm. Eleanor pulled her shawl around her and peered across the empty car park. 'Clifford, why is the pub in darkness?'

'I am unsure, my lady, but I fear we should leave as all is not as we imagined.'

'No, look there's Millie.'

'My lady, I am a dedicated fan of caution, and of staying alive. I repeat my suggestion that we retreat.'

But his words were lost as Eleanor slammed the passenger door behind her. *You've no choice, Ellie, Lancelot's running out of time.* She walked towards the other woman who continually looked around like a terrified rabbit, scouring the inky shadows cast by the moon over the nearby barn cum barrel store and the sprawling pub itself.

Eleanor heard the driver's door of the Rolls click open behind her, the engine still purring.

She called across the gravel. 'Millie, where is everyone?'

'Shut up, you fool! We could be overheard,' her date hissed back in the gloom.

As the two women got closer, Eleanor stared at Millie's make-up-less face and flat shoes, unheard of for one so fashion conscious. Millie grabbed her arm and dragged her into the shadows at the edge of the parking.

'Listen, it's too dangerous to stay here long.' She opened her handbag and pulled out a cigarette. She lit it and took a long drag, eyeing Eleanor through the smoke. 'First up, this has to be between just you and me, but I'm not convinced I can trust you.'

Eleanor stared at Millie, the ghost of her past hovering in the air. They were the exact words her husband had used before he had disappeared on a 'secret mission' for the army. Except, of course, there had been no secret mission, just a secret liaison with another woman. The irony was, it was the other woman who had turned him over to the authorities for selling arms to the enemy. Eleanor had never had the chance to thank her. She eyed Millie coolly.

'Thanks for your vote of confidence.'

Millie looked at her with pure hate. 'For the life of me I cannot fathom what Lancelot sees in you!'

Eleanor had had enough. 'You know, you may not have anything better to do tonight, but I certainly do. I only came here because I hoped you had some information that might help Lancelot, but, silly me, you just wanted to fight.' She turned to leave.

'Wait!'

Eleanor turned back. 'Why should I?'

Millie eyes betrayed her struggle. 'Because… look, you're the only one who seems to be… trying to help Lancelot. The others are a total waste of space. They're just carrying on partying, saying it's what he'd want us to do. He'll hang and then they'll weep that he's gone. It's pathetic!'

Eleanor's stomach lurched at the word 'hang'. She fought down a wave of panic and counted silently to three. 'Millie, have you found out something about the night the colonel was killed that could help Lancelot or not?'

Millie shook her head. 'No. I called you… about Albie, the stupid fool.'

Eleanor blinked. 'Albie?'

Millie hesitated. 'I believe… Albie was murdered.' She stubbed out her cigarette on one of the empty barrels piled around and instantly took out another and lit it. Eleanor waited, her mind racing. Millie took a drag and continued. 'I overheard Albie on the phone trying to blackmail someone.'

Her words rattled Eleanor. 'Are we talking about the same man? Albie? Artistic, melancholy, poetic Albie?'

'Money-grabbing, desperately social climbing, get-me-out-of-the-hellish-life-I-was-born-into Albie, yes. He was so out of his league, so out of his depth financially. I can't imagine what Coco was thinking when she invited him to join us that first night.'

'But he kept up though, didn't he?'

'After a fashion. He was disgustingly tight when it came to buying his rounds. Lucas often got Albie's in for him, he's far too soft. It didn't do Albie any favours.'

Eleanor reeled at Millie's lack of compassion. 'Maybe he was just trying to make a better life for himself, what's wrong with that?'

'I'm all for ambition, but he tried to do it purely on the back of knowing us. He imagined we would be his meal ticket, offer him connections.'

'So you weren't his number one fan, I get that. Why do you care if he was murdered then?'

'Because, stupid, his death is linked to the colonel's.'

Eleanor's stomach churned again. *Did Millie really have a clue that linked Albie's death to the colonel's and... don't dare hope, Ellie... and proved Lancelot innocent?*

Millie looked around and then leaned forward. 'The night Albie died Lucas and I were round at his disgusting apartment.' She brushed her hands as if mentally washing them. 'It's such a dive. Anyway, we decided to leave and go to Johnny's instead, where you can breathe and move about without fearing you might catch something. So we trooped out to the car.'

Eleanor tried to keep up. 'Who is "we"?'

'Lucas and me. Anyway, that's when I overheard Albie. He was on the telephone on the landing. His landlady let him use it in exchange for teaching her nephew once a week.' She shuddered.

Eleanor frowned. 'I thought you said you'd gone out to the car.'

'Listen, will you? Lucas and I did. Albie said he'd follow us in some car he'd borrowed. He whined about having to be back early as he had some hideous work to do at stupid o'clock the next morning.'

'What sort of work?'

'More tutoring I suppose.'

Eleanor considered. 'So if you and Lucas were in the car, how did you overhear Albie on the landing telephone?'

Millie waved her cigarette. 'I left my ciggies on his stupid table and Lucas smokes some horrid brand so I went back up to get them. That's when I overheard him trying to talk like he was a big shot gangster. He was threatening someone.'

'Who?'

'How should I know? Look, I don't want to hang around here any longer than I have to.' She glanced around again. 'I overheard him say, "You think you're so clever but I saw you. So now I want a cut or I'll go to the police."'

Eleanor's eyes widened. 'What happened then?'

Millie laughed hollowly. 'What do you imagine happened? I got out before he saw me!'

Eleanor tried to digest Millie's revelations. 'So how does that fit in with the colonel's death and the jewel robbery?'

Millie sighed exasperatedly. 'Because, you chump, I imagine the "cut" he was talking about was from the sale of Lady Langham's stolen jewels. Why did I think you could help? I took a chance on coming to you, what a dumb idea!' She turned and ran into the darkness.

Before Eleanor could react, an engine roared into life. She spun round as a car screeched out of the barn heading directly for her. Blinded by the headlights, she couldn't see who was driving. If she turned and ran, she would never make it back to the Rolls. Instead she stood her ground. When the car was only a foot or so from her, she jumped to one side. The driver had no time to swerve and the car ploughed into the pile of barrels where she and Millie had been standing moments before and stopped.

The driver's door swung open as Eleanor ran towards the car. Then a single shot rang out, followed by the sound of shattering glass. The car spun away, the driver's door slamming shut as it swerved onto the road and was swallowed up by the night.

Eleanor started after the car and then stopped as Clifford walked up to her, carrying a shotgun. 'What the devil did you think you were doing?'

Clifford stopped, his expression inscrutable. 'I saw the driver attempting to get out of the car, my lady, and fearing he might be armed, shot out the window of the passenger door to discourage the gentleman from leaving the car.'

Eleanor shook her head. 'Really, Clifford, I could have easily reached the car and dealt with the driver before he could get out. Now, we don't even know who was driving the car.' She sighed, letting out her frustration. 'I'm sorry, Clifford, that was probably rather rash of me in hindsight. Thank you for your quick thinking.' She looked around. 'And Millie?'

'Gone, my lady. It seems she was prepared to run, hence the flat shoes.'

Eleanor shook her head. 'And you know what, Clifford? Without her ridiculously high heels, I was taller than her!'

The storm had broken and rain lashed the windows and bounced off the roof of the Rolls. Inside Eleanor leaned back in her seat as they splashed through the fast flooding, deserted lanes back to the Hall.

'How much brandy is there in the glovebox, Clifford?'

'Sufficient, my lady.'

They rode on, Eleanor sipping her brandy and Clifford fussing over her possible injuries.

She peered at her arm and ran her hand over it to double-check. 'It's just a scratch. I must have scraped it on one of those barrels without noticing. Probably the adrenaline and all that.'

He held out a clean handkerchief. 'True, my lady. However, a scratch deep enough to bleed is in fact called a cut. That will require a proper dressing on our return.'

'Nonsense. Anyway, if it does, Mrs Butters can sew me up when we get home. Her blanket stitch is most commendable.'

He waved the handkerchief until she took it out of his hand and wrapped it around her forearm.

'One must also be alert for the signs of delayed shock.'

'Clifford...' Her tone carried a warning.

'Internal bruising can be very hard to spot.'

'Enough!'

'Very good, my lady.'

She stared blankly out of the misted window seeing nothing of the shadowy hedgerows whizzing past. Her hand crossed to the handkerchief bandage. 'It was dashedly lonely at times though, you know, Clifford. All that intrepid adventure stuff is great in doses but in between, it is awfully nice to be...' She tailed off.

'The staff are delighted to have you at home, my lady.'

She felt her eyes well up. It must be the adrenalin, she told herself again. 'Thank you. And thank you for the handkerchief... and, well, your concern for my wellbeing with this cut... and, as I said before, for shooting out the driver's window. Caution probably would indeed have been the better part of valour on this occasion. Live to fight another day and all that.'

'Exactly, my lady.'

Her brain was still churning a few minutes later. 'Can you ride a bicycle, Clifford?'

'It has been a while, but the adage one never forgets is accurate in my case. Actually, I used to race when I was younger.'

'Excellent! Then, when I set off on my next adventure, you can accompany me.'

'You are too kind.' He smiled.

CHAPTER 28

Eleanor trailed her finger through the water, looking up at the figure of the little girl in a pinafore that overlooked the lake. It was the following afternoon. Eleanor, having slept in, had taken the morning at a relaxed rate to recover from the previous night's drama. The storm had moved away in the night, leaving a bright morning with just a few clouds dotted about.

'You know, Clifford, I spent hours staring at this statue on the few holidays I came to stay at the Hall. If I'm honest, I felt as lost then as I do now.' She sighed. 'Back then I wondered if my uncle might have been around more if he'd had a nephew instead of a niece. One who relished catching frogs and newts, who loved fishing and would hurrah over the cricket score.'

'Unlikely, my lady. Your late uncle was a staunch fan of amphibians remaining in their own habitats, not charging about the Hall let loose by grubby young relatives.'

She laughed, then paused. 'But he might have taken more to a ward who shared his interests?'

Clifford tilted his head and stared at her for a moment. 'If you will permit me, my lady, Lord Henley was a gentleman of courageous spirit who lived for adventure. He applauded the bold, young person with the courage to carve her own path. And follow her own heart.'

She dried her hand on her skirt. 'Well, he wouldn't have applauded *my* affairs of the heart, they've all been quite the disaster.'

'I believe Thomas Aquinas would have challenged your statement, my lady. The famous theologian was noted to have said, "Love takes up where knowledge leaves off." Your uncle also greatly admired another trait in others, that of having the attitude of never giving up hope.'

She grinned. 'And a penchant for dressing as a cowboy and adventuring with their butler?'

Clifford gestured to the wicker picnic basket by her side. 'And for eating, my lady.'

'Ah, yes, of course. What has dear Mrs Trotman conjured up for us today?'

They both turned at the sound of huffing, followed by a breathless Mrs Butters. 'Master Gladstone, you terror! Oh, my lady, I'm so sorry, he just bolted. For a lummock, he can fair pelt along.'

Eleanor jumped up and laughed as the panting bulldog nuzzled her outstretched hands. 'No trouble, he's welcome to stay.' She scratched him under the chin.

Mrs Butters straightened her dishevelled apron. 'Joseph is in the greenhouses behind the box hedge if Mr Wilful here starts being a bothersome nuisance, my lady.'

Eleanor watched the housekeeper cross the neatly edged lawns and disappear through the French doors into the morning room. She turned in a slow circle, taking in the Hall, the grounds and the rolling English countryside.

'Gosh, this really is a beautiful spot, Clifford.'

'Indeed, the Hall is in a privileged position.'

'Actually, I rather think that is a better description for me, *I'm* the one in the privileged position.'

'If you will permit me, my lady, I would include myself and the rest of the staff in that group also.'

She beamed. 'That is genuinely heart-warming to hear, Clifford. I am delighted all the staff agreed to stay on since I arrived.'

'The situation is proving palatable enough at present, my lady.'

She peered at him. Yes, there it was, that barely perceptible twinkle again. It had taken her a long while to fathom his relentless dry wit and unwavering deadpan persona. Finally, however, she was beginning to understand him and, better still, to enjoy his company.

A waft of something simply delicious interrupted her thoughts. 'Oh I say, are those mini scotch eggs?'

'Freshly made this morning, with a parsley and thyme bread-crumb, another speciality of Mrs Trotman's.'

'Yummy! Two, please, Clifford. Sorry, Gladstone, old friend, you're not getting the merest morsel of these. But I have a feeling Mrs Trotman has included something for you.' She extracted a bone for the dog. 'Thank goodness murder doesn't ruin our appetites, eh?'

'Most fortuitous, my lady.'

'Do you know some people can't eat when they're anxious? What a nightmare!'

'And some find it affects their sleep…'

'Yes, okay, well spotted, so that's my stress barometer. You, I suppose, don't have one?'

'It is my experience, my lady, that if events take a downturn there are usually a corresponding number of boots and shoes that require polishing.'

She recalled him, brush in hand in the boot room. That was his personal slice of solace, his bolthole. She'd unwittingly intruded into his sanctum before and was aware she was doing so again now by prying into the workings of his very private mind.

'Down to business then, I guess. There's a killer on the loose, and a mountain of confusing clues and a fabulously comprehensive picnic to work through. I can't decide which is going to take longest.'

'Time is not entirely on our side, my lady.'

'I know, the eggs will get cold,' she said, wincing as she picked up another with her injured arm. She caught him scrutinising her. 'It's fine, Clifford. Anyway, whoever was driving that car got frighteningly close to hitting Millie as well as me. Good thing she'd already scarpered… I suppose.'

At his disapproving look, she sighed and accidentally dropped the last half of her scotch egg. 'No!' She tried to grab it but Gladstone was quicker, gulping down the unexpected treat in one swift lunge. 'Dash it! I was enjoying that enormously.' She wrinkled her nose. 'I suppose then the next step is to work out who could have known Millie was meeting me at the Pike and Perch? And whether Millie was in on that stunt with the car trying to run me down or not.'

Clifford reached into the wicker basket. 'Perhaps your notes will aid us.' He handed over her notebook.

She held up the scribbled notes and hastily drawn doodles, one for each suspect, the whole page crisscrossed in a myriad of lines and arrows. Then she pointed at the picnic basket.

'See the difference? Each piece of cutlery, beautifully polished and clipped neatly into its individual place, arranged according to height. The plates all stacked just so. The sherry bottle, label outward, the glasses nestled together and the food packed with infinite care. I know Mrs Trotman made this delectable feast, but she didn't pack it, did she? This has your meticulous hand all over it.'

He nodded.

'You see, your ability to create order out of chaos is mind boggling to me. I think you might actually be a wizard.' She waved the notebook at him. 'I've got all the people and facts here, save for the events of last night. But now when I look at it, it's as though someone has taken all my thoughts and tipped them onto the paper from an aeroplane and then landed so the pilot could run over and kick them all into even more of a muddle. Everything is just a rambling… confusion.'

'And yet you are the one who has made the connections clearer to me.'

'Really? As I said, I'm so lost, Clifford. Honestly, cycling across the world was a...' She looked around. '... a picnic compared to solving this case.'

'Indeed, my lady. However, if a woman on her own is able to circumnavigate even part of the globe, and on a bicycle at that, it shows she has sufficient grit and belief in herself to solve any number of mysteries. And besides' – he brushed an imaginary speck from the row of knives with a soft linen tea towel – 'you are not alone.'

He reached across and turned the basket towards her. He pressed the back corner and a silk-lined, triangular drawer slid out bearing two brandy miniatures and quarter-size crystal-cut balloon glasses.

'Wow! Did my uncle design that?'

'Among many other items we can explore as and when the situation necessitates.' He poured her a measure. 'Tonic, ginger ale, lemon?'

'Neat. And thank you. For the brandy, but mostly for the not alone bit.'

He nodded to the notebook. 'Shall we?'

She stared at the scarf drawing at the top of her page. 'You know, I can't fathom how even Lancelot could be daft and trusting enough to get himself caught up as the scapegoat, or the... what is that term the Americans use?'

'I believe the phrase you are searching for is "fall guy", my lady.'

'That's it.' She rubbed Gladstone's neck. 'Only that is a sobering thought because Lancelot won't fall Clifford, he'll swing if we don't manage to find out who the killer is. Oh gosh! And I've been waffling on about how tasty the scotch eggs were. I really am a monster.'

He reached into his waistcoat pocket and pulled out a neatly folded paper bag, which he unravelled carefully and held out to her.

'Sherbet lemons!' She popped one into her mouth and closed her eyes, shuffling backwards to give Gladstone enough room to sprawl with his head in her lap. 'Now I can concentrate. So, Millie said they, that's her and Lucas, had been at Albie's flat. Which was so cramped and insanitary in her view that they decided to head to Johnny's more palatial and hygienic apartment. She overheard Albie on the phone threatening to go to the police if he didn't get a "cut". A cut of what we don't know, but Millie assumed a cut of the money from selling Lady Langham's jewels.'

Eleanor took a breath. 'Millie left with Lucas to go to Johnny's flat, even though he wasn't there, which seems a little strange. Later they meet Johnny and Coco at this new club, the Hole in the Wall or some such. Apparently Albie was supposed to follow them in a borrowed car, but never did. Instead he stayed at home and got drunk and then decided to drive, by then fully intoxicated, into a canal it would seem. Why?'

'Well, my lady, people do the most illogical things when under the influence of alcohol, so Mr Appleby driving, and crashing, in that state is not so surprising. What is odd, is that he should agree to go out drinking with his friends, but stay home and drink instead, and *then* go out.'

Eleanor nodded. 'That does seem odd. Then again, we know how easily he was upset. Maybe one of them made a remark and he took umbrage? Or maybe he'd run out of money and couldn't afford to drink out and didn't want to say. I mean, I know I'm not financially challenged, Clifford, but the prices at the clubs that lot party at, are steep to say the least. Vertical, in fact!'

'Very true, my lady.'

'Anyway, if Albie was trying to blackmail someone for a cut of the stolen jewels once they were… what's the word?'

'Fenced?'

'Fenced, that's it. If he was stupid enough to try and pull off blackmailing whoever stole the jewels, it seems likely that it backfired on him horribly and they either got him drunk, or forced him to drink, and then shoved him in the car and ran it into the canal.' She took comfort in running her hand over Gladstone's soft warm belly.

'My limited knowledge of Mr Appleby suggests he was a strong scholar but perhaps not best suited to strategy. Do you trust Lady Millicent? After all, she instigated the meeting to confide in you and furnished us with the details of Mr Appleby's seemingly fatal attempt at blackmail.'

'Well, she seemed genuinely agitated about telling me. In her usual charming manner, she let me know that she wasn't sure she trusted *me*.' She chewed her bottom lip. 'Honestly, though, I'm not sure. I do believe she is so infatuated with Lancelot that she would risk breaking the loyalty of "the gang", as they so love to call themselves.'

'Unless I am mistaken, the younger Lady Childs is unlikely to have been wildly keen on Mr Appleby being part of "the gang" though?'

'Perceptive, as always. No, but I agree with Millie in some ways. She made the point that he was forever out of his depth. But what was he to do? He was bright, academically at least. However, there aren't many lucrative opportunities for the son of a miner, after all. And he was desperate to improve his situation.'

'Desperate enough to resort to blackmail?'

'I wish I knew for certain. He didn't seem the blackmailing type, but then who ever does? Here we are again with more clues and yet even more confusion. I guess our only consolation is that if Albie was murdered, it was likely to have been, as we said before, by the same person who murdered the colonel. It's just too unlikely that there are two killers running around, I feel, and unless we have evidence to that effect, let's assume there's only one. And as you rightly pointed out' – she waved a finger at Clifford – 'that can't have been Lancelot because he was locked up when Albie died. We just need to verify the movements of all our other suspects the night Albie died. That's a huge task, Clifford, and one I don't think we can get done before Lancelot's trial.'

'Indeed, my lady. However, our suspect list isn't that extensive, consisting only of the dowager Goldsworthy and her niece, Miss Cora Wynne, the Viscount and Viscountess Littleton, the Childs sisters, Prince Singh and Mr Seaton.' He coughed. 'Perhaps, on reflection, it is quite a list. We do, however, have some more information on that score already, my lady. Lady Fenwick-Langham rang while you were indisposed and informed me that Mr Seaton's parents confirmed he'd been with them all day at a family gathering and that he left them around seven thirty in the evening. Unfortunately, however, Mr Appleby apparently died around one in the morning and Mr Seaton's parents told Lady Fenwick-Langham that he hadn't returned that night. They presume he had been out with his friends until the early hours as usual and then stayed at his apartment outside Oxford.'

Eleanor sighed. 'The trouble is, these blasted bright young things all party together and all provide alibis for each other, but you do not know who, if any of them, to trust. Even if they aren't involved, they'll cover for each other.' She finished her brandy. 'Clifford, what is your normal tipple?'

'A mild porter in the good weather months and a ginger wine in winter, for its medicinal properties, naturally.'

'Naturally. Nothing to do with the case, I just wondered.'

They returned to the investigation and attacked it from every angle they could think of, but a much-needed breakthrough remained elusive. Slowly the warmth of the afternoon gave way to the chill of the evening. Gladstone heaved his squat frame off the rug and stretched first one stiff back leg, then the other. He stared at her and then at Clifford suggesting it must surely be dinner time. Eleanor was just about to suggest they move inside when Mrs Butters appeared on the lawn waving frantically.

Clifford nodded in the housekeeper's direction. 'I believe a visitor has called, my lady.'

'Who the drat is it, do you suppose? Why can't people plan to arrive unannounced with better timing for the poor unsuspecting hosts? I shall send word that I am not at home.'

Clifford turned to her. 'I fear that may not be possible, my lady. The gentleman has himself appeared on the terrace.'

CHAPTER 29

The evening shadows stretched out across the floor of the study as Eleanor, arms folded, faced her visitor.

'Inspector.'

'Lady Swift.' DCI Seldon turned his hat slowly in both hands. 'I must speak to you. Alone.'

She realised that at some point Clifford must have stepped noiselessly into the room. 'I have no problem with Clifford hearing whatever it is you need to say.'

DCI Seldon's expression was hard. 'I do.'

Goosebumps raced up her arms. 'Clifford.' She continued to stare at Seldon. 'We won't require tea, thank you. The inspector will not be staying long.'

'Very good, my lady.' He left as noiselessly as he'd come.

'Well?'

DCI Seldon took a step forward, which brought him in front of her. Struck by the size of his frame, she felt a ridiculous urge for him to embrace her in his powerful arms. He ran his thumb and index finger along his jaw.

'I am here to inform you that last night... Lord Fenwick-Langham escaped from jail.'

Her jaw dropped. 'What! How?'

Seldon shook his head. 'Young Lord Fenwick-Langham may be a fool, but it seems Sergeant Brice is an even bigger one! I take full responsibility. I should have moved him to a more secure jail.'

'But... but why did you come here to tell me? Why—?'

He held up his hand silencing her. 'I won't ask if you already knew of Lord Fenwick-Langham's escape. I will, however, ask you this. Do *you* believe he is innocent, Lady Swift?'

She hesitated. 'My… my heart does.'

'And your mind?'

She said nothing, but held his gaze.

He strode over to the window where the evening shadows stretched out across the lawn. 'Then I offer my sympathies for the decision you must now make. I came here to warn you. If you intend to go to Lord Fenwick-Langham, you need to act fast. I wish I could guarantee your safety to him, and… with him. My men will find him by morning, of that I am sure. If you have any sense, you will be far away from him by then. If you aren't, the minimum you will be charged with is aiding, abetting and or harbouring a criminal. Good evening, Lady Swift.' He turned and walked out.

Eleanor's mind whirled. He could have waited and tailed her if he thought she knew where Lancelot was, but instead he'd tried to protect her by warning her from being caught alongside a fugitive.

She ran to the hall, but he was already walking out the front door. 'Inspector! Wait!'

He called over his shoulder. 'I don't believe in fate, Lady Swift. I have, however, learned that some things are just not meant to be.'

Standing by the window she sensed Clifford's presence.

'It is rather ironic, is it not, Clifford, that the inspector assumes I know the whereabouts of his escaped jailbird, when I have no idea.'

Wordlessly he held out a piece of paper. She took it and looked up in confusion. 'It's an address. I don't… What is this?'

'Young Lord Fenwick-Langham is waiting for you, my lady.'

Her hand flew to her mouth, the paper fluttering to the floor. 'He's… waiting?'

'Yes, my lady.'

'How did you…?'

'It transpires young Lord Fenwick-Langham rang Miss Abigail from a public phone box and asked her to pass the address on to Mr Sandford. Mr Sandford passed it on to Lord and Lady Fenwick-Langham, who sent their chauffeur around with it concealed in a brace of pheasants. I assume they feared the phone wires to the Manor and, indeed, here, might be tapped, as did his young lordship, I presume.'

She hesitated. *Don't do it, Ellie! You don't really love that clown. He's the one playing you for a fool, just like your husband, just like…*

Clifford stepped closer. 'My lady, I assume you are hesitating about whether to go to young Lord Fenwick-Langham?'

She stared out at the growing gloom. 'Yes, but…'

'Do you love him?'

Of course you don't, Ellie!

He voice was quiet. 'Yes. I do.' She turned to Clifford. 'But… but suppose I'm wrong, and he doesn't…'

'Love you, my lady?'

'Yes. Suppose he's just been using me… and he doesn't really have any… feelings for me.'

'Then, my lady, we'll go to young Lord Fenwick-Langham together' – he adjusted his cuffs – 'and I'll kill him myself.'

CHAPTER 30

'We are nearly there, my lady,' Clifford broke into her reverie.

She sighed. 'I wish it hadn't had to come to this. I've only been at the Hall such a short while but it feels… well, it feels like home.' She leaned forward and squeezed his arm. 'Thank you for that, Clifford.' A pang of guilt hit her. 'Will you say goodbye to the ladies for me? And… and Gladstone? I couldn't face the farewells. Tell each of them I wish I could scoop them up and squeeze the life out of them. And I'm sorry that you've all been caught up in this… this craziness.'

'It has been a pleasure from the very outset, my lady. And will be to the end.' He pointed to the glove compartment.

Inside, a brandy bottle lay with two glasses wrapped in a fine red velvet jacket. She poured a hefty measure into the first glass. As she picked up the second, something clinked against the side.

She held up an emerald locket on a delicate gold chain. 'What the—?' She clicked open the clasp and caught her breath at the photo inside. 'Clifford! Gracious, that's me on my uncle's knee.'

'It was your fourth birthday, my lady. Your parents had managed a rare gap between their work projects and spent a delightful fortnight at the Hall.'

She ran her finger over the photo and then read the inscription, engraved on a double-sided inset: *It takes courage to grow up and become who you really are. Your ever loving Uncle Byron.*

Tears streamed down her cheeks. 'Oh, Clifford!'

He took out a clean handkerchief. 'Forgive me, perhaps I should have given it to you earlier. Your uncle entrusted it to me in his final hours. He said I would know the right time to pass it on to you. This, I think, is that time.'

She handed him the first glass and poured a liberal glug into the second. 'To my uncle, Clifford.'

They clinked glasses. 'To his lordship!'

He eased the car off the road and onto a track. 'Ready?'

'Nope.' She glugged the brandy down in one. 'So let's go!'

At the track's end, the headlights illuminated a farm building that appeared deserted and bordering on derelict. Clifford brought the Rolls to a stop and cut the engine and lights. They stepped out, Clifford staying close to Eleanor. They looked around in the moonlight.

'I suspect, my lady, young Lord Fenwick-Langham is not in the farmhouse that looks ready to fall at any moment.'

'Here!' The voice came from behind them.

Eleanor spun around. 'Goggles!'

'Sherlock, you came. I knew you would.' His soft stubble made her tingle with delight.

'Did you? Were you sure I would, because I wasn't.'

She smiled as he tucked a stray curl behind her ear.

'Darling, fruit, I never doubted you. You've already chased me all over the county, what was an extra few miles for a girl as smitten as you?'

'Few miles? We've been driving for hours. You are impossible! And you look dreadful. This being on the run doesn't suit you, you know.'

'Nonsense! My appearance is distinctly roguish, I imagine. No real clue, haven't seen a mirror in days. Tried a peek in the pond over there but you should see the pike, nearly lost my head. Huge beast it was.'

She pulled him up. 'We need to escape, there's no time.'

'I know. Dashed exciting, what?'

'Lancelot…'

'Sherlock, I can't tell you how glad I am that you came. Europe sounded horribly dull without you.'

'Well, let's hope it's ready for us.'

He ran his hand along her chin and brought her face up to meet his. 'What a dashing pair of glitterati we shall be. Those Europeans won't know what's hit them.' He leaned in, his lips just brushing hers.

A cough interrupted them. 'My lady, the man I called before we left will meet me on the main road in a few minutes. You should be safe here until then.'

As Clifford drove off, Lancelot gave her a quizzical look.

'Fake passports, I think.'

He whistled. 'Mr Clifford certainly has some useful contacts.'

He spun round and waltzed her into the hay barn, pulling the door shut behind him. Inside, shafts of moonlight illuminated bales of hay and…

'Florence! How did you get her here?'

The plane stood in the middle of the barn like a gilded dragonfly.

Lancelot grinned. 'Actually it isn't Florence. Same model, though. I came here by motorcycle. It was too dangerous to try and get Florence, and anyone could have heard, or seen, me landing here.' He sighed. 'I will miss her.'

Eleanor shook her head. 'But where on earth did you get another plane from?'

'Ah, well, us pilot johnnies are frightfully pally, you know, like a private club. There aren't many of us, so we help each other out with repairs and parts and so on. This belongs to Hugo Fotherington, a chum of mine, known him since school.'

'And he's given it to you?'

'Good lord, no! The plan is to fly across to the continent under cover of darkness to a private landing strip another chum owns and hide it. Then Hugo'll pop over some time later when all the fuss has died down and fly it back. A plane's like a...' He looked Eleanor up and down. 'A bewitching girl. You just couldn't part with her. It broke my heart to leave Florence behind, but...' He shrugged. 'So what do you think of my bijou pied-à-terre away from home?' He gestured around the barn. 'Delightful what? Mind, after that wretched cell, it seems rather a palace.'

'Delightful.' She took a step back. 'What on earth are you wearing though?'

'Dapper, eh?' He gave a mock twirl. 'I borrowed these britches.'

'Who the heck from?'

'From a most helpful washing line.'

She rubbed her forehead. 'Lancelot, listen, I need to know something before I agree to leave with you.'

He pouted. 'Sherlock, is this going to be that dashedly awkward thing girls do about needing to hear, like, a declaration of undying love, because, well alright, but—'

She leaned across and clapped her hands over his mouth.

'I don't want to talk about anything like that now, you total monkey. We're on the run, you fool. I just need you to be honest with me. I know you tried to steal your mother's jewels, but... the colonel?'

Lancelot took her by the arms gently. 'No, I didn't kill the colonel. Cross my heart and hope not to die.'

Her shoulders sagged in relief. She believed him.

He stroked her cheek. 'Sherlock, I don't know how this will... pan out. You still game?'

She bit her lip. 'This isn't a game, Goggles.' Her eyes searched his face. She started. Something was wrong.

A tongue of flames licked through a gap between the wooden boards. 'Lancelot, move!' She ran to the door and hurled herself at it. It stood firm, throwing her to the ground.

He yanked her up by the arm. 'What the hell's going on?'

'Fire! Someone's set fire to the bloody barn!' She hammered against the door again. 'Jammed. They've jammed it.'

She spun round, looking for another way out. The flames quickly spread inside, forcing them to retreat. The beam above the door gave way, bringing half the hayloft floor with it. Overcome by the heat and smoke, they ducked behind the plane as the tinder-dry bales burst into flames.

'There's no way out, Sherlock, we're trapped.' He cupped her smoke-smudged face and kissed her. 'Dash it, Sherlock, I thought we might have had a future together.'

She revelled in his kiss, but then pushed him back. 'It isn't over yet!'

She scrambled out from behind the plane and grabbed a metal post from the barn floor, swinging it at the rear wall with a ferocious yell. As it hit the thick planks it bounced off, just missing her head.

At that moment the barn doors splintered inwards, sending a shower of sparks over them. The flaming bales were shunted apart by what looked like a scaled-down snowplough blade attached to... her Rolls.

The car jerked to a stop. Clifford leaned out of the window. 'Get in!'

The central beam finally surrendered and the last of the roof caved in. Lancelot pushed Eleanor out of the path of the falling timber and into the car. Before he could jump in after her, the Rolls lurched forward, crashing through the rear wall.

*

A safe distance away from the funnel of black smoke and clumps of burning straw flying through the air, Clifford pulled over.

She struggled up from the floor. 'Lancelot!' Scrambling out of the Rolls, she started running back to the flaming building.

'Sherlock! Where are you going?'

She spun round. Lancelot was standing on the rear bumper, his hands gripping the roof. He hopped off, his grinning face covered in soot, and covered her body with his.

A discreet cough broke the spell. Clifford was standing next to them.

Lancelot looked up and shook his head. 'Clifford, you are simply the limit and beyond! I do believe all those yarns Sandford used to entertain me with about you and Lord Henley were actually true. He told me about a snowplough-cum-ramming device Lord Henley had invented, but I thought it was just another tall tale. And now' – he slapped Clifford on the shoulder – 'I've seen it in action. Nice one.'

'Thank you, my lord, but I do apologise for moving off when I did. I felt I could delay no longer.' Clifford brushed the ash off his suit.

'Clifford, bless you, we will be forever in your debt.' Eleanor leaned forward and kissed his cheek.

For once, words seemed to fail him.

Lancelot chuckled and pulled Eleanor close to him again. 'I do believe you are blushing, Clifford. She really is a terrible mistress, what?'

'However.' She pointed at Clifford. 'Don't ever scold me for graunching the gears again!'

The remainder of the burning barn collapsed behind them with a terrible groan. They all turned and stared.

Lancelot sighed theatrically. 'Well, there goes our chance of a flying escape.'

Clifford nodded. 'Indeed, my lord, without a plane your escape will be that much more hazardous. There is the possibility of catching a fishing boat out of Aberdeen, however.'

Lancelot grinned. 'We'd better get a move on if we're going to make that boat then.' He tried to get in the Rolls but Eleanor blocked his path. 'I say, old girl, we really need—'

'No!' The flames of the burning building reflected in her eyes. 'That's it. No more running!'

He took her hand. 'Sherlock…'

She shook him off. The fire was reflected in her eyes and something had changed. 'Listen, for all the thrill of my so-called adventures, the truth is I've been running away from my problems ever since my parents disappeared. But now I've finally found a place I can call home and people' – she looked at Clifford – 'I can call friends and' – she took Lancelot's hand back – 'more, much more, so… no one, NO ONE is going to take that away from me! Much less try to kill me and my new pals.' She caught Clifford's eye. 'Now we turn the tables!'

Clifford nodded, his eyes twinkling. 'Spoken like a true Swift, my lady.'

Lancelot looked from one to the other. 'Sherlock! I'm the new boy in town here, help me out. What's the plan?'

'The hunted are about to become the hunters. Ready?'

He held up his hands. 'Whatever you say, Sherlock.'

'Clifford, do you have a safe place we can go?'

'Absolutely, my lady.'

Once in the back of the car with Lancelot, Eleanor leaned forward. 'By the way, Clifford, what exactly did my uncle use that device on the front of the Rolls for?'

Clifford eased the battered car onto the road.

'Squirrels, my lady.'

CHAPTER 31

The last twenty-four hours had taken their toll on Eleanor's body, which made snuggling up to Lancelot all the more wonderful. His sleeves were rolled up to his elbows, his strong forearms cradling her shoulders. Looking up, she realised he had been staring at her.

'You alright, Goggles?' she whispered.

'No, I feel most odd. Never known the sensation before, it's like I'm falling.' He kept his voice low.

'Probably a dash of vertigo from all the smoke.'

'It's not that. I'm definitely falling... head over heels for a quite incredible redhead with the most amazing green eyes. If I doze off, do you think she'll be gone when I wake up?'

'Most likely. She'll probably have seen sense.'

'Lady Swift, you are a shocker.'

'Get used to it.' She winked and snuggled back into his side.

The hypnotic rhythm of the Rolls' engine soon lulled her into a deep sleep, broken by Lancelot kissing her forehead.

'Sherlock?'

Eleanor sat up and rubbed her eyes, taking in the dark, over-grown brick arch above and behind them, before stretching the stiffness out of her limbs. They both stepped out of the car and looked around in the moonlight.

'Clifford,' she whispered, 'where are we?'

'In Northington, a hamlet west of Little Buckford, my lady. I believe we will be safe here. Several of your uncle's more... colourful acquaintances hid out here. If you will wait a moment.'

He reversed the Rolls into what appeared to be a solid earth bank, covered in ivy. In fact the car passed through the ivy curtain and vanished. The engine cut out and a moment later Clifford reappeared. 'If you would follow me, my lord, my lady.' He led the way down a rough track to a lone cottage swathed in darkness.

Once inside, with the light illuminated, Eleanor looked around. Clifford pointed to the wicker basket on the simple, wooden table. 'Perhaps you would like to take some refreshments.'

'Rather! I'm beyond famished.' Lancelot rubbed his stomach, opened the lid and cheered. 'Ham and egg pie, a plate of cold meats, two enormous wedges of cheese, sandwiches, three flasks and more. Mr Clifford, I salute you!'

Eleanor grinned. 'Oh dear, the poor jailbird's gone rogue. He does look pretty hungry.'

Clifford poured two large glasses of sherry and handed them one each.

Lancelot gave a thumbs up as he swallowed a hunk of cheese, wrapped in ham. 'Honestly, I could eat a horse, or a large dog at least. I haven't had a thing since yesterday. A chap can't carry off that level of sustenance deprivation for long. What time is it now?'

Clifford pulled out his fob watch. 'Twelve twenty-seven, my lord.'

Eleanor laughed. 'I think there's finally a chink appearing in your impenetrable butler armour, Clifford.'

He raised an eyebrow. 'How so, my lady?'

'Because your perfect timekeeping has let you down. It's not twelve twenty-seven, it's only eleven fifty. See.' She held up her uncle's fob watch. 'It was serviced only last month, so I know it's right.'

Clifford nodded. 'Indeed, my lady, but I believe if you examine it again, you may notice that the second hand is not moving.'

Lancelot leaned across the table and took the watch from Eleanor. 'You're right as usual, Clifford. The bally thing's stopped.

Why would it stop at eleven fifty? Ah! You must have bashed it when escaping from the barn.'

Eleanor pouted. 'I'm very fond of this watch. It reminds me of good times with my uncle.'

Lancelot passed it back to her and grinned. 'Just goes to show there's no point in paying for all that expensive servicing, you might as well just wind it forward to the correct time and it will be as right as Clifford's!'

Eleanor slapped the table and jumped up. 'That's it!'

Lancelot paused, a slice of ham and egg pie in his hand. 'I say, old girl, what is?'

'The answer, of course!'

'To what?'

She looked across to Clifford who was staring at her quizzically. Understanding dawned in his eyes. He turned to Lancelot. 'To proving your innocence, my lord.'

Lancelot looked from one to the other. 'Er... sounds wonderful. Could someone just explain how old Lord Henley's watch stopping proves me innocent?'

Eleanor was too excited to sit down, so she walked back and forth as she explained. 'The whole problem with proving that someone else killed the colonel is that the police believe they know the exact time of his death.'

'Eight twenty-three.'

'Exactly, Clifford. Eight twenty-three, because that was when the colonel's watch had stopped, after being smashed on the fireplace.'

Lancelot frowned. 'So, you're saying his watch *didn't* stop when he died?'

Eleanor shook her head impatiently. 'No, of course it did, fathead! Oh, do explain it to him, Clifford, I need to think.'

'Yes, my lady.' Clifford turned to Lancelot. 'The colonel's watch did indeed accurately record the time of his death, my lord.

However, it wasn't at eight twenty-three. The murderer, having killed the colonel, took the colonel's watch and smashed it on the fireplace, breaking and stopping the watch at, near enough, the time the colonel died. He then wound it forward, thereby providing himself with an alibi and rendering yours, my lord, redundant.'

Lancelot whistled softly. 'By Jove, what a cunning blighter! So he killed the old colonel, broke his watch and set it forward say… fifteen minutes?'

Clifford thought for a moment. 'Perhaps, my lord, maybe slightly less. It would have to have been enough time for the killer to make sure he was back in public view when the body was found, but no more. For every extra minute would have increased the risk of someone other than your lordship finding the body.'

Eleanor, still pacing, interrupted. 'But the killer had to take another risk. You see, the colonel had a fob watch, I've seen him with it before, but it was the sort you could convert to a wristwatch by way of a strap.'

Lancelot nodded. 'I know the sort of thing, always thought it a bit old-fashioned myself, but then so was the colonel.'

Clifford nodded. 'Indeed, my lord, but such watches are very popular with officers of Colonel Puddifoot's generation.'

Eleanor waved her hand. 'Whatever, the point is, at the start of the evening before he was killed, I was talking to him and he wasn't wearing it on his wrist. I'd have noticed it, it was a cumbersome thing.'

'Ah!' Lancelot held up a finger. 'So the killer had to take a chance that no one would notice the watch was now on the colonel's wrist, rather than in his pocket?'

Clifford nodded. 'Exactly, my lord. Had the watch been in the colonel's pocket when the police found it, they might have wondered how it came to be damaged so irreparably. Which means the killer must have known the colonel reasonably well to rely on him having his watch on him in the first instance. But then again, with a man of the colonel's military background and punctual habits, it was fairly certain he'd never be without it.'

Eleanor stopped pacing and spun around. 'That's it! Now we can work out who the murderer, and jewel thief, is.' Eleanor glanced at Clifford. 'Although, to give Clifford his due, I imagine he's already worked that out.'

Clifford half bowed to Eleanor. 'Thank you, my lady, but I feel you should claim that honour. After your brilliant deduction that the murderer wound Colonel Puddifoot-Barton's watch forward, the identity of the killer, and as you say, jewel thief, is now a simple matter of elimination.'

Lancelot looked from one to the other again. 'Okay, I give up!'

It was Eleanor's turn to grin. 'Look, we've actually always known that the colonel wasn't killed at eight twenty-three because if he had been, then the only two people who could have done it were the two people in the room at that time. And that was me and you, Lancelot. And as I know I didn't do it—'

'And I know *I* didn't.'

'Exactly. Then the colonel must have been murdered earlier as we've said.'

'We estimate around eight to thirteen minutes past the hour,' Clifford clarified.

Lancelot frowned, trying to follow the events. 'I understand that means anyone who wasn't in public view, as it were, around that time could be the murderer now, but how do we narrow that down? We can't waltz round asking for new alibis from everyone, can we?'

A cough interrupted them. Clifford was holding out her notebook.

Eleanor smiled. 'Thank you, Clifford.' She opened the notebook and quickly scanned the pages to refresh her memory. She looked at her list of suspects, skipping Lancelot's name. 'Right, Lord Hurd we've already ruled out. Our first real suspects are the dowager countess and Cora. However, they came over just after I fell, which is about when the murderer would have had to have lured the colonel up…' She stopped, her hand flying to her mouth.

Lancelot looked at her quizzically. 'What's up, old girl?'

'I've just realised that the murderer was probably looking for an opportunity to draw the colonel upstairs and my face planting in front of the entire ballroom was probably exactly what he needed! In fact, the inspector said it had distracted everyone, including his men.'

She looked at Clifford who nodded, and Lancelot, who looked on eagerly, his mouth full of Mrs Trotman's ham and egg pie.

She sighed. 'Oh well, nothing we can do about it now. Where was I? Oh, yes, that eliminates the dowager countess and Cora. Also Viscount Littleton helped me up, and the viscountess was there too, though she, like the dowager countess, wasn't exactly sympathetic.' She looked down at the notebook and put a line through the four names.

Lancelot finished his slice of pie. 'So who does that leave?'

'Well, we've already cleared you.' She grinned at him. 'So that leaves your bright young things gang. We've suspected all along that the jewel thief, and then the murderer, was one of them. And another thing, I've just worked out what's been nagging at my mind. It's something the inspector said. He told me another reason the jewel thief had to be you, Goggles, is that the safe hadn't been blown and there simply hadn't been time for anyone to pick the lock.'

Clifford and Eleanor looked at Lancelot, who flushed at their accusatory gaze. 'Look here, do you think I'm…' Comprehension dawned in his eyes. 'I say, I have been a chump. I told the gang I was going to steal Mater's jewels and one of the girls, I can't remember which, started ribbing me, saying I couldn't do it because I probably didn't even know the safe code. Well, of course I did, the parentals trust me, you know, so I repeated it from memory just to show them.' He shrugged.

Clifford coughed. 'Which means they all knew the code.'

Eleanor held up a finger. 'Ah! But as we discussed, neither Coco nor Millie are strong enough to bash the colonel over the head, so they can be discounted. That leaves us with Albie, Johnny and Lucas. That's right, isn't it, Clifford?'

'Yes, my lady. And if we assume that the person who murdered Colonel Puddifoot-Barton also murdered Mr Appleby…'

'Exactly, we can exclude Albie, which leaves Johnny and Lucas. Now, Pickerton, the second coachman, told me that Lucas had to leave early to attend to some emergency. However, Pickerton didn't actually see him leave, so he could have had time to kill the colonel before he left.'

'Or doubled back, snuck into the house again and killed him?' Lancelot said.

Clifford nodded. 'That might have been tight on timing, my lord, but also possible.'

Lancelot looked back and forth between them. 'Look, here, don't keep a chap in the dark. Which one is it?'

Eleanor ignored him. She paced the kitchen. 'The killer has been one step ahead of us at every turn. We need a plan, Clifford.'

He frowned. 'I have a rudimentary idea, my lady. However it has two potentially serious flaws.'

'Well, what are they?'

He coughed. 'The first is that it would place you in a possibly dangerous, if not perilous, situation.'

Lancelot jumped up. 'Hold on, Clifford! I think she's been in enough danger.'

She turned to him. 'Do you have a plan, clever clogs?'

'Er, no.'

She waved him down and turned back to Clifford. 'And the second flaw?'

'It relies on us procuring an elephant gun, as sadly your late uncle did not feel the need to include one in the equipment kept here.'

She slapped her leg. 'Dash it!'

'I can get you one,' Lancelot said without looking up.

They both stared at him in surprise.

He winked at them and grinned. 'Who's the lynchpin now then, eh?'

CHAPTER 32

Somewhere out in the elegant entrance hall, a mantel clock softly chimed two. A light breeze rustled the floor-to-ceiling silver curtains, letting in a wisp of cool, pre-dawn air. The chesterfield sofa creaked as Eleanor adjusted her position. She'd sat there long enough to take in every inch of the room from the central spiral staircase to the open galleried bedroom. The country mansion, set in its own parkland, had been converted into luxury flats for gentlemen of independent means and normally Eleanor would have admired how tastefully it had been done. Tonight, however, she had more pressing matter on her mind. *This is taking forever, Ellie!*

The click of the front door made her freeze. The sound of a man's dress shoe on the black-and-white marble hall flooring followed. The steps paused, then crossed the thick circular rug of the adjacent reception room.

Johnny Seaton stopped in the doorway, surprise on his face. He quickly recovered his composure, sliding his white silk scarf from his neck and hanging it over the gold stand of the floor lamp beside him.

'This is a surprise, Lady Swift.'

Eleanor nodded, her face grim. 'I had to see you urgently. The night porter wasn't sure when you'd return, so I asked him if it would be okay if I waited for you.'

He slid off his jacket, leaving his bow tie hanging loosely around his neck. 'I see. Good evening, by the way, I do believe I missed that bit. And apologies for keeping you waiting. I was catching up with a couple of chums from Oxford. A fine steak and an even finer Romanee-Conti.' He grinned. 'Quite the bachelor night, you might say. Now, I'll knock up the cocktails and you tell me to what I owe this delightfully unexpected pleasure.' He took a slow waltz across the room, taking an extra turn around the central gold inlay table. 'What'll it be?'

'Look this is really important, but, okay, I'll have an Angel Face.'

'Well there's a thing, an angel on my sofa. But tell me, dear girl, you didn't come here to drink cocktails, did you? What are you really doing here at two in the morning?'

Eleanor leaned forward. 'I know who the jewel thief, and Colonel Puddifoot-Barton's murderer, is.'

He turned and flipped the stopper from a decanter with his thumb. 'Good lord, it seems Lancelot was right about you, you really are quite the sleuth. One Angel Face, one Hanky Panky.' He passed her a glass and then sat on the adjacent chesterfield and slung one leg over the other. 'Now, spill the beans, who is it?' He raised his glass and she raised hers in return. 'And why have you come here to tell me? Flattered though I am.'

She placed her drink on the table. 'Johnny, this is serious. I believe you're in danger.'

He took a swig of his cocktail. 'Why me in particular?'

'Because he knows you're on to him. Just like Albie was.'

Johnny's casual manner deserted him. He leaned forward. 'Albie? You think Albie was... murdered?'

She nodded. 'Not think, *know*. By the same person who stole the jewels, killed the colonel and framed Lancelot.'

Johnny looked visibly shaken. 'Poor old Albie,' he muttered. 'I should have said something, but...' He looked up at her. 'It's Lucas, isn't it?'

She nodded. 'You knew, didn't you?'

He nodded wearily. 'I wouldn't say knew, more suspected. And only recently, really. Things just didn't add up. The jewel thief always seemed to strike when the gang was around, and Lucas and his old man know so much about gems. What clinched it was—'

'When you saw him climb that church steeple?'

He nodded again. 'Everything just sort of fell into place. But I had no idea he'd killed Albie, I genuinely thought it was an accident.'

'Well, I realised that you suspected Lucas, and I've seen the guarded looks Lucas has been throwing your way, so I'm sure he knows you've rumbled him. And there's more.' She leaned forward. 'Lucas mentioned something to me. He told me that he suspected you of somehow being mixed up in the jewel thefts and colonel's murder—'

'Why the—?'

Eleanor held up a hand. 'Listen, Johnny, we haven't got time. The police found jewels hidden in Lancelot's car and Lucas—'

'Don't you mean his plane?'

Eleanor stiffened. 'His… his plane?'

Johnny nodded. 'I thought the police said the fool had gone and hidden the loot in his plane.' A shadow of doubt passed over his face. 'Maybe I was wrong.'

Think, Ellie! She forced herself to sit back. She took a sip of her drink, her mind whirling. She nodded at his empty glass. 'You might need another.'

He stood up. 'You?'

She shook her head. 'I'm fine, thanks.'

He turned to the bar, mixed himself another drink and sat down. The sound of slow clapping interrupted them. They both looked up to see Coco descending the spiral staircase.

'Congratulations, Eleanor. You're really quite the master at this.'

'Coco!' Johnny rose and looked between the two women.

Eleanor stared at Coco, her mind now racing even faster. Somehow she kept her voice level. 'Gosh, Coco, I didn't have you pegged as one of those peculiar girls who likes to spy on others.'

Coco laughed drily. 'No, I guess you didn't. That's because you might be able to fool a man, especially one with an over-inflated libido.' She shot Johnny a hard look. 'But you can't fool me. You're obviously used to using your charms to get what you want. Maybe that's how you made it round the world, batting your lashes and flashing your thighs?'

Eleanor smiled, desperately improvising, trying to gain time. 'Whatever it takes, Coco. You'd understand that, I'm sure.'

'Oh yes. And you'll understand this then.' Coco pulled a gun from beneath the folds of her dress. Eleanor swallowed hard as Johnny joined Coco's side.

'So sorry, Eleanor old thing,' Johnny said. 'But as you can see, I'm already taken.' He slung his arm around Coco's shoulder. 'Shame though, it would have been awfully fun to compare notes on the two of you.'

Coco kept the gun trained on Eleanor. 'You see, there're some advantages to everyone thinking you're just a vacuous bright young thing, good for nothing but partying.'

Johnny nodded. 'In reality, my dear Eleanor, Coco's quite the brains. She's the mastermind behind the whole operation. I'm simply the handsome executor of her daring and delicious plans.'

Coco waved the gun at Eleanor. 'Of which, this is by far the most delicious. Lancelot will swing for all our previous little acts of mischief and we'll simply change our "modus operandi", as your dreary butler would no doubt call it, and carry on. It will take the police years to connect the two sets of thefts, if they ever do, and realise they hung poor old Lancelot by mistake. Oh, Eleanor, we owe you a huge thank you.'

Eleanor's voice was cool. 'For what?'

Coco laughed. 'Don't be so modest. You made the whole thing not only possible, but downright child's play. You antagonised that handsome detective so much that he didn't believe a word you said. He even threatened to arrest you. Oh, you're too much.'

Eleanor cast her eyes down, muttering, 'Yes, I suppose I did.'

'And all your interfering has done is help put a noose around your lover boy's neck. A frightful bish, wouldn't you say?'

Eleanor looked up, her eyes glinting. 'So tell me, what's your terrible habit, that you need *so* much more money than your doting parents already throw at you? What happened to the sweet girl with a bright future?'

Coco grimaced. 'Oh don't try and play the psychological game with me, I'm not Johnny.'

At his confused look, she shook her head. 'She tricked you into revealing that you knew where the jewels had been found.'

Johnny's face lit up in understanding. 'Well, I'll be blowed!' He stared at Eleanor. 'So... so no one knew?'

Eleanor shrugged. 'The police never told anyone. I only knew because I have a... source who passed the information on. But I was sure it wasn't you...'

'And only the thief and killer would have known.' Johnny bowed to Eleanor. 'Very impressive.' He looked thoughtful for a moment. 'I get it... you'd narrowed the jewel thief and murderer down to Lucas or me, so you worked out all you needed to do was find out which of us knew about the jewels being planted in Lancelot's plane.' He whistled softly. 'Impressive.'

Eleanor said nothing. It would have been impressive if that had been the case. As it was, she'd simply got the wrong man.

'Impressive?' Coco held her arm straighter as she trained the gun on Eleanor's forehead. 'I think the hole in her skull the bullet from this Webley Revolver is going to make will be a lot more impressive.'

Eleanor swallowed hard. She noted that her hands were shaking. Forcing herself to remain sitting she tried to keep Coco talking.

'So why come to me and ask for my help when it seemed you'd got away with everything?'

Coco laughed. 'So you didn't suspect me, of course. I knew you'd stick your nose in to try and save your precious Lancelot. And because you trusted me, I was able to find out what you knew.'

'So why did you need to send Johnny to follow me after we met at the Blind Pig? It was you Johnny, wasn't it?'

Johnny nodded. 'Not really my type of thing, I'm more of a slow shoe shuffle type of guy.'

Coco grimaced. 'You were useless, Johnny. She rumbled someone was following her straight away.' She turned back to Eleanor. 'I wanted to keep tabs on you and make sure you weren't smarter than we thought. Unnecessary really, as you obviously weren't.'

Johnny laughed. 'Well, certainly Lancelot wasn't. The minute we found out he'd escaped we knew he'd try and rendezvous with you, Eleanor, and then skip the country. By plane, of course.'

Coco nodded. 'Even he wasn't stupid enough to go near his own plane because the police would have been all over it.'

Johnny nodded back. 'Which meant he needed another. So, I just rang round. There's only a couple of chaps who have that sort of pocket money within a reasonable distance of here. And bingo! The Right Honourable Hugo Fotherington told me he was lending Lancelot his plane and I told him I was helping Lancelot escape, so he told me where the plane was.'

Eleanor frowned. 'But why set the barn on fire? Why not let Lancelot go? His fleeing would have made him look doubly guilty.'

Coco yawned. 'Maybe, but I hate loose ends. And besides, Lancelot wasn't the threat. You were.'

Eleanor flinched.

Coco continued. 'You just don't know when to stop, do you? You'd have persuaded him to return at some point with some stupid plan to prove his innocence and we couldn't have that, could we?'

Eleanor shook her head. 'But why, Coco? Why all this stealing in the first place?'

Coco laughed drily. 'You disappoint me, Lady Swift. You think you're the embodiment of the modern woman, but frankly you're a total parody. I, on the other hand, am a truly liberated woman. Why should I rely on my parents for money, when I can go and get my own?'

'By stealing other people's jewels?'

Coco shrugged. 'Why not? Stealing from the privileged classes isn't stealing. Most of them have so many trinkets that they don't even notice when one or two go missing.' She cocked her head on one side. 'You know, your morals are as quaint and outdated as your fashion sense.'

Eleanor shrugged back. 'I quite like some old-fashioned values… especially ones about not committing murder.'

Coco rolled her eyes. 'Really, you are *so* Victorian. That old fool, the colonel, brought it on himself. Meddling in stuff that had nothing to do with him. He saw himself as some kind of vigilante hero, the idiot. He was simply a casualty of war.'

The hairs on the back of Eleanor's neck stood up. 'I wasn't talking about the colonel. I meant Lancelot. If he… hangs, you'll be as responsible for his death as much as if you'd put the rope round his neck yourself.'

Coco's eyes darkened. 'I wish I *was* the one putting the rope round his neck! Who the hell does he think he is? He broke Millie's heart when he rejected her.'

A wave of anger washed over Eleanor. 'You're wrong, Coco. You can't break something that's not there.'

Coco stepped towards her, fury on her face.

Well done, Ellie, she's only the one with the gun! She held Coco's gaze, finally understanding. 'So this whole thing really had nothing to do with stealing jewels and everything to do with getting revenge on Lancelot?'

Johnny nodded. 'Quite right. The original plan was just to have Lancelot arrested for stealing his mother's necklace. Of course, we soon worked out that that plan wouldn't work as his doting parents would simply refuse to press charges.'

Eleanor frowned. 'So you came up with the idea of planting the jewels in Lancelot's plane?'

Johnny nodded. 'Yes, but Coco decided it wasn't enough to have poor Lancelot done for something as minor as theft, even on a grand scale.'

Coco kept her eyes, and gun, fixed on Eleanor. 'And then fate played into our hands…'

Johnny lit two cigarettes and passed one to Coco. 'The colonel suspected that someone in our group was the jewel thief. The old fool started making a nuisance of himself. It was only a matter of time before he went to the police.'

Coco smiled sweetly at Eleanor. 'We knew that he would be at the ball, so it was the perfect opportunity to get rid of the interfering old fool and pin the crime on you know who.'

Johnny took a long drag on his cigarette. 'It was easy to set Lancelot up as the fall guy, he was made for the job. Only trouble was' – he took another drag – 'the plan seemed dead in the water when Lancelot got cold feet after hearing the police would be there.'

Coco interrupted. 'Or it would have been if Lancelot wasn't as gullible a fool as the colonel. I told Johnny to wait until he was alone with Lance, then offer to create a diversion to distract the police so Lancelot could steal the jewels safely.'

Eleanor frowned. 'But you didn't create a diversion, did you Johnny? I did. You lured the colonel into the upstairs study after stealing the jewels. Then you bashed him on the head with a candlestick.'

Johnny chuckled. 'I couldn't believe our luck when I heard Lancelot had picked the thing up.'

Eleanor swallowed her anger again, forcing herself to keep calm. 'And the clever part was winding the colonel's broken wristwatch forward, what, fifteen minutes?'

Johnny grinned. 'Ten, old girl, couldn't afford to leave the old duffer's body lying around too long. Too much chance of someone else like you stumbling across it.'

Eleanor smiled grimly. 'True. And after he was arrested, one of you planted Lady Fenwick-Langham's jewels in Lancelot's plane.'

Coco applauded, even more slowly this time. 'You've got it all worked out. Such a shame it won't do you any good.'

Eleanor held Coco's gaze. 'And you'll sleep tonight, will you, knowing you put a bullet in my brain?'

'Perfectly.' Coco licked her lips and raised the gun to Eleanor's head.

'Coco, we don't have time,' Johnny said. 'We've only got a few minutes before it takes effect.'

Coco shrugged. 'If you're a good girl, Lady Swift, it won't come down to a bullet. Johnny is a stickler for his pad being just so and bloody bits of Eleanor all over the soft furnishings would spoil the refined ambience, wouldn't you say?'

Eleanor frowned. 'So how are you going to kill me? A fatal blow to the head like the colonel?'

Johnny smirked. 'No, that was altogether too boorish for my liking. I am, as you so shrewdly noticed, far more sophisticated than that as a rule.'

Her eyes shot to her glass. 'A few minutes? You've... you've spiked my drink, just like poor old Albie!'

Johnny tutted. 'Poor old Albie? He brought it on himself. He really shouldn't have tried to blackmail us. All his life he was out of his depth, socially, criminally and' – he laughed – 'literally, in the canal.'

Eleanor shook her head. 'So Millie was telling the truth when she said she overheard Albie trying to blackmail you?'

Coco winked at Eleanor. 'Yes. And now, angel face, it's time to go to heaven.'

'What have you given me?' Eleanor's heart was pounding.

'Phenobarbital,' Coco said. 'I can see the headline: *Lady Swift's tragic suicide over inability to save her lover from the gallows.*'

Eleanor was aware of Johnny having moved round behind her. He yanked her arms down and bound her hands behind her back. She went limp as Johnny tied her hands, making sure she kept her hands as far apart as possible. 'Whoa, Eleanor, old girl! You really can't hold your drugs, can you?' He swung her up over one shoulder, her head lolling against his back.

She heard Coco's voice. 'Right, it's all clear out by the car. Shove her in the back seat. And get a move on.'

The back of the car felt icy and damp. Coco shuffled in next to her, bracing herself against the passenger seat, the gun still held tightly in her hand. Johnny slammed the door and roared the engine into life. Unable to steady herself, Eleanor's head hit the front seat as the car lurched forward. The car lurched again as Johnny changed gear, pushing her back into the rear seat. The car's tyres sprayed gravel as it barrelled towards the gates.

Coco was leaning forward, over the front seat, talking to Johnny. Seizing her chance, in one fluid motion Eleanor pulled her knees up to her chest, slid her bound hands under herself and over her feet. With a deft flick of the rope, she whipped it round Johnny's neck, pulling him back against the front seat. Instinctively he let go of the wheel with both hands and grabbed the rope. Before Coco could react, the car swerved violently, knocking her away from Eleanor and into the door. Looking ahead, Eleanor quickly jerked the rope off Johnny's neck. Released, he swore and reached for the wheel. Too late to stop the car ploughing into the corner of the gatehouse and coming to a sickening stop.

The crash had lifted the front wheels off the road and caved in the bonnet. Johnny was slumped unconscious over the steering wheel, the windscreen cracked and bloody. Coco, swearing violently, was already half out of the car.

But Eleanor was quicker. Catching Coco's trailing leg with the rope, she sent her sprawling onto the gravel drive, the gun flying from her hand. Eleanor was right behind her. By the time Coco had struggled to her feet, knees bleeding, Eleanor had kicked the gun out of her reach. Coco glared at Eleanor, disbelief in her eyes. 'But, you—'

Eleanor smiled pityingly and shook her head. 'Did you really think I'd drink anything put in front of me? How many times do you think people have tried to spike my drink? Really!'

With a howl of pure hatred, Coco lunged at Eleanor. Eleanor easily sidestepped her, revealing an ornamental pond, which Coco fell headlong into. She emerged a few seconds later, spitting water, weed plastered over her face and clothes. She lost her footing on the algae covered bottom. As she disappeared under the water again, a voice shouted out, 'I say!'

Blocking the gates was the Rolls, Clifford sitting impassively at the wheel, Lancelot standing behind the open passenger door, shouldering an enormous elephant gun. 'This thing is dashedly heavy you know, I think I've lost all feeling in my arms!'

Eleanor stared for a moment and then a smile spread across her face. Clifford and Lancelot were supposed to be chasing down Lucas while she warned Johnny. Clifford had obviously worked out after they'd dropped her off that they'd got the wrong man and dashed back.

She called out, 'I don't think we'll be needing it just now, thanks, but maybe keep it handy.' She indicated Coco, who had given up trying to stand and was crawling up the opposite bank onto the lawn. 'In case she has any more fight left in her.'

CHAPTER 33

Eleanor stared out of the window of the Rolls, surprised at how light-hearted she felt as she lifted the veil from her face.

'Clifford, I've never been to such an uplifting service. What a wonderful celebration of a life that was.'

'Indeed, my lady. Your presence was greatly appreciated.'

'What? Me? But I only said a few words.'

'The perfect words. Mr Appleby's parents were greatly moved by your reading of his poem.'

'A wonderful poem, and turn out too. I believe the families he tutored were all there.'

'Plus several childhood friends and two of his professors from Oxford, my lady.'

'How strange that we form an image of someone in the narrow snippet of life we meet them in. Albie was obviously much loved in his own world.' She tickled Gladstone's ears as he sprawled half on her lap and half in the footwell. 'The colonel's funeral was also very uplifting. I was really glad for the chance to hear all the good things people said about him, especially Lord Langham, as I never really got to see the colonel's better side. However, that's enough funerals for me for a while.' In between trying to avoid Gladstone's many slobbery kisses, she looked around at the passing scenery. 'It really is beautiful here, Clifford, but you know I was born without any patience at all. I'm desperate to know where we are going.'

'Not going, my lady.' Clifford swung the Rolls to the right and turned down a neatly gravelled track, lined with horse chestnut trees in full bloom. 'Arrived.'

'There she is!' Lord Langham's hearty voice boomed across a swathe of immaculate grass that ran up to the side of an ornamental lake. On the central island stood a magnificent white stone folly, its six central columns supporting an ornate domed roof. Lady Langham gave an enthusiastic wave as Eleanor stepped from the Rolls.

Before Eleanor could speak, Lady Langham engulfed her in a loving hug. Lord Langham stood behind his wife, patting Eleanor's shoulders. Finally, stepping back, Lady Langham clutched her handkerchief to her chest. 'My dear, dear girl, we haven't had a chance, what with Lancelot coming home and all these funerals to attend, to really thank you for saving our boy! We will always be in your debt.'

Eleanor felt quite overwhelmed. 'Well, with Clifford's help. And yours, of course. Speaking of Clifford.' She spun round. 'Ah, there you are.'

He handed her a leather travel bag. 'I took the liberty of bringing you a change of clothes, my lady. Funeral attire is perhaps not best suited to a celebration.'

Having changed into her olive-green twill trousers and emerald blouse, she rejoined the others to find them busily unpacking a mesmerising amount of food from a series of wicker hampers.

'Gracious!'

Lord Langham took her arm. 'The memsahib had the spiffing idea of throwing a special bash to show how grateful we are. She had a host of elaborate ideas and then telephoned Clifford to bring him in on the surprise.' He leaned in and whispered, 'I believe he may have saved you from something with posh frocks and canapés, masterfully dropping the hint that a picnic by the lake in easy togs is more your thing, old girl.'

'Good old Clifford,' she whispered back.

'Damn fine butler. Anyhow, Lancelot was coming, but the blasted police nabbed him at the last minute. Something about signing another statement, I think.'

By the time Clifford had restrained Gladstone from jumping into the lake for the fourth time, the party had eaten heartily and Lady Langham seemed finally to have banished the worry she had carried during the 'terrible business' as she referred to it.

'So, my dear, Mr Seaton and Lady Coco Childs, will they…?'

Eleanor nodded as she swallowed a delicious piece of egg and bacon flan. 'They will both stand trial next month. Inspector Seldon was sure he'd find more than enough evidence now he knows where to look. Coco won't say a word, but Johnny gave a full confession.' Eleanor shook her head. 'He was infatuated with Coco. Bizarre what some men fall for. Of course he loved the excitement of the jewel thefts and the notoriety they gained in the press. I think he saw himself as some sort of Raffles, pathetic really.' She patted Lord Langham's arm. 'I'm so sorry about the colonel. That was Coco's idea, she knew he was on to them and cajoled Johnny into ridding them of him.'

'Poor old Pudders. Good man, underneath all his bristles, of course.'

Lady Langham put down her plate. 'But, my dear, what has become of Lady Millicent Childs? Was she in on it? I always heard the sisters were very close.'

Eleanor drummed her fingers on her cheek. 'She is either the most incredible actress or she really wasn't aware of the whole scheme. She has sworn to Inspector Seldon that she only met me at the Pike and Perch to pass on the information about the phone call she'd overheard in order to help Lancelot. She said she was too scared to go to the police. And Coco did confirm that Albie was trying to blackmail them, so…' She shrugged. 'I imagine we'll never really know.'

Lord Langham swallowed and wiped his mouth. 'Speaking of actresses, your performance at that am-dram affair was first rate!'

Lady Langham nodded. 'Indeed it was. But tell us, what about that prince fellow they were all running around with?'

'Lucas? I agree with Inspector Seldon, I don't think he had any inkling of what Coco and Johnny were up to. However, the whole thing's obviously shaken him up. He's decided to pack in all this bright young thing business, finish his studies at Oxford and return to India before he ends up losing his life or his father's trust, which he said was worse.'

Lady Langham squeezed Eleanor's hand. 'Well, that seems to be that. Our son's back at home and that's all that matters.'

'Of course. Only…'

Lady Langham looked at her quizzically. 'My dear Eleanor, after all you've done for us, I hope you'll never hesitate to ask for our help… or tell us what is on your mind?'

'No, no, it's just that… well, this whole thing kicked off because you were in a spot of bother, financially speaking…'

Lord Langham chuckled. 'Kind of you to try and save our blushes as ever, but no need. We were indeed in a dashedly awkward spot financially, and you'd think we still were, what with the police returning Augusta's jewellery, so we never did get the insurance money.'

Lady Langham released Eleanor's hand and patted her husband's. 'Your prince wasn't the only one, Eleanor my dear, to be shaken up by this terrible affair. Harold and I had a long talk in the rose garden. Our actions put our son, and you, the two people we care about most in the world, in grave danger.' She waved aside

Eleanor's attempt to interrupt. 'Don't deny it, we acted selfishly and immorally. So the minute the police returned my jewels, we sent them up to London to be auctioned.'

Lord Langham grunted. 'And the rah-rah set can look down their sniffy noses and gossip behind our backs as much as they like.'

They all turned at the roar of a motorbike racing up from the direction of the Manor. Lancelot appeared, standing up on the foot pegs and waving wildly. Eleanor rose and ran to meet him as he skidded to a halt and threw his bike against one of the horse chestnut trees.

'Sherlock!' he cried, scooping her into his arms.

'Hello, Goggles.' Eleanor beamed, unable to keep the silly grin from her face.

Lancelot fished in his jacket pocket. 'You really are the cat's pyjamas at this sleuthing lark, you know. Thanks, darling fruit.' He kissed her and held out a small tissue-paper-wrapped package.

Eleanor took it and peeled off the paper. 'Oh, a leather notebook.'

Lancelot grinned. 'Like that Holmes fellow had. In case one day you might need to help some other chump who was too much of a fathead to pull himself out of a hole he'd dug himself.'

They joined Lord and Lady Langham and Clifford handed everyone a glass of champagne.

Eleanor raised her glass. 'To true friends!'

Over in the folly, Clifford ruffled Gladstone's ears as if needing a distraction. Harold poured another glass of champagne and insisted Clifford take it. Raising his glass, Harold cheered, 'To true friends!'

His wife leaned against his shoulder, staring at Lancelot as he wrapped his jacket around Eleanor's shoulders. 'And maybe... just maybe, more than friends. Cheers.'

A LETTER FROM VERITY BRIGHT

Thanks so much for choosing to read *Death at the Dance*. I hope you enjoyed reading it as much as I did writing it. If you'd like to follow more of Ellie and Clifford's adventures – and maybe find out if Ellie and Lancelot's romance blossoms – then just sign up at the following link. As a thank you, you'll receive the first chapters of Ellie's brand-new adventure and be the first to know when the next book in the Lady Swift series will be available. Your email address will never be shared and you can unsubscribe at any time.

www.bookouture.com/verity-bright

And I'd be very grateful if you could write a review. Reviews help others discover and enjoy the Lady Swift mysteries as well as providing me with helpful feedback so the next book is even better.

Thank you,
Verity Bright

    @BrightVerity
    veritybrightauthor
    veritybright.com

A LITTLE MORE ABOUT
THE LADY SWIFT BOOKS

We're often asked where the ideas come from for the Lady Swift books. Well, Verity Bright is actually a wife-and-husband writing team, so we are very fortunate to have two minds to dream up our ideas. And two people to research them, because many of the events and places mentioned in the books are real.

For instance in book one, *A Very English Murder*, Ellie arrives in England having taken the first commercial flight from Cape Town to London. This was a real flight (although it actually went from London to Cape Town), that did actually take forty-five days with all but five of them spent in deserts where they'd crash-landed trying to fix the plane and get supplies.

In *Death at the Dance*, while Little Buckford is a fictional village, Ellie and Clifford travel to the real ancient university town of Oxford and visit DCI Seldon in the magnificent town hall built in 1897. And in the upcoming book, Ellie takes advantage of a real change in the law of the time that allows her to stand for Parliament, but not vote.

The characters are also a mixture of fact and fiction. For instance, I (the husband of the duo) actually used to be a butler and a little of that may have come out in Clifford, although I was never as cheeky! And my wife was something of an adventurer in her younger years, so there's definitely a touch of her in Ellie.

We live in a small village in the Chilterns on the edge of the Cotswolds where life does seem to have gone on unchanged in many ways since Ellie's time. There's still a Lord of the Manor, they shoot and play polo every weekend the rain allows, and the local café serves traditional Buckinghamshire dishes like Bacon Badger Pie. All this seeps into the settings and feel of the Lady Swift books and hopefully adds to your enjoyment.

Best
Verity

ACKNOWLEDGEMENTS

Huge thanks to my editor, Maisie, and the team at Bookouture who guided *Death at the Dance* through to publication in difficult times.

Lightning Source UK Ltd.
Milton Keynes UK
UKHW010219311021
393102UK00001B/182